A WEST CORK MYSTERY

ROY McCARTHY

A WEST CORK MYSTERY

A DARK, BROODING SUSPENSE SET
AT THE HEART OF RURAL IRELAND

First published in 2015 by
Roy McCarthy
Email: roy.mccarthy@gmx.co.uk
www.backontherock.com

CreateSpace paperback   ISBN: 978-1505608588
Also available as an ebook

Cover design by Design for Writers
Typesetting by Chenile Keogh

NOTES FROM THE AUTHOR

This is a work of fiction and all characters and events, except for those noted below, are the product of the author's imagination.

In Chapter One Tom Barry was indeed the commander of the 3rd (West) Cork Brigade of the Irish Republican Army during the Irish War of Independence and the subsequent Civil War. The events of Bloody Sunday in November 1920 and the Kilmichael Ambush a week later are a matter of public record.

The Whiddy Island disaster at Bantry in January 1979 was regrettably a true event. May those that lost their lives rest in peace.

The myths and legends of Ireland are manifold and which of us can declare for certain to what extent they are true or false. A good and very entertaining source of background reading is *Fairy and Folk Tales of the Irish Peasantry* by the Irish poet William Butler Yeats (1865–1939). I have drawn liberally on Yeats' research.

For the history of old Ireland I used primarily Eleanor Hull's *Pagan Ireland (Epochs of Irish History)*.

My thanks to author Dianne Gray for sparking the original idea for this book, also Sudesna Ghosh for her invaluable help and advice and Lucy Jouault for her proofreading.

Roy McCarthy
January 2015

1

'God bless all here!'
Michael Cullinane unlocked and pulled ajar the wooden door. Like a bird fearing a cat he craned his neck and peered around the door into the night. The fresh country air swirled through the gap diluting the warmth inside. That was the least of Michael's worries. He had only unlocked the door as he knew the consequences of not doing so would probably be worse. These were dangerous times in Ireland.

'Who is it? What do you want?'

'My good man, excuse our rough methods ... go, go!'

The door was pushed wide open with force and Michael staggered backwards, fell on his backside and banged his head on the floor. Through the resulting fuzziness he saw two roughly-dressed figures, rifles at the ready, run past him into the hallway. No subtlety, heavy boots resounding as they crashed their way through the rooms on the ground floor. Doors slammed, furniture banged.

Above him, as his head cleared somewhat stood another man, calmer, revolver in hand. After a cursory glance this one turned his attention from Michael and, trotting over to the foot of the staircase, he looked up. Seeing no one he waited at the foot, tense, listening.

Michael began to struggle to his feet, to stutter questions. The gunman quickly pointed the revolver at his head.

'Stay down!'

Michael sat back down and waited, trembling. In his fright however he was somewhat relieved that the gunman was an Irishman, and with a Munster accent. Presumably his cohorts, who continued to rampage within, were Irish too. If it had been the Tans he'd likely be dead by now, and the women.

'Nothing sir!'

The riflemen, breathing heavily, returned to the hallway.

'Upstairs then, careful now.'

'Please sir, your honour,' Michael began.

'Stay easy man, only the enemy need fear these men.'

A minute later screams, those of women. Eyes wide, Michael made to get up again but was stayed once more by the gimlet-eyed gunman.

The screams subsided to sobs. More banging of doors, heavy thump of boots. The two riflemen reappeared on the stairs.

'No one sir, two women only.'

'*Two* women?' The gunman turned to Michael, a ghost of a smile perhaps appearing, eyebrows raised.

'My wife, sir. And her sister!' Michael replied indignantly.

The gunman considered for a moment, then went to the still-open front door. He whispered something that Michael didn't catch, but he heard running footsteps disappear towards the back of the house. The gunman returned.

'Now then, get up. My apologies for the rough entrance. One cannot be too careful these days, I'm sure you'd agree?'

'No sir, thank you sir ...'

'Tom, call me Tom. And this gossoon here is Liam and the other is Sean. Now, we are tired and hungry. Can you recommend a comfortable hotel hereabouts?'

Liam and Sean broke into laughter and Michael, though somewhat uncertainly, joined them.

Soon the men of the Irish Republican Army were settled around the hearty turf fire. Indeed they were exhausted and cold and extremely grateful for a spot of comfort and warmth. There were five in all and Michael's wife Mary and her older sister Niamh bustled around preparing a meal. The smell of goat stew wafting in from the kitchen reminded them just how hungry they were as well as cold and tired.

They were all Cork men but beyond that they volunteered little information. Michael and the women knew better than to probe. Each knew that, in these troubled times, walls had ears. Information shared was likely to be shared again.

In a guerrilla war it was vital that all but the blandest and most public news was kept close to one's own chest, for everyone's sake. Michael, although undoubtedly a good Irishman, was still vulnerable to interrogation by the enemy, and this could not be risked.

The goat stew and hunks of bread went down extremely well and at last the men were both warm and replete. Comfortable beds were prepared for them – the women would share and Michael would make do with a chair. Presently the four volunteers were fitfully asleep. However a freedom fighter in an occupied land never sleeps peacefully and their rifles were loaded and ready, by their bedsides.

Tom, the leader, chose to remain awhile with Michael by the fireside. They sipped glasses of Paddy whiskey. The clock chimed midnight and Tom, choosing his words carefully, spoke a little of what had brought them to the house.

'Well now, you heard of the doings up at Croke Park the other day?'

Indeed Michael had. On a dreadful day the British Auxiliaries had murdered 14 civilians during a football match in reprisal for the killing of a number of their Intelligence men earlier that same day in Dublin.

'Well we decided that the Auxies needed to suffer for that. And indeed they did. A few days ago, we wiped out a couple of truckloads there near Macroom.'

Indeed the news of a great IRA victory at Kilmichael had not been long in traversing the length and breadth of the country. But the Black and Tans and the Auxies had not been slow in making their own random reprisals. Thus it was that Michael and his family, in an isolated spot, lived in constant fear, and in the hope of a victory, or peace by whatever means.

'Anyway,' Tom continued, 'we had to skedaddle out of that pretty quick. It's by keeping to the fields and the old ways through the bogs that we've managed to elude the Tans. Our only bit of a rest was last night, up there at Cronin's in Gougane Barra. There we split up. I think we might more or less have given the bastards the slip, at this point.'

'And how will it all end Tom? The people live in terror.'

'I can't say Michael, but there won't be peace until the British see sense and withdraw.'

'There's talk of a settlement.'

'Talks have got us nowhere Michael.'

The two men gazed into the fire, each with his own thoughts. Michael was now certain of the identity of his guest.

'Well, Michael, I must join my men. But I am grateful for the hospitality, and thank the women too. You are all good Irish people. God save you.'

'And you too Tom Barry! God save you and your men.'

As he rose Tom Barry drew his revolver and pointed it between Michael's eyes.

'Michael,' he said calmly, 'if anyone learns that we have been here today you are surely a dead man. Now goodnight.'

2

'Well I guess we could swing by again tomorrow, take another look.'

Miranda Hunter smiled and reached over to squeeze her husband's hand. Around them subdued conversation, the clink of cutlery and the busyness of the only waitress that appeared to be on duty in the tiny restaurant. It was the couple's first evening in Killarney and they had been lucky to get a table after rocking up on spec late in the evening. Not that there weren't other dining opportunities in the popular tourist town. But this little place down a side street had caught their attention. It had seemed perfect to both of them even before they had scanned the menu, or ventured inside.

The house had made her heart leap earlier; she couldn't get it out of her head. They had pulled over to consult the map. They weren't lost or in any rush. In fact it was quite the opposite. Rather than rush through the Irish countryside like their compatriots tended to do, they wanted to slow down a little. They wanted to take their time; maybe take a detour or two before their scheduled overnight stop.

And then Miranda had seen it, tucked behind an untrimmed hedge and several leaf-heavy trees. A gate leading into a weed-infested gravel drive. A grand, dignified looking property clearly fallen on hard times. And, alluringly, a 'for sale' sign planted somewhat unsteadily inside the shabby gate.

They hadn't hung around for long, heading off for their

overnight stop at Killarney, arriving the pretty way via Glengarriff and the National Park. But, despite the many distractions, Miranda's mind kept drifting back to the house behind the trees. Sad and neglected, it appeared to be calling to her.

'Thank you Joe. I know we're not house hunting or anything so you're a darling to humour me. I'd just like to see it once more, get it out of my system.' They smiled lovingly at one another and sipped their wine.

Miranda was correct. They weren't looking for a house; they already had a nice one in Martha's Vineyard close to family and friends. However, neither of them was averse to the idea of living and working elsewhere, at least for a while. Joe was a successful author and in-demand writer for a number of magazines in Boston, Chicago and New York. With the wonders of modern communication he could ply his trade from any base that he so chose. Miranda also had portable skills, being a teacher of mathematics. Newly-married, Joe in his late twenties, Miranda a little younger, it wouldn't have come as a surprise to their friends if they were to move away from Massachusetts at some stage.

Both Joe and Miranda were settled and happy. They were moderately wealthy, both through Joe's success and Miranda's inheritance. Miranda didn't need to work but dreaded becoming a lady of leisure, a lady that lunched and played golf.

Neither wished for children. Miranda hadn't any maternal instincts whatsoever. She found that odd in herself. But there again she noted that more young professional women were choosing to remain childless, or at least were delaying starting a family until later than used to be the case. So maybe she wasn't so odd at age 25. Whatever, she was open to the prospect of living away from her childhood home if the opportunity presented itself.

This was a first trip outside of the United States for both of them. Married for just a year they had decided to treat themselves to an overseas trip. Ireland hadn't, by any means, been top of the list. Neither of them had close connections to the country, though many of their acquaintances claimed Irish forebears, real or imaginary. But President Obama's visit to the home of his ancestors had sparked their interest. Then there was the 50th anniversary of President Kennedy's assassination. It had only been a few months before that event that he had made a historic visit to Ireland, the first US President to do so.

So it was that Joe and Miranda acquired passports and arrived in Ireland in midsummer. And their first few days had confirmed to them what a good choice of destination it had been.

Dublin had been fine. They had spent the first couple of days seeing the many sights the capital had to offer. Eschewing the guided tours they had set their own itinerary with Kilmainham Gaol, Phoenix Park, the National Museum, Merrion Square and St Stephen's Green winning their approval. They were the only people around in Henrietta Street as they inspected the oldest Georgian buildings in the city. Some of these were now barely still standing but they were redolent with history, firstly as grand houses, later as tenements as Dublin decayed after the Act of Union. On the other hand Temple Bar at night dismayed them and they sought less debauched venues for eating and drinking.

They hired a car. Joe assured his wife that he could handle a manual drive. And, after jumping the car into the back of another in the hire car yard, and after ten minutes instruction by a worried employee, they jerkily headed off down the country.

Joe had never been too handy with machinery and suchlike. He was a Clark Kent lookalike with his dark-rimmed glasses and neat haircut. Tall and slim, conservatively dressed, Joe was all brain but struggled when it came to sorting out practical issues. But he was romantic. He loved the world, the written word and, importantly, he loved Miranda. He wouldn't have thought of loving her at all only that she'd practically thrown herself at him during a charity barbecue held in their home town of Edgartown. She'd had enough of beefy, sporting jocks that treated their women like ornaments. She wanted to settle down with a quiet man who would give her unconditional love. Almost to Joe's surprise, he fell in love. And it was only after they were wed that Miranda realised how successful and wealthy a writer he was.

Miranda herself thought she was a bit like Sandy in *Grease*. Pretty in a so-so sort of a way, quiet though able to converse happily and intelligently with friends. Average height and happy to be able to look up at her man, most comfortable when in her teaching role, exploring the world of figures. Her hair was fair and always neat, straight and never passing her shoulders. Yes, she considered herself a Sandy, or perhaps Etta Place, the girlfriend of the Sundance Kid.

South from Dublin they headed, Joe gaining better control of the car by degrees and mostly remembering to drive on the left. They loved the Wicklow Mountains, Glendalough and the pretty towns of Wexford and Kilkenny. No time to see the city of Cork but, as they headed for Killarney, like many before them they fell in love with the countryside of County Cork.

And now, as they relaxed over coffee, still the neglected

house continued to pop into Miranda's head, unbidden. She told herself that it was one of thousands and that her infatuation would probably disappear upon closer inspection. But for now it called out to her across the miles.

Later, hand in hand, they watched with fascination the starlings swooping over St Mary's Cathedral. Nearby they could hear the music and laughter from a bar. Down here in the south-west of the country they unwound, falling into the slower rhythm of life, the rhythm of the land. Rural man's clock is governed by the seasons, by the weather, by the crop cycles and by the life cycle of farm animals. None of these elements rush about in haste; each takes its turn and man follows. And at the end of the working day there is rest and relaxation.

That night, Joe and Miranda fell asleep peacefully, the almost perfect silence broken only by the comforting chime of the cathedral bell tolling midnight.

On the Cork side of the border, Dunmurry House settled down for another night, caring not if the weather was fine or foul. It had lived through every extreme many times over, and had survived passably well. It was of sturdy construction and from time to time someone would come along and make repairs and improvements. Modern plumbing and wiring had given it a new lease of life over the years. Then there was insulation, damp proof courses, cement pointing and weatherproofing. It was a fortunate property.

Across the county Cork, across Ireland, many such buildings had not survived. Some lay in sad ruin, open to the ravages of cold, damp Irish winters and to the rapacious growth of grasses, plants and trees during the short summers. They had been abandoned by their owners – indeed in many cases the owners were untraceable. Others had been attacked and burnt in more troubled times, causing their inhabitants to flee and never return.

Men and women had loved at these old homes, children had played. No longer. And with each brick that fell away the building would lose a little more of its memory, of the things it had seen and heard. No one would ever hear the stories.

It was sad, but a kindness of sorts when machines roared up and razed all traces to the ground, mercifully killing the old building in a quick day. A fine new house would arise from the dirt, built with the best of materials and fitted with all modern amenities. A new family would arrive and park multiple cars in the driveway. The new house would begin to store its own memories in place of those recently erased.

Dunmurry was fortunate indeed. Tonight the summer breeze caressed the overgrown trees that hid the property from view. The careful listener might discern the occasional sound in the undergrowth, or the sudden, sharp cry of a bird awakened from a bad dream. But then all would fall silent again in the gentle West Cork night.

And the old building was content in its security. It would be nice to have someone living there again but Dunmurry had memories enough within its walls to last it awhile yet. And if those walls could speak, what tales they might tell.

Full Irish, none of your cereal and pastries rubbish. Not for the duration of this vacation anyway. Miranda worried that the cholesterol would manifest itself in spots or pimples but for now they both seemed unaffected. Sausages, delicious and bursting with flavour, not objects of indeterminate origin plucked from the deep freezer. Mushrooms which might have been picked from the fields just an hour ago. Tomato, fried eggs, crispy bacon. Plenty more for the asking plus limitless toast. A couple of cups of coffee and they were ready to hit the road again.

'So, come on dear. Let's get back to your old house then we can move on with our tour.'

'You're too good to me. I love you.'

Joe edged the car through the hotel car park between the tour coaches which were loading up, and the young Americans congratulated themselves that they had chosen to be independent. The signpost for Kenmare beckoned them forwards and they felt rather superior as they let the roof down on their two-seater BMW and let in the warm Irish morning.

Miranda had stopped worrying about Joe's driving. He had more or less got the hang of it now and she was able to drape her arm out of the open window and enjoy the breeze and passing scenery interrupted only by the occasional 'shit' as a gear was missed.

They were largely retracing yesterday's tracks but it didn't really matter. They had no return flights booked and no deadlines to keep. They were thinking of another week or so to allow them to see Galway and Donegal before returning to Dublin and the flight home. They were determined to enjoy the country, its places and people at a gentle pace, not relentlessly trekking from one destination to another.

From what they had observed of the coach tourists, it was always about the next destination. Even as a coach party arrived at one place the maps were being studied to figure out where they were heading next day. There seemed little intention of actually enjoying being in a particular place beyond posing for a few obligatory photos, for proof to those back home. The most important thing was ascertaining the exact time of dinner at the hotel.

Being the height of the summer, the traffic on the main roads was heavy. Many were the tailbacks behind tractors, caravans and slow-moving cars driven by men in hats, on the winding roads. While Joe concentrated on the road Miranda had time to gasp anew at the hills, forests and lakes with their many shades of green. It was no wonder that Killarney was so popular despite its rather tarnished reputation as a tourist trap.

By degrees the BMW meandered up to Moll's Gap and Joe and Miranda joined the hordes queuing up for sustenance at the roadside amenity. All admired the stunning vista set out before them in the continuing fine weather. Many days it was misty and one could barely see beyond the stone wall, but today the Cork and Kerry mountains were displayed in all their splendour. Rolling hills and valleys, lush with vegetation, reached up to rockier heights. Silvery rills tumbled down the slopes, emptying into larger streams. The more ardent gazers, or those with binoculars, might pick out the odd farmer in the otherwise natural splendour. He might be on the slopes, striding along with his stick, calling to his dog who, with huge enjoyment of his task, collected the odd sheep or two who had wandered too far.

The coaches filled, their occupants impatient to be off. Engines started, but a few strays dallied along with Joe and Miranda, reluctant to return to the fold. They had escaped, if only temporarily. They leaned on the roadside wall looking at the timeless view.

'Hey, see that sheep right up there?' Joe pointed into the distance.

'What one, where? All I see is a bunch of fields and rocks. Oh, yes. One on its own.'

'What do you think – is he trying to sneak away from the rest of the flock?'

'She. Sheep are she. Could be. Maybe she's thinking 'Hey, I don't have to run with the flock. I'm going to see what's around the next hill, see if there's a better life".

'Yeah, maybe there's a place where the gorse is more succulent, where there are no dogs to nip your backside. Where I can be free!'

'And maybe there is a place where above-average sheep end up if they manage to escape. A sort of sheep land where they sit and read books and order dogs about.'

The laughed companionably, still unwilling to rejoin the traffic.

The few watchers at the wall might have considered the fit, hardy farmer, the quaint looking house down the valley there. Soon he would be heading back, a hearty lunch calling. His wife, all business in her apron, had perhaps prepared a nice stew. Maybe an apple pie with fresh local cream. And didn't they both have a great life out there in these idyllic surroundings? What might it be like to emulate them – perhaps without the hard work? To live here peacefully away from the city with its drugs and knife crime, its poverty, its slow loss of the social fabric that they had known when they were younger. 'Yes! Buy a place in the countryside – in Ireland, one day. I'll do that.'

One by one the coaches pulled away. Joe and Miranda followed, though knowing they'd soon be stuck behind them once more.

*

It was after midday when they descended the road into Kenmare in the county of Cork. The BMW still growled impatiently, eager to leap ahead at speed, but there was little chance of that as each time Joe pressed the gas it brought him all the quicker to another S-bend or up against slow-moving traffic.

They stopped at a pub outside Kenmare for coffee and sandwiches. The parasols over the wooden trestle tables waved a gentle invitation to passers-by, to tourists in particular. The bartender was well used to American customers and, though it was unlikely they would pass his way again, he greeted them warmly and made them feel welcome. Miranda was struck, as in previous days, by the unmistakable smell of the Irish public bar, a mixture of polish and alcohol. And no bar was ever without at least one old lad, parked on a stool at the counter, or perhaps away at a table studying the horses. And there was always the black pint with the creamy head in front of him. Then, as sure as night follows day, the barman would place the fresh pint in front of the drinker, seemingly unordered, just as the last drops of the previous one disappeared down the throat.

Refreshed, the couple drove on into the early afternoon. The town of Glengarriff appeared and disappeared, Garinish Island and the Blue Pool for now unvisited. Onto Bantry, nestling in Bantry Bay, and the turning for Drimoleague.

'OK, so straight down here? Ten miles or so I'd guess.'

Miranda kicked herself for not marking an X on the map, but it had only been later that the house had started calling to her. Nonetheless they were both fairly certain that they were retracing their steps correctly. Her map reading had been generally fine throughout the trip, her sense of direction good. But maybe it wasn't this road they'd taken yesterday. It was different. What if ... yes, they were close, she could just tell.

'There! That's it!'

At Miranda's exclamation, Joe braked hard, skidded to a halt and stalled the engine. Miranda braced, waiting for an impact from the rear. But there was no vehicle behind, or indeed in front. There was perfect silence. Magically the summer traffic had been left behind back there somewhere.

It was the same property all right. Joe restarted the car, checked his mirrors and performed a 180 coming to a halt again outside the gate. They unbelted, opened their respective doors and climbed out. Together they leaned against the twin wooden gates that guarded the gravel drive. Several layers of paint peeled off the gate – purple, green, cream. The drive curved up to the front of the property through the trees and the overgrown lawn. The building itself was half hidden from view by the march of nature. But Miranda sensed it was inviting them in.

Joe rattled the latch on the gate and looked at Miranda enquiringly.

'Well, shall we?'

'I guess so. No point in coming all this way not to. Do you think anyone will mind?'

'It's for sale,' pointed out Joe, indicating the estate agent's sign, 'I imagine the owner would be pleased for us to look around.'

Joe lifted the latch and they stepped inside, the gate hinges complaining at the unaccustomed movement. He shut the gate behind them and they proceeded up the gravel path, eyes on the building as it slowly presented itself to them.

'D'you think anyone's at home?'

'There's no car anyway. Doesn't look as if anything's been driven up here recently.'

They drew near to the house. It was a stolid building made of stone in the old manner. Of considerable width, the ground floor walls were painted white though the brightness had long faded to a sad grey. A porch with a side door leading to the main entrance door broke up the straight line of the front aspect. Timber-framed windows indicated several ground floor rooms. The one distinctive feature of the building was the tiled, pitched roof from which projected three attic windows. The tiles extended over the front porch. At first glance the building looked in fair condition though the many-tiled roof actively needed attention.

They tried the porch door but it was unsurprisingly locked. Peering through the windows and net curtains they saw that the cosy-looking rooms were unfurnished and that the large kitchen, though intact, was desperately old fashioned.

They walked around the building with some difficulty, pushing through plants left to grow unhindered. At the back there was a pair of glass balcony doors giving entrance to the main, large living room.

It was clear that nobody had lived here for many months.

But, much as the house itself interested them, Miranda in particular, it was the view from the back that made them gasp. Beyond the large garden the ground fell away to south and west, a landscape of fields, hills and the occasional dwelling. Its gentle but majestic beauty took their breath away.

'Joe, isn't it just beautiful?'

'The view or the house?'

'Both, everything! Imagine living here!'

"Imagine living here in the middle of winter, honey. The rain and wind howling in off the Atlantic, more tiles being blown off the roof. Miles to get to the nearest store. Probably no broadband. Then it would be 'why did we leave Massachusetts, honey?'".

Undeterred, Miranda pulled out her iPhone and tapped in the Bantry estate agent's details from the leaning sign. The weary-sounding agent was not surprised to get the call. He fielded a steady stream of enquiries about the property, especially from Americans. None had come to anything and he was reluctant to traipse out the road yet again to show these new enquirers around. However, encouraged by the offer of a small finder's fee he agreed to come out from Bantry later.

With a couple of hours to wait and feeling peckish, they jumped back into the car and headed east. The traffic continued to be light until they approached Drimoleague, a small town about 10 miles away. They pulled up and decided on a spot of lunch at the Drimoleague Inn. As with everywhere they had visited in Ireland they were made to feel welcome. The place was quiet enough, it being midweek, and they were able to settle down at a comfortable table in one of the bay windows. They ordered a selection of sandwiches and, whilst waiting, they were poured some proper strong coffee.

For the very first time the notion of living away from their home state and country was out in the open between the pair. It was a safe topic while it remained theoretical. But now it was clear that Miranda was the one who wanted to talk about the possibilities while Joe played Devil's Advocate. Neither wanted to upset the other, they had an easy and loving relationship, but it was clear that Miranda would have her work cut out to persuade Joe to make what would be a significant life change.

Miranda tried to play down the magnitude of such a move, and to play up the fact that they would only be a few hours of flight time from the States. She tried to convince him that they would not lose touch with their friends and families. Joe could be in New York or Chicago almost as quickly as it presently took him to travel from Edgartown to those places. And if it came to the worst then they could just as easily sell up again. Nothing need be permanent. Certainly there were no great work considerations as Joe accepted that he could write just as easily most anywhere in the world.

But Joe was more open to the idea of trying Dublin for a year or two, renting or buying a property in leafy Ballsbridge, or down along the coastal suburbs in Dalkey or Killiney. Miranda saw sense in the compromise but her heart was set. The house – Dunmurry the agent had called it – attracted her like nothing else had on the trip. She couldn't explain it in terms logical enough for Joe to understand.

Perhaps once she'd seen the interior and had been quoted an outrageous price, the attraction would wear off.

Back at the house, the agent was on time. Business was slow and the prospect of a cheque in his pocket together with the slim chance of a sale had outweighed both his lethargy and his plans of locking the office up early before heading for a pint.

He was clearly no stranger to the porch door, or the heavy entrance door inside and they swung open easily at a turn of the key. All three stepped inside, into stagnant and musty air. The house was huge, made even more so by the lack of furniture. Clearly the main living room was to the right as they stepped into the hall. It was very big, reaching from the front to the back of the building. The glass doors they had seen earlier from the outside allowed the afternoon sun to flood the room, showing up the dust on the old-fashioned mantelpieces, radiators and wallpaper.

Miranda saw great possibilities of renovating the room, decorating, refurnishing and reflooring. Basically, bringing the whole place to life. Joe saw a sad, deserted place that could never be brought up to modern standards. Miranda saw the awesome landscape to the south. Joe saw the overgrown jungle that was the grounds.

There was another smaller room to the left then, on the other side of the hallway, more rooms together with the large, outmoded kitchen. Venturing upstairs (the agent preferred to enjoy a cigarette outside instead) they found a surprising number of what might have been bedrooms together with two bathrooms. Miranda dreamed, Joe's lips were pursed together.

Outside they inspected the grounds. There were sheds and outbuildings tucked away which they hadn't noticed before. A lawn, remnants of flower beds, vegetable patches maybe, a couple of sad garden ornaments. A head-high hedge guarded the southern boundary. An overgrown and crumbling concrete path threaded its way along the eastern edge from the house down to the southern hedge with evidence of an exit to the fields beyond.

They had both seen enough. The price that was quoted was more than they had imagined but was still easily within their reach. The agent pocketed his finder's fee and headed back to Bantry. Joe and Miranda Hunter headed back to Killarney, Miranda with one last, wistful look back.

That evening she pushed Joe to the limit, urging him to at least consider making a low offer on Dunmurry House. They might get a bargain if the owner just wanted to get rid of the place. Joe ummed and ahhed, not convinced but never saying no. Later in bed Miranda tried one or two new tricks and at last Joe weakened.

The next morning he protested that the decision had been obtained under duress but nonetheless he allowed Miranda to call the agent. The offer was noted by the agent who said that he would pass it along to the owner. Miranda extracted a promise from the agent that they be given the chance to improve on any other offer that might come along; she couldn't bear to think of someone else buying Dunmurry.

3

J oe and Miranda spent a further five days in Ireland. There
wasn't a single hour during which Miranda didn't think
about Dunmurry. Still it called to her, the further away
they travelled. If her phone bleeped or pinged she hoped it
might be a message from the estate agent. She was determined
though, not to keep nagging Joe about the matter, or to keep
talking about it. There would be time enough for that when
they heard about their offer.

Instead, she admitted that there might be other places in
Ireland that she would appreciate and enjoy! They decided
on a change of plan having now booked their flight back to
Boston in five days time. After Killarney, they had booked
ahead at Dingle Town with a view to driving around the
Dingle Peninsula. However, they were advised that, whilst it
was beautiful out that way, it was also rife with motor traffic
at the peak season. They were not keen to sit nose-to-tail for
hours so the plans were changed.

Booking ahead at Lahinch they drove up easily through
County Kerry, soft top down, a Chieftains CD keeping
them company. Then across the River Shannon by ferry into
County Clare. Not caring to follow the crowds to Bunratty
Castle and Durty Nelly's, they tootled along the western
coastlands via Kilrush and Kilkee, stopping frequently to
savour the slow pace of life before being thrust back into the
rat race of Dublin and Boston.

They overnighted at Lahinch and spent the following

day exploring the moonscape that is the Burren; 'not water enough to drown a man, wood enough to hang one nor earth to bury one.' They did some walking among the rock, conscious of the weight they were putting on sitting in the car and consuming the best of food and drink whenever they could.

Galway City was their next stop – a five-star hotel overlooking Eyre Square with a drive through Connemara the following day. They called in to see the cottage which featured in the 1952 romantic comedy *The Quiet Man* with John Wayne and Maureen O'Hara.

Finally, they were done. From Galway, Joe put his foot down for Dublin and 24 hours later they were back in Edgartown, Massachusetts. After a few days off, Joe started writing again. He was syndicated in several magazines. He was also involved in a research project and was also at the second draft stage of his second novel.

It being summertime Miranda had time on her hands. She caught up with friends who were eager to hear about each other's holiday adventures. Miranda spoke warmly of Ireland but started to forget about Dunmurry the longer time went on.

In September she renewed her gymnasium membership – she was horrified to find that she had put on 16 pounds since the end of the previous school term. She hadn't noticed whilst wearing casual holiday attire but her work trousers pinched her hips and her jawline was becoming fleshy. She threw herself into a fitness routine and was joined most days by her friends Jodie and Carmel. The aerobics machines, spinning, swimming. After three weeks she felt fitter and fresher, better in herself, more confident.

Miranda and Jodie tried a bit of jogging to break up the routine and to get fresh air into their lungs. They made the most common of mistakes and charged off at the speed of Olympic champions, such was their confidence. After the second occasion, they dragged themselves painfully back to the gym and informed the staff that they weren't suited for running and were sticking to the indoors. However, they were persuaded to try again, this time under supervision. One of the part-time staff was an old runner and it was Charlie who showed them how to warm up properly then to forget about speed until they knew what they were doing. And, at a much reduced pace, they unsurprisingly found that 20–30 minutes was not as impossible as it had seemed at first.

And within a short space of time the women proved themselves to be competent runners who looked forward to their runs rather than dreading them. Joe even joined them on occasion when Miranda could persuade him to leave his desk. Joe was naturally fit and had no difficulty in keeping up with the girls and joined them in the juice bar afterwards.

Then, just as they were settling back into their old routines came the call that they had stopped expecting. The estate agent in Bantry called Miranda to tell her that, if the Hunters were willing to confirm their offer, Dunmurry House was theirs. The owner had been let down too many times and he was now willing to sell at a price he considered a bargain. He wanted a non-refundable deposit of 10% to secure first option.

Immediately, a mental image of the house came back to Miranda. She had shut the image away but now it came back to her as sharp as ever. Joe, however took a dim view after the lapse of time.

'Too late honey, the moment has passed. We've both moved on.'

'Oh, Joe, not necessarily. We're doing nothing different now than we were during the summer. Why not consider it?'

'We're settled here, think of the upheaval.'

'We're stuck in the mud here you mean Joe. Darling don't you remember what we talked about? How a spell elsewhere might do wonders for your creativity, for our lives generally? Those things still apply now.'

'Hmm, we did enjoy Ireland didn't we? We'll talk about it then, chew it over for a week or two. No rash decisions, OK?'

'Thank you darling, that's all that I want from you.'

Miranda was delighted and made sure to tell the agent that, yes, they were still interested and not to sell to anyone else. Then they talked. To each other. To family, friends – Jodie thought it a strange idea but she couldn't quell Miranda's enthusiasm. Mentally she was making plans to leave already but she still had some persuading to do.

Then Joe surprised her one evening. He could see that a downright refusal would be devastating to Miranda. He loved Miranda and didn't wish to hurt her without good reason. And, the longer time went on, the more Joe realised that this wasn't a passing fancy. She wouldn't be happy, no, *they* wouldn't be entirely happy as a couple unless he agreed to go along with her on this. There would always be resentment.

And financially it was a sound decision. They had lots of money tied up in property bonds, among other investments. It was simply a matter of liquidating part of that to invest directly into the Irish market. And, in the midst of a deep recession, it was unlikely that a property such as Dunmurry would come onto the market again at such a low price in future years.

Joe realised it was simple inertia on his part. He was well capable of making the break from the home region he knew best. He would settle elsewhere and, as Miranda kept reminding him, plenty of people regularly flew the Atlantic for both business and pleasure. He wasn't about to lose anything.

So Joe agreed. No 10% deposit though and a large Dublin-based practice would carry out the survey, just so there was no chance of collusion between drinking buddies in the small town of Bantry where everyone probably knew everyone else.

Miranda was on tenterhooks, expecting any day to hear the purchase had fallen through or that the owner had changed his mind. But the survey came back basically sound, though with a long list of improvements, some imperative, others advisory. Joe and Miranda discussed everything and came to joint decisions, but Joe insisted again that an international firm of lawyers with an Irish office be retained to see to the formalities.

And at last, in the week before Christmas, the Hunters became the legal owners of Dunmurry House, Caherogullan townland, Bantry, Ireland.

Joe and Miranda wrapped up their affairs in Martha's Vineyard, though even Miranda knew that they'd be back from time to time. Permanently? Who could tell? Their house in Edgartown was entrusted to a letting agent.

They engaged the Dublin surveyors to commission and supervise the most pressing work needed at Dunmurry in their absence and, after protracted farewells mingled among the seasonal socialising, they flew to Dublin early in January. They hired a more practical SUV with which to convey their belongings and headed down the country. They checked into the Maritime Hotel on the quays in Bantry town, a booking that the hotel had been delighted to facilitate in the bleak midwinter. A little disoriented, the Hunters started to adjust to their new life.

Padraig straightened himself up, put his hand to the small of his back and, with his other hand, extracted a grubby handkerchief from his pocket and mopped his brow. Maybe he'd go inside, make himself a nice cup of tea. There wasn't a huge amount to do in the garden this time of year anyway. Maybe it was time to listen to the advice of that social worker busybody. Every month she came, no matter how unwelcome he made her. And she was dedicated enough in her role to march up more frequently if she had a mind to. Padraig stopped short of barricading his door against her. At least he could deal with this one. If he got too uncooperative they might send someone else. They might even try to remove him to a care home, God forbid!

So maybe he ought to rest more. Not that he needed to, but other people seemed to think he did.

Leaning on his fork he surveyed his work. The soil in the flower and vegetable beds had been turned time and again. The lawn had been trimmed a couple of months beforehand and hadn't needed touching since. His fences and trellises were in good order. Yes, maybe a cup of tea and then check on the tomatoes and peppers in the shed.

But first he squinted curiously down the road and through the trees. The estate agent's sign had been taken down before Christmas and the builders had been backwards and forwards since. He could hear muffled banging even now. Padraig was curious and thought he might have a little walk that way later, see what was happening.

Of course such a fine property wouldn't be left empty forever. Someone had bought it and was doing it up. Just as it had been done up before, several times. He only hoped that the owner didn't have a notion to divide the house into apartments that would house any number of people. There would be fine carry on if that happened and Padraig knew that it wouldn't work. Oh no.

Padraig continued to mull over the matter of the big house. He had seen some changes during his time at Dunmurry Cottage. He'd find out soon enough who the new people were. They would wander down this way, hesitate at the gate, speak to him politely. They would want a chat no doubt with an old countryman, their neighbour. Well that was fine because he enjoyed chatting to strangers, watching them hang onto his words as if he were the fount of all wisdom. Eejits.

Not that it was any of his business what went on up at Dunmurry House. No business at all. And anyway, things may be different up there now. These were modern times and things may have changed. Well, whatever. Whoever moved in would find out for themselves soon enough.

Joe and Miranda settled down to life in Ireland. The gales and rain sweeping in over Bantry Bay was far removed from the beautiful weather they had experienced the previous summer. The rain would lash at them as they took their morning jog along the quays. At such times it was tempting to have second thoughts about their decision to relocate here. The town of Bantry itself offered little, especially in the winter months. Lively enough during the summer, the town closed in on itself out of season. It was a bleak and depressing enough place.

The town had had its season in the sun. For 15 years, the oil terminal on nearby Whiddy Island had brought prosperity and the town thrived and preened as the local economy boomed. But the great disaster of 1979 had finished all that. Not for the first or last time, a multi-national corporation had provided jobs and given the economy a leg-up. When it was over, it was seen to have been a temporary fix; no lasting, indigenous industry or legacy had been created. The profits had been upstreamed elsewhere and little or nothing had been invested for the long term in Ireland. The town fell back once again on its fishing and tourism. And in the winter, there was precious little of either.

But Joe and Miranda had not been looking for paradise, which was just as well. They were, however, eager to move into their new home. They were pleased that, in their absence, the most pressing of the external repairs had been carried out. It was now structurally sound and the deterioration was halted. Now they were working with a Dublin interior designer to make the place habitable.

Miranda would spend an hour or so each day on the phone with the designer, as they discussed the plans. Online, he would display his ideas for colour schemes, furniture etc. And Miranda would throw in her ideas. Sometimes Joe would look up from his work and join in the discussions but was generally content to leave it to the other two.

By mid-February they started to plan their move to Dunmurry. Although there was still work to be done the house had become completely modernised and was ready to be lived in. They treated themselves to a fortnight in Cyprus, a sunny antidote to the Irish climate. Then, towards the end of March the day arrived. They handed back the keys to their suite at the Maritime Hotel. The owner was sad to see them go, not only because of the drop in his income stream but because he had found them good, agreeable company.

Padraig leant on his spade and watched as the new owners moved into Dunmurry House. A youngish couple, as far as he could make out – maybe the man was older. No children from what he could see. That they had money was not in doubt – he had already noted the non-stop comings and goings of tradesmen for the last number of weeks. Now their posh car, then a large van bringing the rest of their belongings, left no doubt.

He knew that this day would come and he was quite serene now that it had. It was true that, occasionally, he imagined that the house would be forgotten. It had been empty for so long that it might be its destiny to crumble away like so many had in Ireland; former grand residences that had become too expensive to keep up. Mortgaged to the hilt, the paintings and other valuable items auctioned off, the staff let go one by one, and finally the old major, or whoever, persuaded to give it up. No family interested in its fate, the bank losing interest in the asset that it had acquired. The same old story.

But Dunmurry lived to fight another day, saved by new owners. Padraig wondered if they would consider their investment a good one in the months to come.

The steaks were cooking gently in a garlic tomato sauce.

Everything was under control. Joe went to the fridge and extracted a bottle of 2002 Moet and a couple of flutes. They held hands and walked into the south-facing sun room. Although it was still early in the year, the room had retained what warmth the fitful sun had offered. Its remaining light was sufficient for them to pick out the relief of the land as it fell away towards the south coast. It was their first night in the house.

Miranda smiled as the cork popped and Joe filled their glasses.

'Well honey, here's to you, me and Dunmurry House.'

'You, me and Dunmurry House! Cheers Joe. And thank you.'

They sat in the cushioned wicker chairs and tried to take in their surroundings.

'Kinda hard to imagine this is all ours; the house, the view, just being in Ireland,' Miranda contemplated.

'Yeah, funny that a year ago we knew nothing about Ireland. Now we're actually living here. Remind me honey, how did all this come about?'

Miranda laughed. 'You know what, I can't remember. Yes I know! Remember that old documentary about John F Kennedy and his Irish roots? I did a little reading after that.'

'And about the same time I got to read a bit of Joyce, Yeats and that. Wrote an article on it.'

'Did it really snowball from there?'

'Must have happened that way. It's not as if we have any other connection.'

Miranda got up to turn the steaks and sat down again. Joe topped up her glass. She continued.

'Now that we're here I want to learn a little more about the country, this area in particular. The Famine, War of

Independence and all that. I'm going to look out for those old castles, ruins. And I've always had a thing about old graveyards!'

He laughed.

'Sure, go ahead and I'll join you in between projects. The accountant is horrified at the bills we've racked up on this place. One of us needs to keep working.'

She got up and hugged him.

'Well you're the best there is honey, and you love your work. Maybe I'll get bored again soon enough and look to start teaching again. I guess math is math most everywhere.'

The toasted garlic dips were perfect as were the steaks, cooked medium. An expensive bottle of red wine was shared, the last of it accompanying the cheeses of which two were local.

Then they had an early night. They were both physically and mentally exhausted from the long day but managed a fond, gentle session of lovemaking after which Joe's eyes closed, not to open again for nine hours.

Miranda lay awake for a while listening to the night sounds – the breeze in the eaves and in the leaves, occasionally the birds of the air and unidentifiable small creature noises. She thought that, two hundred years ago, most everywhere would have been perfectly silent. No mechanical or man-made sounds, no cars or aircraft. No farm machinery. Just the sounds of nature.

The sounds of the house; little creaks and sighs, comforting. The same little noises that had continued all through its lifetime. The old walls and timbers must have been witness to a lot of happenings down the years. Could the walls retain those memories in some form? And what if walls could talk?

They had not enquired as to the history of the place, only that it was built in the early 1900s. Many years then. Who had lived here, died here? She would find out. Drowsily she smiled to herself and thought how lucky and happy she was. She would make Dunmurry a happy place for both of them. In the meantime, she had a strange feeling that they were not completely alone here, but that possibility intrigued rather than worried her. As she finally drifted off she looked forward to uncovering any secrets that the house might care to share.

The next morning, their first at Dunmurry, was a typical West Cork day. A 'soft' day they called it in these parts. Cloudy with a persistent drizzle that threatened to last the day, though with no more than a light breeze to speak of. Joe and Miranda had no illusions about the Irish weather. On the contrary, the rainfall was all part of the make-up of the country, part of its fabric.

They had had quite enough of full Irish breakfasts at the Maritime. Yes, there had been healthy options but the fry-ups had been hard to resist. Both of them had put on weight again and dreaded to think what their cholesterol readings would be. So today it was cereal with fresh fruit, toast and jam. Soon (they said) they would start jogging again and maybe join the local golf club, once they had settled down.

But for now, Joe headed to his office which he'd had designed for him on the ground floor on the west side, off the main sitting room. He had several projects in hand to review and progress. Miranda was determined to get some fresh air and stretch her legs. The dishwasher loaded, she found her light rainproofs and walking boots. She poked her head around the office door to tell Joe she'd be no more than an hour and then stepped out into the dreary day.

The front of the house was looking so much better now, she decided. After the essential building works had been completed the brickwork had been completely repainted white to bring it back to the colour it had been previously. They were both very pleased with the way the property looked now.

The trees had been cut back, the lawn mowed and neatly trimmed and edged. The drive had been thoroughly weeded and treated to another load of gravel. A bird bath and sundial, neither in good condition, had appeared as the undergrowth had been cleared. Given a power wash, they were left to stand as before to await weather that might bring them back to their intended uses.

Unlatching the gate, Miranda hesitated before turning right. To the left lay Bantry town and they had worn a groove up and down that way recently.

Drops fell from the trees. The quiet road ahead glistened. If there were birds awake, they weren't making themselves heard. Perhaps they sat together in morose rows high in the branches like holidaymakers peering through guest house windows wondering if it was going to clear up. The air was clean and fresh so Miranda let her rain hood down to better enjoy the sensation.

Fields lay to left and right, some under cultivation though this morning there were no workers in sight. She walked on and shortly came to a lane leading through the fields to the left. Then, behind a hedge, a chocolate box cottage! Absolutely and totally Irish, she thought. The sort of building that featured on a thousand postcards. And the garden in front a picture of industry with rows of vegetable plants, beautifully maintained.

The sign on the small gate read 'Dunmurry Cottage'. She wondered if there was then a connection to Dunmurry House. She resolved to research the matter on the internet or perhaps the library in Bantry – no doubt there was a 'local studies' section.

She walked on past the cottage in the direction of Drimoleague with only the occasional car swishing by in the rain. She and Joe would need to jump in the car and drive out down this way to see if there were any nice pubs or restaurants this side of Drimoleague town. The latter she doubted but both of them had gotten to enjoy the sociability of Irish bars where there was always conversation to be had, and sometimes music and a bit of craic.

She walked a couple of miles and turned back. Nothing much to see or do down this way she thought, though it was great to be out in the fresh air. The trouble these days is that everybody needs to be doing something and doing it now. Times past, unless there was work to be done then people relaxed, walked, chatted. No TV or internet, just a bit of radio maybe. Mind, she pondered, she was in a fortunate position to be able to walk along country roads with no concerns.

Coming again to Dunmurry Cottage she saw now that, with the easing of the rain, an old man was in the front garden. Short and stout, balding under his peaked cap. He poked with a garden fork, fiddled with his plants.

'Good morning!' Miranda shouted as she came to the cottage.

Padraig looked up, taking stock of the stranger. An American. This would be your woman from the big house he decided.

'Good morning to you, Miss,' replied Padraig and bent

to his work again, not overly keen to be friendly though he knew it was expected.

'I wonder, could you tell me if there is a good pub nearby, somewhere that serves food?'

Padraig straightened up again by degrees, leant on his fork and contemplated this smart young woman. He decided on obfuscation while he got her measure.

'Food, is it? Now, I wouldn't have started from here Miss. Bantry now is the place for food, so I'm told.' He extended a gnarled hand in the vague direction of Bantry. 'Then if you've a mind, there's Drimoleague town.' The hand indicator swung through 180 degrees. 'It's a fine big town, so I'm told, and God willing they'd feed you there. Now, there's Shanahan's back the way a mile,' the hand swung back again, 'but the woman there's dead these last eight years and there's no one to cut the sandwiches I'd be saying. Now, would you be from Dunmurry House, Miss?'

Miranda was relieved to get a word in edgeways.

'Yes, yes I am. Me and my husband just moved in. I'm Miranda!' She briskly extended her hand over the gate. Padraig looked at it dubiously as if a market trader had offered him a green tomato. Then, cautiously, he took two steps forward and briefly grasped the small, female hand with his rough, work-worn fingers. She continued, 'Have you lived here all your life?' She looked over his shoulder at the cottage.

'Yes, indeed Miss!'

'Then you know lots about the locality.'

He removed his cap and scratched his spotted head through the thin hair.

'Well now, there's little enough to know but it would be a long day before you'd find the man who'd bate me at the local knowledge.'

'Maybe you could tell me a little some time? Something of the history, of Dunmurry House maybe?'

Padraig went into one of his long pauses. His visitor was best not knowing everything and the safest course of action was to pretend to be busy and let her go on her way. But it was a long winter and few were the chances he had of a bit of chat with anyone, and fewer still the opportunity to entertain a fine young woman.

'Then, Miss, if you'll accept a cup of tea in my poor home I'll tell you a little of what I know. Will you come in?'

Miranda followed the old man into the cottage and settled down to listen.

4

Will you boys stop horsing around and get down here this minute!'

Margaret Fitzgerald wondered how she ever kept her sanity. Why had she been blessed – cursed was the better word – with three boys? There was no sign that they had heard a word. Laughter, noise, the sound of running feet upstairs, continued unabated. Margaret looked at the top of her husband's head. He was engrossed in the Sunday Examiner, puffing away at his pipe, not a care in the world other than what he was reading in the international news columns.

'James, for God's sake. Will you instruct your children to come downstairs now!'

'Huh, what?'

James was well able to zone out the familiar sounds of chaos but his wife's semi-hysterical plea found an unwilling ear. He was miffed, much preferred not to be disturbed until it was time to set off. And, to be fair, this was the way things usually happened. Margaret arranged things so that he wasn't usually called upon to interfere in the running of the household. It generally ran smoothly without his interference, and for that he was glad.

Sighing to indicate his irritation at being disturbed, he folded the paper so as not to lose the column dealing with Italy's abolishment of the monarchy. He headed up the stairs.

Two minutes later silence reigned, apart from suppressed giggling, as the boys lined up for inspection, in order of age. Jim, the oldest was 10, Donal 9 and Jonno 8. All were dressed in their Sunday-best white shirts, grey shorts, grey socks and black shoes.

Donal and Jonno had their black hair Brylcreemed to their heads. Jim was unaccountably a ginger top and he insisted on keeping it short, crew-cut style like the American soldiers he read about in comics. Their mother gave them the once over, wiping smudges from faces with a handkerchief, adjusting and tucking in shirts, straightening socks.

'Well now, that's better. Just stay like that for an hour and maybe you'll get ice-creams after church. Now, into the car.'

The family trooped out of the front door and clambered into the black motor car; the boys in the back, Margaret in the passenger seat and James of course driving. It was a rare if not unprecedented thing for a woman to be seen driving Ireland's roads in the 1940s. The engine spluttered into life and they lurched along the drive, stopping to allow Jim to jump out and perform his gate-opening duties. Then they turned left for Bantry and gained speed along the narrow road.

The county council had made up the road as far as Dunmurry though not to the standards applying to the main roads. They therefore proceeded at 30mph, the optimal speed so as not to shake the occupants to pieces. There was little traffic, especially this far out from town. They eased past occasional donkey- and horse-drawn carts, James quieting the engine so as not to startle the four-legged beasts. A bicycle or two, a gentleman riding a horse. On another day, they would have seen the country folk along the road going about their business, maybe fetching water or milk, delivering messages and suchlike but Sunday was for Mass or church for most people.

As they reached the outskirts of town and the main road, it became much busier with everyone heading in the same general direction. Car horns tooted, people called and waved, children happily greeted others who they knew from school. Church or not, Sunday was a holiday and welcome at the end of an often arduous working week.

The Fitzgeralds eventually reached the Protestant church of St Brendan The Navigator and the churchgoers parted to let the car into the parking area. It juddered to a halt, its innards sighing with relief. The family exited and there was the usual greeting of friends, inconsequential chat about the weather, a few words with the vicar as they made their way inside.

It was an unwritten rule that certain families and personages got to sit nearer the front. Accordingly the Fitzgeralds ostentatiously made their way down the centre aisle, James nodding to acquaintances on either side as they went. They filed into the second row from the front on the left, the boys strategically arranged so that none of them sat together.

A significant number of the churchgoers at St Brendan's were the well-to-do of Bantry society. Many were landowners, or owned a sizable property, or were businessmen from the area and their families. In many cases they were of British stock, or perhaps Old Irish who had prospered down the years. Several families were recent incomers glad to be starting a new life away from the austerity of Britain. That land was just beginning its long recovery from the war which had drained it of many of its young men and much of its economic resources.

Not all of the congregation were, of course, equally well off financially. All contributed to the collection according to their means. Those at the front threw notes into the plate, their children a silver coin or two. As the plate travelled towards the back of the church, coppers started to appear but even the most impoverished old souls took pride in contributing something, however little. And so the worthy Protestant congregation bent to their weekly devotions and raised their voices in prayer and song.

Over at St Finbarr's gathered the Catholics who made up the majority of the town and surrounding areas. There were some notables among the Catholic community too, of course, and they were respected by all. Mostly though St Finbarr's was the place of worship for the ordinary Irish folk, those whose families had inhabited the area and worked the land since before anyone could remember. And such was the paucity of written records it was anyone's guess how long the lineage stretched back in most cases.

The Great Famine of the 1840s would have greatly affected the population hereabouts but the deaths, migration and emigration of those times were likewise charted mainly by word of mouth. Those stories, year by year, became more unreliable. One man's account was as good as the next and who could gainsay the old chap in the corner of the pub who claimed Brian Boru as an ancestor?

At St Finbarr's the elders of the community arrived first, then the families, large and small, dressed in their Sunday best and scrubbed well behind the ears. All filed inside in good time for the entrance of the priest and his altar servers. Presently, the church was almost full.

Then, last of all, came the young men of the town. Many of them cared not a jot for the Mass but few were unwilling to gamble their souls by missing. They would do the minimum necessary to attend and to be seen to attend. If the priest were to question their whereabouts, there would always be someone who could vouch for them.

The church itself now being full, the latecomers, relieved not to have to go in and be shown to a vacant seat, gathered around the open door. They lit up fags and muttered alternately in prayer or about the match to be played later that afternoon.

The crucial moment of the Mass was the Consecration. The bell sounded and the bread and water was transformed into the body and blood of Christ. If you got this bit it was alright, you had ticked the box. At the ringing of the bell, heads would drop and hands clasp together, fags hidden away for a minute or two. When it was over there was general relaxation once more.

No rush at the end as the congregation streamed out. Sure the pubs weren't open until 12 o'clock. It was time now to say extra hellos and to catch the beady eye of the parish priest should he emerge to mingle with his flock. The business bit of Sunday was done with.

At St Brendan's the Fitzgeralds emerged and chatted to all and sundry, the boys now allowed to chase around with their friends. Eventually, as the crowd thinned, the boys were herded up into the car. Mindful of people still milling around, James drove carefully until he neared the quays, then he suddenly sped up.

There was commotion in the back.

'Ice cream, ice cream!'

It was an old game. James screeched the car to a halt to a chorus of hurrays. Margaret led the boys in the happy charge and they joined the queue that extended out the door of the small shop.

The Fitzgeralds drove, light of heart, back to Dunmurry House. Whilst James picked up where he'd left off with the paper Margaret bustled around preparing dinner, to be served at the traditional time of 2 o'clock. The boys, liberated from their formal attire, played their various games in and around the house.

Dinner came and went. James went upstairs awhile for a nap while Margaret set to work with the dishes. Presently she might be able to sit down for an hour before preparing for tea.

Jim and Donal announced that they were going out.

'Fine. Be back before dark or there'll be trouble. Mind the river and the railway now.'

The river and railway ran to the south of the property. The railway would be no less busy today for it being a Sunday. Plenty of city folk liked to take a spin out to Bantry on a fine Sunday, to walk along the sea-front, watch the boats and eat ice-creams or sea food snacks from the vendors on the quay.

The boys shouted for Jonno but he shook his head. He was tired. Somewhat relieved the older ones didn't argue and ran off down the long path at the back of the house and out of the gate. They were sure to meet their friends down by the river. Jonno was six now but still needed to be looked after. A bit of a nuisance when the older ones were sometimes pushing their own boundaries.

Jonno lay on his bed and, after trying to read a comic, slept for half an hour or so. Then he awoke feeling better. It was a bright day outside and with school tomorrow, he didn't want to miss out on the rest of the day.

He headed off down the path towards the gate. His mother saw him go. He would be back with the others a little later looking for their supper.

But, as Jonno closed the gate behind him, he frowned and pursed his lips. He wasn't sure if he wanted to find his brothers and their friends. There weren't any boys of his own age. He wanted someone to wrestle with or to race against – he was the smallest and always came last. And anyway, Jim and Donal didn't really want him there.

So Jonno's feet took him east, alongside the river. The boys didn't come this way very often. It was a bit boring and they'd never found much to do. Jonno found a stick and whipped the reeds and grasses that grew alongside the slow-moving river as he slouched along. He crouched and watched the fish and tiddlers which darted to and fro, splashed the water with his stick to startle them. Then he stopped to wave as the train came through from Drimoleague, crowded with Sunday trippers and was pleased when plenty of the passengers waved back. Within the hour the same train would be heading back to Cork.

He walked some more until the path began to get rather muddy, then decided to turn back. No new friends down this way. How boring. Why did they live here anyway, out in the country? No shops even. Dublin was full of shops, he'd seen pictures. You could buy anything there. Maybe when he was old enough he'd run away to Dublin.

He came to a point where another path cut up to the right, away from the river. He had always been told not to wander but he wasn't too far away from the house anyway. And sure enough the little path took him through a wall onto the road which ran past their house. He knew this for two reasons. First, there were no other roads around here, just tracks and ageless boreens. Second, he had emerged right opposite Dunmurry Cottage where the old man lived.

Decisions. Jonno idly wondered whether to just follow the road the 100 yards or so home or to retrace his steps back to the river. The train would be coming out again from Bantry any time now. Or maybe he'd be bold and go down the lane behind the old man's little cottage. It wasn't as if he was going to the fairy fort or anything.

The fairy fort! They were all under strict instructions never to go there. Their parents had told them, and the old man at the cottage had said the same, one time he had found them hanging around. No reasons were given but Jonno had never known his brothers go there, and he himself certainly hadn't. It was in a field down that lane.

He decided to wander down the lane a little, then come back and go home. He was getting hungry. The lane was no more than a boreen with cartwheel tracks leaving a grassy middle bit. Jonno headed idly down the boreen, swishing his stick as he went. No fairies would mess with him, he'd swish them with his stick like this, swish!

To the left was a potato field, a little while yet before they would be ready for lifting. To the right a grassy field in which sheep peacefully grazed. Jonno bahh-ed at them but got no reply, just blank looks. He sighed and slouched onwards.

There, that must be it. Over in the far corner of the sheep field was a grassy mound with what looked like a few hawthorn bushes growing on its slopes. All around the land was flat, just this little hill tucked in the corner where the hedges met. Jonno stopped and stared. Were there really fairies there? He didn't think so. Fairies were just in story books for girls! Little white things with wings and sparkles in their hair waving wands with magic fairy dust. Still it might be fun to try to catch one, or swish it with his stick.

The hedge and wire fence was no barrier to a six year-old boy and he soon emerged onto the grassy field, startling the woolly inhabitants who cantered away in consternation. Jonno took no notice of them. Still swishing his stick bravely he marched towards the fairy fort, eyes peeled for fairies.

As he got closer his paced slowed, his heart quickened and his eyes sharpened. He listened intently. Nothing. He stepped the last few yards to the mound as quietly as he could. The mound was shallow, not much higher than the boy himself. Slowly he walked around it, noticing nothing. He arrived back at his starting place and sighed. He wished he had gone with his brothers after all.

Still, now he was here he might as well climb to the top. And so he did, weaving between the rather straggly hawthorn bushes. He reached the top and turned around to view the land, and a fine view it was too. He could easily make out his own house from here, peeking from behind the trees. He wondered whether or not to tell his brothers that he had been to the fairy fort. Would they snitch on him? But it was no good having a secret just to give it away to anyone. No, he'd keep his secret until he found a friend his own age. Maybe they'd come here together.

Fairies were no longer on his mind as he started down the slope again, but then! He saw something with the corner of his eye. Something had moved. He turned his head to stare at the spot where he fancied he had seen the movement. Nothing, or maybe a bird or a mouse. He set off again.

But again something moved. Something red! What was it? Jonno jumped off the slope and walked quickly around the mound towards where he thought he had seen something. Then he heard a noise, like a little girl giggling. It came from above. Startled he looked up. And there, behind the bush at the top of the mound sat a little man. The little man looked at him and laughed his giggly laugh. He had on a red cap, green jacket and brown trousers and boots. He was tiny, just about half of Jonno's size.

Well, small boys might run from giants and tigers but not from little men.

'Hello,' said Jonno tentatively.

The little man giggled again, and then replied, 'Hello,' in a strange, squeaky voice.

The two looked at one another.

'What's your name?' asked Jonno, breaking the silence.

'My name? Jack, of course. And you're Jonno,' said Jack in between giggles.

'Is this your house?'

'Well, to be sure, this is my house. How kind of you to visit.'

'Thank you. We're not allowed to come here you know.'

'Why ever not?'

'No one has ever told us. Can I come up and sit with you?'

'Indeed you may.'

So Jonno climbed the mound again and sat down between the giggling Jack and the topmost hawthorn bush. He looked at Jack and said

'You're very small.'

'Of course. We couldn't live under the ground if we were tall like you.'

It was the first time anyone had thought Jonno tall and he felt strangely proud.

'Are there more of you?'

'More? Yes of course.'

'Who are you? Where do you come from?'

'You are the curious boy aren't you? I'm one of the fairies, the good folk.'

'Oh! You're different to what I thought.'

'Not many from the outside see us, that's why.'

'Where do you come from?'

'Well now, that's a good question. The truth of the matter is that we are fallen angels. We were not good enough to be saved yet not bad enough to be lost.'

Jonno didn't understand this at all, but he was beginning to like the little man.

'Can I bring my brothers and friends here to meet you?'

'Why, yes. Of course! But before you go, you must meet my wife. Come this way.'

So Jonno followed Jack down from the top and there, leading into the mound, was a narrow tunnel. Jonno was sure he hadn't seen this before. Still laughing and giggling Jack led the way. And Jonno followed.

The Fitzgeralds left Dunmurry within the month. The search had continued for many days. The distraught family together with neighbours, Gardai and many volunteers combed the lanes, woods and fields for miles around. The river was searched for several miles downriver. But Jonno had just disappeared. No one had seen him since his mother had watched him open the gate that Sunday afternoon. When all hope had been lost and the last searchers had gone home James and Margaret decided that they couldn't live at Dunmurry House any longer. They left the property in the hands of an agent and left to try to rebuild their lives in Dublin.

5

It was the Murphy sisters, Kathleen and Olive, who had finally bought Dunmurry House for the moderate asking price. In the depressed years following the Emergency there was not much money about and not everybody was keen to live in the West Cork countryside. Some well-to-do families came to view the property but no firm offers were made. It was just a little too far from Bantry Town for most.

It was also the case that, even before the Fitzgerald affair, Dunmurry had something of a reputation. Even the original builders in 1901 had been none too happy working here and had left the site well before dusk descended. Old ones and storytellers would say that the good folk inhabited the land around Dunmurry and often created mischief. The local inhabitants would never disturb the fairy fort in the field behind Dunmurry Cottage for fear of angering the inhabitants. Too many strange things had happened down the years if you were to pay heed to those who would romance away beside the log fire in a Bantry pub for the price of a whiskey.

The Murphy women took no heed at all. They were no nonsense middle-aged spinsters from Cork city. They had made a pretty living out of buying and selling property in the city. They paid a low price to owners, waving the cash in front of them as an incentive. A superficial decoration job later, the property was back on the market at a handy profit, together with a cut from their recommended lender. But now they wearied of the daily cut and thrust and had sold the business. They saw a bargain in Dunmurry House, and also a quieter way of life which they both hankered after.

No motor car for them. They were quite content with their horse Hercules and trap. On a Wednesday, market day, they would spend the day in Bantry shopping, having lunch, socialising. Maybe even an early evening drink or two before heading home. On Sundays they were regular churchgoers, St Brendan's of course. They took out memberships for the golf club and, during summer months, played once a week.

Otherwise, they were happy enough in each other's company at Dunmurry House. They would sew, write and cook, Radio Eireann playing a mixture of classical, big band and jazz from the corner cabinet. They were early to bed and early to rise.

Often they would walk, alone or together, gathering wild flowers, herbs and berries, the latter to be used in the making of jam or, indeed, pies. Thus, it was one fine morning that Kathleen set off through the back gate with her basket. A little footbridge took her over the river to the railway line. Crossing over the line to the hedge alongside the farmland a profusion of flowers grew, pollinated by the many bees and insects, there for the taking. The train from Bantry puffed into sight, next stop Drimoleague, then onwards to the Albert Quay in Cork. Kathleen watched and waved as it trundled by and disappeared down the line. Then she recommenced her gathering.

Presently she looked up in surprise. She had been joined by a young boy, no more than six or seven. Kathleen was sure that she hadn't seen him around before. Indeed there were few enough children living in the area these days.

'Good morning young man!'

'Good morning. Please can you help me find my brothers?'

'Your brothers? Where are they? Are you lost?'

There was no answer. The boy just looked at her.

'Cat got your tongue? Where do you live?'

The boy waved vaguely in the direction of Dunmurry House, perhaps beyond. He spoke again in a strange, reedy voice.

'Can you help me find my brothers?'

For answer Kathleen said,

'Run away now, over the bridge. Your brothers are sure to be close by. Be off with you!'

The boy continued to look at her, expressionless, then slowly turned away. Kathleen commenced once more to survey the plentiful flowers, picking the choice ones. She turned her head once to ensure the boy had crossed the line and bridge but, oddly, he was already out of sight. She looked briefly about her, shrugged her shoulders and thought no more of it. Vaguely she noted the vibration of the rails as another train approached.

Some time later an exasperated Olive stomped through the gate at the bottom of the garden. It was well past dinner time and Kathleen had not put in an appearance. This was most unusual and unsatisfactory. She would give her sister a piece of her mind. Calling out her name, Olive crossed the wooden bridge and looked up and down the length of the railway line. Nothing. Crossly she marched a few steps westward, where she found Kathleen. Her dress, as brightly coloured as the flowers, gave her away. Her body, quite lifeless, lay alongside the hedge as if thrown there by a great impact. Her eyes stared open, her basket several yards away, the flowers scattered.

Olive lived on at Dunmurry for several more years, even taking a husband for a brief time. There being no divorce mechanism in Ireland they travelled to England to be officially unwed. Things were never quite the same after that. To her own annoyance Olive grew lonely. One day she loaded up the trap for the last time and turned a surprised old Hercules to the east on their final journey back to Cork city.

6

Miranda perhaps outstayed her welcome at Dunmurry Cottage. She was mesmerised by Padraig's storytelling. The old man seemed delighted to have company and was in his element as he sat back in his old armchair which seemed to mould itself around his body.

At first Miranda excitedly asked questions, but soon realised that she would get best value out of simply listening. Padraig spoke quietly but with enthusiasm. When he had finished a story, or a segment, he would lean back and think, his mind elsewhere. Then he would start again.

In these silences Miranda would think that maybe the old man had had enough of her company and would stand up to take her leave. But, just as often he would raise his hand and say, 'Wait there now awhile, Miss. Here's another thing.'

Padraig spun tales of the townland and some of the characters that had lived hereabouts down the years. There was the woman who had kept cats and, when she died, the cats stayed with her body and died alongside her one by one though there were windows open. The man with his donkey and cart who happened to have every item for sale that you might wish for. On the rare occasion he hadn't got it he would return the very next day with the item required. The tinkers that would roam the county in their colourful horse-drawn caravans. The menfolk would fix your pots and pans by day. By night they would play cards, drink and quarrel around their camp fires. Their dogs would keep watch, barking wildly at any stranger that drew near. Then they licked the faces off them once they were welcomed in by the tinkers.

Those were the times when the farmers used to milk the cows and take the churns of milk down to the roadside. There they would be picked up to be taken to the creamery, the churns returned later. Every man had a bike, and plenty women too, for it was the only means of transportation for many. Life was lived at a steady pace, governed only by the seasons and the work to be done between dawn and dusk.

The countryside thrived on gossip, there being little other entertainment. Two women passing on the road would always stop and wring the latest news out of one another. If one woman reported a child had a cold, by the afternoon the little one was at death's door. If a young wan was seen looking at a boy at Mass the gossips would almost have her at the altar within a week. Nothing could be said or done but everyone in the district knew about it within the hour. And these the days before all your televisions, telephones and internets.

But what Miranda really wanted to hear was about Dunmurry House, its history, the people who had lived there. Padraig proved surprisingly vague on the subject, evasive even it seemed to Miranda. 'About a hundred years ago' was his best stab at the age of the house, but didn't argue when Miranda said she was sure it was constructed in 1901. It had been considered a 'safe house' during the War of Independence and the Civil War that followed. Members of the guerrilla flying columns and anti-Treaty fighters would find food and shelter there in what was a fine house owned by an Old-Irish landowner with no apparent political connections, and his family.

Owners had come and gone, said Padraig. It had been a

hotel one time, a convent house another time. He couldn't remember the names of the various people, he said.

Seeing the old man was tired she eventually took her leave, thanking him for his hospitality. She said that he must stop by Dunmurry House one day to meet her husband. She was surprised and slightly offended that Padraig's eyebrows shot up and he politely but firmly said that he wouldn't dream of disturbing them in their fine house.

Puzzled, Miranda returned home.

Not for long. Joe was ready to go for a run. He'd finished an article to his satisfaction and had sent it off to a highbrow New York magazine which paid him handsomely for what he considered was 'old rope' that he could knock out at the drop of a hat with little or no research. Just now Joe's followers seemed to be hooked on his accounts of life in Ireland, and he could write such stuff almost without thinking. Nevertheless he fancied a break before embarking on his next, rather more demanding, project.

Miranda was happy to join him and quickly got her gear on. She now loved running and was always convinced that she had a pound or two to lose. They set off towards Drimoleague, deliberately steadily at first. They would automatically hit their optimal pace as their rhythm kicked in. Almost immediately, they were back opposite Dunmurry Cottage but Padraig was nowhere in sight. Most likely asleep thought Miranda. Still breathing easily Miranda started to tell Joe about the old man, and the information he'd given and the stories he'd told.

Joe listened politely enough and laughed and commented in the right places. But he really didn't share Miranda's fascination with the past. His life, his work was in the present and looking to the future. Sub-consciously he drew a line under each day, put it behind him and moved on ever forwards. As they ran together, their feet now matching each other's rhythm, Miranda talked of the past. Joe mentally shuffled his work projects, ideas, timelines, deadlines. He changed tack and considered his investment portfolio. The purchase of Dunmurry had been a shift out of property company shares into direct property investment. No big deal. And it had enriched both of their personal lives, for the time being. But, for Joe, it was primarily a financial investment. For Miranda it was already much more.

They ran easily for 25 minutes then, by agreement, they stopped and turned around. Checking their watches they now decided to step it up and aim to do the return trip in just 20 minutes. Joe was the stronger runner and would be expecting to make the target. Now there was less chat. For one thing the increasing effort made it impossible to do anything other than gasp a word or two at a time. For another it required concentration on the job in hand, an awareness of body position, foot strike rate, positive relaxation, arm drive to deliver the best possible running outcome. They ran side by side facing what little oncoming traffic there was. It really was the quietest of roads serving mainly local traffic, including delivery vans and lorries servicing the small towns and townlands in this part of the county. The main road to Cork to the south was the one that carried the most traffic – it was fast and dual carriageway most of the way.

Imperceptibly, their pace increased despite now running into the westerly breeze. Strike rate and breathing quickened together. Joe as usual was the stronger but Miranda dug in, determined to match him for as long as she could. But as

Dunmurry Cottage came into sight he pulled away and she immediately slowed, rhythm and impetus lost. Breathless she joined him on leaning on the old gates, gasping, checking her watch. Joe had beaten the target by seconds, Miranda more than a minute outside, but they were both happy with their runs.

Showered and changed, Miranda made them both a light lunch. Joe was getting very partial to the Irish brown soda bread and this with slices of beef, ham and cheese went down very well with the coffee. He went back to his office refreshed. Miranda mooched about, did some tidying and cleaning though they had a regular cleaner. She picked up a book or two but couldn't get into them. Finally she closed her eyes and slept awhile.

As a consequence that same night she slept fitfully. Joe snored peacefully beside her. Half-awake she lay on her back listening to the breeze play in the trees, to the occasional voice of a creature, one of many who frequented the nearby copses and farmland. No other sound. What a long way they were from the USA! They had settled well even though it was still early days.

Miranda considered that, in all probability, they wouldn't see out the rest of their days here at Dunmurry but it suited them well at present. She loved the house and the surrounding countryside. Joe was writing as well and as productively as ever. She, Miranda, was quickly settling down into the Irish pace of life where any task not immediately necessary was deferred until the following day. Joe couldn't afford that luxury but still appeared to be content.

Her iPhone told her that it was just past twelve, the

witching hour. She decided to get up and make herself a cup of herb tea. It never failed. Quietly she slipped out of bed, found her dressing gown on the chair and slowly felt her way along the balcony rails and then down the stairs. She flicked on the light as she reached the kitchen.

Drowsily, she made herself a cup of chamomile tea and brought it through to the big main room. By the light of a reading lamp she flicked through the pages of yesterday's Independent. The country's economic woes interested her in a detached sort of way. She and Joe were fortunate in that they weren't really affected by adverse trade figures, austerity budgets, new taxes. Their accountant ensured that their earnings attracted the least possible tax, and their move to Ireland had assisted this though it hadn't figured in their decision. The IRS …

Miranda froze. Her eyes widened and were drawn towards the wall to her right. She saw nothing, heard nothing. But something was there, quite clearly. From the wall the 'something' moved across the room in front of her, slowly. And although she saw or heard nothing Miranda followed its progress. It stopped. Then after a few seconds it continued and then seemed to exit the wall to the left.

Miranda was transfixed. She shook her head, closed her eyes and re-opened them. Had she fallen asleep briefly and dreamt something? No, she had been reading the newspaper and then … something had made its way across the room right in front of her. It had made no sound and she hadn't actually seen anything. A person? She couldn't tell. She wasn't frightened. Wasn't a woman meant to run around hysterically at this point?

She ought to tell Joe right away. But what would he say? 'Honey, you saw nothing and heard nothing? Hey let's call the cops. Look, you nodded off for a second there, had a little dream. Too much cheese. Now come back to bed.' No, Joe wouldn't believe her and it was best to say nothing or he might start worrying about her.

So, maybe they weren't alone at Dunmurry. Somehow that realisation didn't surprise her. A house more than a hundred years old. So much must have happened here. The original walls were still in place. What if those walls could talk? What if the walls had a memory? What if something of past times were to escape those walls, that memory, from time to time?

What had happened here? Padraig had skipped over the details though he surely knew more than he was telling. He had lived down the road all his life. The old Irish folk had the uncanny means of extracting your life history from you within five minutes so it was impossible that Padraig didn't carry such knowledge in his head. He was as bright as a button despite his great age. Why hadn't he told her more? Was it to protect her, or to protect himself in some way?

Miranda studied the room again, finished up her tea. She was intrigued. Would the 'something' come again? She hoped it would, and maybe more would be revealed in time. After all, hadn't they come to the ancient land of spirits, fairies and leprechauns? She couldn't wait to solve this little mystery.

Miranda carefully slipped in beside Joe. They had no secrets but this one was best kept to herself, for now anyway. Within seconds she was sound asleep.

7

Dunmurry, 1954–1975

Olive had left and, after another period of neglect, Dunmurry House was bought by an order of nuns for use as a care home for wayward girls and young women. Thus began the darkest of periods in the house's history. The place was universally hated though few were the stories that escaped from that miserable place. Girls and young women were sent here by the county council and indeed sometimes by their own families. They had fallen pregnant outside marriage or had otherwise been judged immoral and unfit to live alongside decent people. Often it was enough to have been caught using make-up or perhaps kissing a boy after a cinema show.

Once handed over to the nuns, the young women were of no further concern to the authorities. They would be looked after and taught a lesson at Dunmurry and that was the end of it. It was mostly their parents who were glad to see the back of them. They had brought shame on the family. Sending the recalcitrant child to the nuns was the best thing they could do to redeem themselves in the eyes of God and of their neighbours. And sure didn't they have plenty of other, good children to worry about?

The regime at Dunmurry was a harsh one. A bell rang at 6.30 each morning and the girls were expected to be downstairs by seven for prayers.

There were usually six nuns in residence. In the early

days, Sister Agnes was the eldest nun and nominally in charge. Due to her age and frailty, however, the real power lay elsewhere. As long as Agnes was consulted on important matters, she was content to leave the day to day running of the establishment to Sister Bernadette.

Each of the nuns in residence took turns to deliver the morning service. The girls were forced to kneel on the hard, wooden floor of the big room, listening and responding to the prayers. Then, with relief, they would clamber to their feet to sing the appointed hymn for the day, following the words in their prayer books.

Immaculate Mary thy praises we sing
Who reignest in splendour with Jesus Our King
Ave Ave Ave Maria
Ave Ave Ave Maria

Not singing loud enough or whispering to the next girl was likely to draw a slapped cheek from one of the nuns patrolling the room.

There was always a sermon, and it always had the same central theme. The girls had only one chance of redemption and that was prayer, obedience and hard work.

Breakfast followed. Tables and chairs, cleared away for the morning service, were reassembled and the girls sat down. It was two local, respectable women who were employed as the kitchen staff. They slammed down the bowls of porridge, chunks of bread and teapots on the tables. Never a change – porridge, bread and tea. Nonetheless the girls made sure to finish all that was offered as nothing else would be forthcoming.

Talking was not allowed but the sound of a heavy hand

against head was common as the girls risked a bit of news or gossip. Mostly there was silence though, as the girls well knew that all misdemeanors were quietly noted for further and greater punishment down the line.

Then to work. There were three main work details – garden, house and laundry. In a rare demonstration of humanity, or more probably practicality, the more heavily pregnant were spared the garden. Instead, they either worked in the laundry house or the main residence itself. The laundry was not only that of the house itself. The home took in paid work from residents of the surrounding countryside. In this way, the grant from the county council was supplemented while making work for idle hands.

The laundry house was situated in the gardens behind the big house, down near the river. Water supplies were hauled up from the river by bucket, the girls forming a chain gang. A concrete platform jutted out into the river from where the girls would stoop to dip their buckets in all weathers.

A van would collect the dirty laundry from the customers in the morning and would deliver it, clean and neatly folded, during the afternoon of the following day. The two big boilers bubbled away non-stop, the sweating girls loading and unloading, putting the garments, bedding and so forth through the mangle, until every last drop had been extracted.

'Here. These are ready. Stack them with those others there.'

'Is there much more to come? Jesus there's loads!'

'Breda O'Shaughnessy! I heard you blaspheming. In your free time later you'll kneel in front of everybody and say a complete round of the Rosary. Do you hear me?'

'Yes Sister.'

The clothing would then be hung on washing lines,

outside for preference but, with the propensity for rain in the south-west of Ireland, in the drying room if necessary. And many were the panics to unpeg the clothes hung outside after optimism over the weather had proved wrong.

Whatever the logistics and problems encountered the laundry had to be ready in time for delivery to the customers. The nun in charge (they would rotate, no one wanted the job) would become more and more hysterical if time was getting tight. This transmitted itself to the girls and the pace of work increased, nerves got fraught and mistakes crept in. Most times though, the work got done satisfactorily and a measure of relaxation was allowed towards the day's end.

Garden detail was the hardest and it suited the strongest. Nevertheless, on a fine day, the girls welcomed being in the open air. They might be working hard but at least they were not sweltering in the laundry house, or worse, confined in the hated house itself.

To the front of Dunmurry House were lawns, flower beds, the impressive gravel drive and a hedge running from the gate and along the road, turning at right angles at the property boundary. From there, the hedge ran alongside the lawns and behind the main house and the laundry buildings before petering out as it approached the river.

At the south-facing rear most of the land was given over to vegetable growing. Some of the produce went towards feeding the establishment but mostly it was considered too valuable for that. The vegetables, each to their season, were bagged and sold to wholesalers who would in turn sell on to retailers and maybe the larger hotels in Bantry and its environs.

From morning to night the girls toiled. They dug, planted, weeded, raked, pruned, cut, tended, harvested and bagged. For most of the year they worked in all weathers, watched over by the gimlet-eyed nuns. Their hands would be blistered, muscles ached, backs often in agony for hours afterwards. In winter when there was less to do outside, they would be found indoor work. If there was no work it was either invented or the same work, such as cleaning and polishing, done a second time.

Needless to say, the interior of Dunmurry House was always pristine. The residents swept, scrubbed, polished, wiped. If ever a spot or stain or, God forbid, a dustball remained, or if a nun ran a finger along a picture rail and discovered dust, there was trouble for she who was responsible.

A day never went by when two or three of the girls didn't get a taste of the tawse. For offences real or imaginary, Sister Bernadette would deliver a minimum one, usually more, strike on the hand or leg. Sometimes a hard-faced younger nun was tutored in the punishment, inevitably being urged to lay on harder.

Tears cut no ice with the nuns. If ever they had human feelings of sympathy, their training and subsequent apprenticeship had dispelled all such emotion. Their idea of the love of God was that all should suffer in this life to be worthy of entering His Kingdom. It was their duty on earth that those entrusted to their care followed a narrow path of hard work and obedience. The question of happiness or sadness was neither here nor there.

A sandwich at midday and a basic evening meal were nonetheless highlights of the girls' day. Before bedtime, there was a rare relaxation of the regimen and the girls were allowed to read, talk quietly, or walk in the grounds if it were still light. Eight-thirty was bedtime, nine was lights out. No talking allowed in the bedrooms which each held a number of narrow, cot-like beds. Whispers were of course exchanged, at the risk of being caught should a door suddenly open in a spot check.

The time between lights-out and sleep was the worst. Sobs could often be heard in the quiet of the late evening. All were here against their will and most had been unexpectedly taken from a good life, a good home. Most had grown up as happy, carefree country girls, often with brothers and sisters. Life in rural Ireland was hard and they'd had only the basics, but that had always been enough. Each day was a new and exciting one – school friends to see, siblings to play and wrestle with, a mother to give cuddles and fix a grazed knee, a hard-working father to nuzzle up to as he smoked his pipe after a day in the fields.

But now they were all alone, apparently forgotten. Of course they knew that they'd done wrong and must be punished – weren't they reminded every day? But it was hard, so hard, not to be allowed to see their mother and father at least. Surely they still loved them? But if they did why didn't they come and take them away from this awful place? They'd learnt their lesson. They'd thought it was a lark to wink at the boys and to go down the lane with one or other of them. They didn't realise it was a bad thing. They'd seen the grown-ups kissing and no one said anything. It had been a mistake, they had done wrong, but this was so hard.

The poor girls who had fallen pregnant at least had an escape route. When their time drew near they would be packed off to somewhere called The Laundries in Cork City.

There they would have their child, love it, care for it. They would be looked after themselves and a house would be found for them. Then, in due course, they would take the child back to meet its grandparents and everyone would be happy.

That was what they were told.

But for the others there seemed no end to the nightmare. Those that plucked up the courage to ask about their future invariably got the tawse for answer. Occasionally a girl was suddenly not there any more. She had been replaced. Dunmurry could only hold so many residents. If a young woman was sent there, and there was no place, one had to be found. It would be then that Sister Bernadette would consult with Sister Agnes and decide which, if any, of the girls was worthy of being released from care. In this way a young woman might suddenly find herself on the roadside with her worldly belongings in a small suitcase, thumbing a lift to Bantry and an uncertain future.

Yes, the time between lights-out and sleep was the worst. And, from time to time, pure misery and the want of a little comfort and love meant that beds were shared and tears spent on each other's shoulders.

Of course, there were ways and means of ingratiating oneself with the nuns. This way the tawse came less often, you got an easier work detail and perhaps a bigger helping at the evening meal. The best way was to suck up to the nuns, offering them gifts, flattering them, snitching on the other girls. Occasionally girls would leave their bed at night returning an hour or more later. Rumours would have abounded if conditions had allowed.

Sundays were dreaded. Work was light and, if the weather

was fine, there was maybe the chance of an accompanied walk along the river or the lanes. But it was the day Father Dick came to say Mass. The Mass and sermon was fine. Most of the girls enjoyed reciting the Latin prayers and the formulaic progress of the ceremony was a small link to the outside world of their past. Parents and friends would, all over the country, be reciting or singing the same words at much the same time.

Credo in unum deum
Patrem omnipotentem, factorem caeli et terrae
Visibilium omnium et invisibilium
Et in unum Dominum Jesum Christum

But as Father Dick's closing sermon came to an end the dread increased. Two of the girls – to the relief of the others – would be instructed to assist Father Dick in disrobing in the private room adjacent to the big room. However, the disrobing was always accompanied by a spanking for having been 'naughty' during the week. The older girls well knew was going on and any new one, alarmed by the priest's behaviour, was coached by the elder how it would be all over the quicker.

'Now, Susan is it? For your behaviour, off with your knickers and over my knee here.'

'Pardon? But Father I haven't misbehaved … I …'

'Now! Or it will be double.'

'But Father…'

'Susan, do as Father says, now. It doesn't hurt much.'

'Good girl Niamh, easy strokes for you today.'

This way the ordeal was over with quickly. The girls would be dismissed. A little later the nuns would line up to say farewell to Father Dick as he got into his car to drive back to town. He looked forward to Sundays at Dunmurry.

8

'But why Ma? I'm sixteen, I'm not a baby. And Mary-Jo and Roseanne are going.'

'Look my girl, I've said no and I mean no. And your father agrees with me. No one with morals frequents that establishment.'

'Morals! Listen to yourself Ma! It's bloody 1970. No one talks like that any more. It's only a dance for Christ's sake!'

'Don't you blaspheme in this house my girl, do you hear? I'll have Father Kelly out the road to you and all the neighbours will know about it. Now go to your room!'

'Oh fu… blast Father Kelly! He knows nothing about anything of the modern world. What does he know about having fun? Cop yourself on Ma, the world has changed.'

'You brazen harlot you, speaking ill of a priest! I wish I could wash my hands of you. What did I do to deserve the Devil in my house?'

And with that Maggie Spencer sunk onto the kitchen chair, sobbing into a tea towel, her shoulders moving silently up and down. Orla looked at her mother with exasperation. On the stove, potatoes bubbled away in one saucepan, cabbage in another. A pair of bream lay, wrapped in newspaper on the chopping board awaiting beheading, de-scaling and boning. On the windowsill a grimy transistor radio, permanently tuned to Radio Eireann, played a mixture of showband and popular tunes, punctuated now and again by national news items.

This Friday evening scene had hardly changed in all of Orla's 16 years, she thought. Outside the front door the wet, darkening streets of Dunmanway town slished with the sound of passing traffic. The start of another dreary weekend.

Sighing, the red-haired, rather tall girl decided on alternative tactics. Unwrapping the fish she opened the cutlery drawer and found the long, sharp fish knife. This was half its original width having been honed weekly on the back step by her mother, and her mother before her.

'Sharpen the knife!' came the voice from the chair, the automatic response to the removal of the fish knife from the drawer. Orla drew the knife across the step, zing, zing, zing. She darkly imagined drawing it against her mother's throat. She thought they'd never eat fish again if the knife were to be lost or broken. No other would ever do.

She hated preparing fish, and rarely offered. She preferred to slouch in a chair reading a magazine. But she needed to do something to get back in her mother's good books. She would literally die if she had to spend another wet weekend in this town without a bit of excitement.

The matter under heated discussion was the weekly dance at the Lilac Ballroom in Enniskeane. A glitzy venue, the Lilac was the present destination of choice for the young men and women for miles around. It offered music, dancing and companionship – all of which were in short supply in West Cork.

Short supply that is, unless you counted the dances that took place at various church halls. Orla had been to plenty of these, together with her friends. And they were fine if you were happy to ignore the eagle eye of the priest who presided over the occasion. The boys would eye the girls up and vice versa. Occasionally they would dance with strict rules and conditions in effect. Arms length, no roving hands, most definitely no smooching or kissing. Sure, it was well-known what went on later in the dark lanes outside, especially if the boy had paid the girl's entrance fee. But to be discovered was to risk being denounced from the pulpit, identities barely disguised, so it was hardly worth the effort.

The Lilac was where it was at, where the cool cats hung out, where a bit of craic was to be had. Orla was determined to go with her friends.

The first fish was scaled to her satisfaction. She picked up the second, cleared her throat and produced her little-girl voice.

'Ma?'

'No. You have my answer.'

'It's not what you think. There's no drink and it's all strictly supervised.'

'Strictly supervised, my hat! And would all present be sober then, there being no drink for sale?'

'Ma, no one is allowed in with drink taken. It's exactly like the church dances.'

'My eye! And then why do all the blackguards and gurriers for miles around make a beeline there instead of to the church dances?'

'Ma, we'll be going with Rory and John. They're no blackguards are they? I'll be very safe.'

There was a period of silence. Starting on the fish heads, Orla sensed the tide turning. She kept the pressure on.

'Ma, we'll go in Rory's car and come straight home afterwards. I don't want to be late anyway because I want to get early Mass on Sunday.' 'Jesus,' Orla thought, 'if she buys that then anything's possible.'

'And then there's all that lovemaking. You don't know

what manner of lout will be there preying on young girls from good, Catholic homes.'

Orla pursed her lips and suppressed a sigh. Lovemaking indeed. A girl would be lucky to get a kiss.

'Ma, I've got no interest in boys. I'm too young. I just want to be with my friends, listen to the new bands, dance. Please Ma?'

She went to her mother who still sat on the chair and hugged her around her shoulders and kissed her hair. Her last throw of the dice.

'Well so, we'll see.'

'Yay, thank you Ma, you're the best!'

Happily, and before her mother could change her mind, Orla skipped back to the chopping board to finish dealing with the bream.

ENNISKEANE, WEST CORK 1970

She stood, mesmerised. The big neon light sign above the hall flashed, promising a great time to all who would pay the entrance fee and come inside. Her friends Roseanne and Mary-Jo, both of whom were old Lilac hands, lit up fags and scouted all around them, taking in the scene.

The lads had gone for a quick drink and they wouldn't be long, they said. Rory had driven them all out from Dunmanway in no time at all, swinging the Vauxhall Viscount with abandon along the, largely unlit, country roads. There was plenty of parking in front of the hall and, as eleven o'clock approached, the place was getting busier as more cars arrived from the surrounding countryside.

The girls hung around by the car, wrapping their shawls closer around their shoulders against the cold breeze. They fidgeted about, anxious to get inside. Occasionally one or the other would see and greet a friend, mutually admiring dresses, hairstyles, saying 'hi' to friends of friends.

Orla knew no one apart from her two friends, and of course Rory and John. She was nervous now, not quite knowing how to act, unsure of herself in these strange surroundings. She had on her best dress, a grown-up dress showing off her pale shoulders and a lowish neckline, though not so low as to bring on more tribulation from her mother. It had been a compromise purchase but Orla was happy with it. She had slapped on the make-up liberally, heavy on the eye shadow as she had seen the older ones do. She now pulled out her lipstick from her handbag and applied a little more, checking in her compact mirror and surreptitiously pursing her lips to see the effect. She sighed. She considered her face too thin, nose too sharp, cheekbones too high. Which boy would ever ask her to dance – a blind one maybe? But already there were admiring glances from both boys and girls at the striking tall girl with the red hair.

At last the local pubs seemed to be emptying and, to Orla's relief, Rory and John reappeared refreshed and ready for action. The five of them joined the queue which had suddenly formed outside the doors which led into the foyer.

Orla had her half-crown ready, it was double for the men. It was money that Orla could ill afford. All of her group seemed to be paying their own entrance so that way there could be no misunderstandings afterwards.

They paid their money and took a ticket. Mary-Jo reminded Orla to keep the ticket as a pass-out, in case she went outside later and needed to regain entrance. Now they could hear the band, and the music hit them as they pushed through the swing doors into the hall.

At the far end was the band, presently playing an Irish dance-tune set. This was expected early in the night and only two couples were taking advantage to swing each other around the floor.

'See ya later,' said Rory and John and they wandered over to where the men were standing. Orla followed Mary-Jo and Roseanne across to the opposite wall to join the women. There her two friends chatted animatedly to others they knew, Orla joining in when she could. She didn't want to be the wallflower that no one talked to. Some, though very few, of the women smoked cigarettes. Orla had never tried one and had no intention of doing so. By contrast most of the men puffed away creating a foggy, slightly mysterious atmosphere over the dance floor.

At the end of each set – three tunes – the band paused for a few minutes and sipped from bottles of water. Some of the women headed off to the toilets or to the café-bar. Orla looked across the smoky room at the men. Almost all men these days had long hair, in complete contrast to the clean-cut looks of the showband who were getting ready to play again. Most had jackets and ties though, and flared trousers were all the rage. The men were laughing, joshing, horsing about, showing off. Just like the church hall after all, thought Orla. But she nevertheless noted that the men would cast their occasional glances across the room, sizing up the women. In much the same way, she fancied, that the farmers would assess the cows in the market square. She hoped that she might catch the eye of a nice one.

The band struck up again and, to cheers, the leader announced a set of pop songs. Taking his cue the singer launched into the first number, joined by many of the assembled crowd.

'Oh Sugar, Oh Honey Honey ...'

The girls commenced jigging on the spot; the first of the men bravely crossed the room.

'You are my Candy Girl ...'

The prettiest girls were the first to be asked. And, just as inevitably, they politely refused. 'Sorry, I'm not dancing.' The older, more experienced men took the early rebuffs without demur and went along the line until a girl would step out with them.

'When I kissed you girl I knew how sweet a kiss could be ...'

Soon the dance floor became less of a no-mans-land. Some of the women, still partnerless, danced around their handbags. A proportion of the men were now dancing, with varying degrees of style or none at all, cavorting, smiling, inviting their partner to be impressed with their moves.

'Like the summer sunshine pour your sweetness over me ...'

'Thank you,' the girl would say at the end of the set and would retreat back to her fellows without further ceremony, head high. Even if the lad was a dish a girl wouldn't risk her reputation publicly by pairing off that early in proceedings.

Orla got a dance on the third song of the set. A young, spotty lad but she supposed she ought to be polite and start to make an effort. She swayed her hips to 'Bad Moon Rising', gazing vacantly over the lad's shoulder, ignoring his efforts to smile and make eye contact and, as the set drew to a close, she retreated back to the line with a 'thank you'.

'Come on, let's get a drink.' Roseanne led them upstairs to the bar area. Soft drinks only, which explained why the men tended to dally elsewhere before the dance. They bought Tanoras and sat at a table overlooking the dance floor.

'I hope that Pat fellah asks me out again. He's gorgeous.'

'Well I dunno. There's not many here tonight I'd look at twice. Be as well sitting at home with me Ma.'

The night wore on. The songs became livelier, the crowd less inhibited. Even the most sorrowful wallflowers were asked to dance though even they had the dignity not to cling onto their welcome saviour.

But then the last, slow set was announced and it was all to play for. Though Orla had been 'up' a number of times by now she had met no one interesting. Still, she hoped that she might partner a nice lad for this last set and maybe progress to a kiss or two outside before the drive home. At least then she'd have something of interest to say to the others afterwards when they'd be gassing in the back of the car.

But her heart fell when she saw Spotty making a beeline for her. She was sure that one or two other men had their eye on her as well but he was almost at her side. No one wanted to be left at the wall at this stage. Already there were a few stranded and loveless who were making for the exit as if they didn't have a care in the world. As did many lads who had only been there for the music and the craic really.

Mary-Jo and Roseanne had disappeared. Orla resigned herself to her fate, no one was going to save her so she gave her best attention to her eager beau. Yes, a bit spotty, but not unpleasant, nice smile, teeth, Patrick he said. They one-two-three'd around the floor among the other couples. He danced nicely enough, tried to hold her closer. She gently resisted. He bent his head to hers and, as she angled away he nibbled her neck. It tickled and she giggled. He laughed too and planted an unexpected kiss on her unwary lips. She smiled and returned the kiss. It was a nice sensation, gave her the shivers, and Orla thought this was the best she was going to get. She hadn't had that many kisses from a boy and was quite unpracticed. Certainly at the church hall Patrick and Orla would have been prised apart by now. As the last number drew to a close Orla consented to Patrick holding her ever closer.

The main lights were switched on and the band said goodnight. Orla looked around but her friends were nowhere to be seen. Never mind, they wouldn't go anywhere without her.

'Well goodbye Patrick, thank you for the dance.'

'Thank you Orla, I'll see you outside. Do you have a coat to get?'

Outside she looked around again. No sign. She walked towards where the car had been. It wasn't there. She started to panic. They'd left her here, in the middle of nowhere. God, who'd give her a lift home, who was going her way?

Startled, she realised Patrick had followed her. Why was he still here?

'Problem Orla?'

'My friends have gone, left me. What do I do?'

'Where do you live?'

'Dunmanway. Have you got a car ... could you ...?'

'Course I can, anything for a lovely girl like you. My car's over here.'

Relieved she followed, away from the bright car park and down the street. It was darker away from the club and Orla was thankful she was not alone. They came to a battered Cortina.

'Here we are, jump in.'

Once inside, Patrick leaned across her and locked the door. Orla thought nothing of it.

'So, Dunmanway?'

'Yes please. This is so kind of you.'

'It is really. Do I get a kiss in return?'

She hesitated. But why not? It was only a little thing. She leant towards him, puckered her lips and closed her eyes. Their lips met once, then twice. Orla was quite enjoying herself really, feeling very grown up, but now she ought to be getting home. And when Patrick's tongue touched her teeth and he pulled her closer, breathing heavier, she pulled away.

'Okay then.'

Patrick turned the key and they quickly accelerated away down the main street, Orla happy to see the road sign for Dunmanway. Then the town lights were left behind and the road ahead was in darkness. Suddenly Patrick braked and turned sharply left off the road into a driveway, a gap through the roadside hedge. Well away from the road he stopped and switched off the engine. Orla was horrified and frightened, not believing this was happening to her.

'Patrick, what are you doing? Please, I want to go home, now!'

'So, do you have the fare?'

'No you know I haven't. Look, take what I've got.'

'That's better, show me what you've got Orla.'

Patrick leant across. Too late the frightened girl realised her door had not been locked for her safety. He pulled her shoulders, her slim body towards her and kissed her roughly.

'Patrick, please no. Leave me. Let me go, I'll walk home, just …'

He didn't answer but pulled her to him again. He was stronger, much stronger. This time he bent to bite her neck whilst his right hand pawed at her breast. She screamed but there was no one to hear. Still it annoyed him and he slapped her face twice, reducing her to frantic sobs.

Still holding her firmly with his left arm he now tore at the shoulder of her dress, ripping it away and exposing her chest. Breathing heavily he forced her back against the door and started loosening his belt.

'No Patrick, please. I've never done this before. You can't … please just let me, you know …'

He didn't hear. His eyes were bright, his breathing heavy. She felt him drag her dress up to her thighs and push himself onto her.

'Orla, Orla …'

Desperately using what strength she had left she twisted her body. He growled in displeasure and frustration, but it had given her the chance, unbeknown to her assailant, to find what might be the door locking switch. Praying to herself she threw the switch and, praying once more she grabbed the door handle. To her utter relief the door swung open. She half-fell out of the door onto the muddy driveway. Patrick, his trousers around his knees tried to pull her back but it was impossible. He threw her legs out so now she was completely sprawled on the ground.

She screamed, louder than she thought was possible. She screamed again as she got to her feet and headed for the road as fast as she could, her shoes long gone. No one was listening, and if they were, they were taking no notice.

The car started, the headlights shone brightly. Patrick spun the Cortina round and headed straight towards her as she stood and watched, horror-struck. Something told her that he wasn't going to stop and she somehow threw herself aside as the car roared by. Lying in the wet grass and nettles Orla watched, as if she was sitting at the Broadway Cinema watching a film, as the Cortina swung onto the main road and roared away into the night.

Crying her eyes out with a mixture of terror and relief she limped into the road praying that a car would come by soon, though it was now well past two o'clock. Her abiding terror was that the next car would come from Dunmanway direction – Patrick returning to find her. No car came and she started to walk, shoeless, back towards Enniskeane – maybe there was someone left at the Lilac that might help her. As she approached the first of the town streetlights she was elated to see, driving towards her, the Vauxhall with her friends.

She broke down and sobbed her story as they drove home. Indeed it trumped those of her friends, their minor escapades forgotten as she relieved the attack. It transpired that they had been cruising the town looking for her. If only she'd waited in the car park none of this would have happened.

The best that could be done now was to get Orla home. They would all go together to the Gardai to report the matter in the morning. And so ended Orla's first and last night out to a big dance on a Saturday night.

DUNMURRY 1970

By 1970 Sisters Agnes and Bernadette had long departed the care home but others of a similar stripe had taken their place. Dunmurry was no less heartless and sad a building – it could hardly be called a home. Orla Spencer suddenly found herself therein one day. The Guards had half-believed the trollop's story, her parents hadn't. She had come home from the dance in disarray, shoes and handbag gone, dress torn asunder, bruises on her chest, love-bites on her neck. Her friends had tried to cover for her, saying she'd been attacked. But no one had been apprehended and the facts were plain. She had got into a man's car after the dance and that was that. Orla had screamed the Garda station down refusing to be medically examined.

Orla hated her mother for disbelieving her, and now she took to deliberately annoying her. She slammed doors and broke cups to pleasing effect. Knowing her father wouldn't touch her she started using coarse language, all the more when she saw her mother's red face and, eventually, tears. Deliberately she started to flaunt her blossoming charms and came home drunk one night regaling her speechless mother with the imaginary details of what she'd just done with a boy in the churchyard.

The priest came to talk to her but by now Orla was getting used to a life of defiance. As the good priest warned of the perils of disobedience and wantonness Orla pulled out a packet of Carroll's No.1 and lit up in front of him.

Her parents, especially her father, had never wanted it to come to this but the affronted priest would have it no other way. Orla found herself imprisoned at Dunmurry. She twice managed to escape, shocked at her predicament and determined to turn over a new leaf. However, on each occasion she was caught without reaching her home and throwing herself on her parents' mercy.

Of course the nuns gave her a hard time; beatings, lengthy cold baths, enforced hours of supervised prayer, solitary confinement with only the Bible to read. Alone in her bed Orla didn't cry; rather she hardened her heart against the world. Where once there was a spirited young girl just trying to act grown-up there was now a sullen, defiant woman, harbouring her grievances, old before her time. She accepted her surroundings for the time being knowing that they couldn't keep her for ever. She would bide her time then, when the time was right, she would have her revenge. On everybody.

The first spring of Orla's confinement at Dunmurry was turning into summer. She dozed and tossed fitfully one night, unable to sleep. Damn, if she only had a packet of fags, even a magazine or something to read other than the Bible. Before she knew it she would be polishing the fecking floor again without the benefit of a night's sleep. Damn the nun bitches that wouldn't even allow them a glass of water in their rooms.

Thirsty, she climbed out of bed, opened the door of her small room and padded down the corridor to the bathroom, feeling her way along the walls in the dark. Having found the bathroom and quenched her thirst she hesitated in the corridor. A cup of tea now, that would be the thing. And a nice, strong cup, not the dishwater they were served with their meals.

Orla cautiously made her way downstairs, her eyes getting accustomed to the dark. Where there were no curtains the bright moonlight lit up the rooms. Quietly, quietly. Though she didn't fear the nuns as most of the others did she would rather do without further beatings from them.

Reaching the kitchen, she dared to switch on the light. But before she could locate the tea Orla's eyes lit upon something else. A bottle of Paddy whiskey standing there in a cupboard, tucked away behind various packets and tins. Smiling, Orla fished it out. Well, who would have thought it. They taught and preached all about sin, the temptation of the Devil, the power of true repentance. They beat it into you did the nuns, those that harboured no vices. And all the time they had drink hidden around the place!

Orla was no stranger to drink. She didn't like the taste much but she had found it gave her a good, warm feeling. And it helped her to sleep, more to the point. Better than tea which would have her up again peeing in an hour. So, she uncorked the top and tipping the nearly-full bottle to her lips, took a sip. She coughed and spluttered a little, then took another sip. There, that was enough. She replaced the cork and put the bottle back on the shelf.

Returning quietly to her room, Orla drew back the curtain. The sky was cloudless, the moon bright somewhere up above the house, so bright only the most vivid of the stars made themselves visible. Beneath her window the pristine lawn, gardens and driveway. Beyond the grounds the dark road running off to Bantry on the left. Drimoleague, Dunmanway and beyond to the right. Beyond! Cork city even where her father used to take her when she was young, when she was happy. She remembered train journeys as a child, buses once the trains ran no more.

Beyond! To Dublin even. Trains and buses ran regularly to Dublin. And from Dublin there were boats to England, planes to America. Why would she stay in Ireland, the bloody damp nun and priest-ridden place?

Not so damp tonight though, quite pleasant even. Why wouldn't she go for a walk? Feck the nuns. They'd never know and she'd only be gone half an hour. Yes!

Quickly, she put her work jeans on, a shirt and jacket. Wide awake by this time, holding her clumpy garden shoes in her hand, she tip-toed her way back downstairs. The main door would be locked. The nuns kept all the doors locked at night and had the keys, but the authorities had warned against the danger should there be a fire. The nuns had reluctantly compromised by leaving the key in the door that led from the kitchen to the side path. Orla and the other girls knew this but the nuns weren't too bothered. The regular escapees were inevitably caught and returned within the day.

So out through the kitchen Orla went, hesitated, returned to get the bottle of Paddy, and set off on a moonlit walk. She put on her shoes and, to save the crunching noise, kept to the grass as far as the gate. Lifting the latch quietly she slipped out onto the road. And, remembering the Paddy in her other hand she took another little sip, replacing the cork once more.

Which way? The moonlight lit up the tarmaced road in both directions. She had been picked up on the Drimoleague road the last time, the Bantry road the time before that. It didn't matter. She turned right towards Drimoleague, and her home town of Dunmanway beyond that. Would her parents take her back in if she kept walking as far as their house? But tonight walking east for ten minutes or so would be good practice for the day she would leave Ireland – this was the way to go.

'I see the bad moon arising, I see there's trouble on the way …' she giggled and waved the Paddy at the bright moon above. God, it had been months since she'd heard any pop music. The bitch nuns sometimes had the radio on in the kitchen but not when any modern music was playing.

It was quiet, so quiet. Everything was asleep, the birds, farm animals, creatures of the fields and woods. The moonlight picked out the hills to the north where the mountainy men lived, according to her father. The empty road lay ahead. No cars, no lorries. It had become busier these last few years what with the oil terminal works down at Whiddy, but for now the West Cork countryside slept silently.

Orla came to the boreen which ran behind Dunmurry Cottage towards the north. A few minutes more and she would turn back. Should she continue east or take a few steps down this little lane. God, what a nothing place this was – fields, hedges, ditches, more fields. What was the difference anyway? She turned left, the moonlight guiding her way and took another sip of Paddy.

'I hear the hurricanes ablowin, I know the end is coming soon …'

Fifty steps and turn back. One, two, three … Out came the cork again with a little 'pop'. Funny, she was holding a cork in Cork, which came first, Cork or the cork? Thirty-nine, forty, forty-one … Something caught her eye across the field to the right. She stopped and peered. Some manner of a mound or fairy fort. At least it was something different to look at. Might get a nice view from the top. Yes, then she'd go back.

And so Orla made her way across the small field towards the fairy fort, for now she was sure it was such. She had heard and read tales about fairy forts when she was younger. It was where the good people lived and no farmer or landowner would dare disturb it or else their crops would forever struggle, their animals easily sicken.

'Don't go round tonight, well it's bound to take your life, there's …' Orla's voice had dropped to a whisper. As she drew nearer the fort she sensed a movement. A rabbit maybe. She stopped some 30 yards away, peering curiously. No sound, but definitely movement. Shapes coming and going on the slopes where the fort was silhouetted against the silvery night sky.

Cautiously, she drew closer, not afraid. Ireland is a land of legends and fairies though many in the modern world have turned their backs on such things that have no meaning to them. Well, the modern world had turned its back on Orla. She would take comfort and companionship where she might find it.

As she drew nearer, the shadowy movements ceased. Another step or two and she made out a figure in front of her, a small figure maybe half her height, about ten feet away.

'Good evening Miss, and welcome.' The figure spoke in a high-pitched voice and performed a little bow as he did so.

Orla had never been addressed so gracefully and her heart sang.

'Well, good evening yourself.'

'Will you join us in the dance?'

'What's the occasion?'

By this time Orla could make out the little man. A ginger beard, red hat with a broad brim and green jacket. Some manner of trousers and black shoes.

'I've gone quite mad,' thought Orla, 'here I am talking to a leprechaun as if he were my next door neighbour.' As if reading her thoughts the little man continued.

'Sure aren't we all mad, Miss? It's Midsummer's Eve, didn't you know? Will you join us?'

So Orla followed the little man and gradually others appeared. They appeared to be dancing in circles and lines. But then they caught sight of Orla and the music and dancing stopped. More little men, but only the first wore the red hat. They were otherwise all dressed up in much the same fashion. Little women too, but instead of trousers they wore floor-length skirts. They all looked up curiously at Orla, doing or saying nothing as Orla hesitantly waved at them in greeting.

Then a fiddler among them struck up and the dance recommenced.

'Come!' said the little man who had greeted Orla, and he reached out for her hand.

'If I'm to dance with your honour then I should know your name,' Orla stated primly.

'It's Jack of course,' said Jack, 'come!'

And so Orla joined the dance that Midsummer's Eve when the good people are at their gayest and most accessible. On and on they danced, around the fairy fort, up and down and over the top. The fiddler kept the tempo high with jigs, reels and slides. Orla danced with each of the men in turn, the women too. She was transported and couldn't remember a time when she had been happier, even as a child.

As the moon dipped and became less bright the dancers started disappearing two by two. Orla found herself once more alone with Jack, for Midsummer's Eve is when a daring fairy might seek a mortal bride.

Later the next day the searchers found an empty bottle of Paddy at the fairy fort, but the nuns claimed to know nothing of it. The search was scaled down some days later. Orla Spencer was never found. It was assumed that she had run away to England or elsewhere. To this day her elderly parents still wait for the telephone to ring.

9

Miranda was fascinated by the 'something' in the living room. On the following two nights, she sneaked downstairs again after midnight. Exactly the same thing happened. Whatever it was, the manifestation would appear at one wall, travel across the room and stop before continuing across and exiting the opposite wall. Still she saw, heard and smelt nothing. There was nothing to touch or taste. It was her sixth sense.

Of course she wasn't able to keep her secret for very long. Once she was convinced that she wasn't going mad, she had to say something to Joe. On the fourth night her watch alarm went off at 12.30. She had the coffee ready and now went back upstairs.

'Joe, hey Joe.' She shook his shoulder.

'Hey, what, what's up?'

'Joe, get up. I want to show you something.'

'Huh? It's the middle of the night. What?'

'I know, sorry. Humour me, get up.'

Grumbling, he got up, threw his dressing gown on and followed Miranda downstairs. She led him to an armchair, sat him down and fetched coffee. Ignoring his grumbles and questions she switched the main light off, leaving a muted side light only, and came and sat beside him.

'Just wait and watch. It might be a little while.'

He played along, said nothing, sipped his coffee. Minutes passed. Miranda started to wonder once again if her mind had invented all of this. A few more minutes and she was about to admit defeat as Joe started to yawn and fidget. Then it happened, just as before.

'Look, there!' she whispered.

'Uh, what, where?' he replied in a low voice.

To Miranda the manifestation was quite clear, but Joe saw and sensed nothing. She looked into his face and he looked back, blankly, and shrugged his shoulders.

Miranda cleared her throat as the strange visitor paused in the middle of the room, as it had done previously. There was a much longer pause than usual before the visitor moved on and exited in exactly the same place as before.

She looked at Joe.

'You saw nothing, sensed nothing?'

'No honey, I'm afraid I didn't. It's clear you did though. I don't doubt you. You've done this before?'

'The last three nights. I was afraid to tell you.'

'Hey you are clearly more receptive than me. I know things aren't always as they seem. I wonder if your friend will stick around?'

'Thank you for not thinking me crazy. I just wonder what I ought to do now.'

'Maybe do nothing, why should you?'

Thereafter, Joe left Miranda to her own devices. For the next few nights exactly the same phenomenon occurred, then she didn't feel the need to go downstairs each night – nothing was changing. Certainly it worried neither of them. It was like their new life on the edge of Europe had invited in these little curiosities.

They were otherwise settling down very nicely. Joe was writing well, Miranda had made initial enquiries over substitute teaching, not that they needed the money. She was still busy arranging the large house to her satisfaction and deliveries of household goods and accessories arrived daily. And in the evenings Miranda would often drive them down to the Drimoleague Inn. Joe was getting a taste for the Murphy's stout and the bar meals saved Miranda cooking. All in all, they were loving life.

At the end of June Joe returned to the States on a business trip, but Miranda elected to stay in Ireland. The urge to revisit friends and family had lessened and she felt most at ease and indeed reinvigorated here in Cork. It was where she now regarded as her home, at least for the foreseeable future.

They had both been absorbed into the small local community without any outward difficulties. This was the new Ireland, a country that had finally learnt to look outward beyond its own shores. European Community money had transformed the country's infrastructure. A journey from Bantry to Cork used to be a trial along winding, single-carriageway roads. Now, sure you pointed your car in the right direction and kept your foot down until you arrived at the South Ring Road less than an hour later. And from the capital of the so-called People's Republic you could jet off anywhere; and of course anyone could jet in.

In recent years the phenomenon of immigration had been seen in Ireland for the first time. It was no longer a surprise to see a black face in the street. Ethnic communities had sprung up in every city, town and village transforming the formerly insular nation.

And of course these days everyone had satellite and cable

television and the world was brought to everyone's living room. Whereas not so long ago a local telephone call involved a complicated procedure involving a local exchange operator, now the Irish telecommunications industry was among the world's best.

All remaining vestiges of mystery attaching to the green and misty island on the edge of Europe had been swept away.

Joe and Miranda found that they were fitting in perfectly.

Miranda squinted out of the kitchen window and pulled a face. However, light rain was part of the Irish summer and not thought of as unwelcome. She needed some fresh air and was well equipped for wet weather. Today, she decided, she would walk by the river for an hour before lunch. Rainproof coat and sturdy boots, essentials for both of them, were always close to hand. Then a rather stylish black hat with a peak that she pulled tightly over her head. No bother that she would need to shower and dry her hair again afterwards. If she bothered even. It wasn't as if she was going anywhere special later.

The aluminium door closed silently behind her and she locked it, almost as an afterthought, and pocketed the key. The pathway down towards the river followed the perimeter of the neatly-kept lawn, past the outbuildings. Strange, she thought, it was only after she and Joe had decided to use this outbuilding as a storage and laundry area that they learnt that this had been its original use, back in the days when Dunmurry had been a girls' home. Certainly it was big enough to have served the purpose.

The rain pattered down on the hedge and the leaves of the trees as she made her way through the large garden.

Reaching the far end she pushed through the wrought iron gate that guarded the south face of the property. The gateway was arched by foliage that the garden people had battled with during the house renovation and which, without constant attention, threatened to engulf the aperture once again.

It wasn't a well-worn path but it was clear enough to lead the way down to the river through the long, wet grasses. She reached the old bridge and paused for a while, perusing the lazy river as it made its way eastwards. It would eventually feed the Bandon River and make its peaceful journey across the county to Kinsale.

Miranda clumped her way over the bridge and turned west along the path of the old railway line towards Bantry. Although the line had been disused since 1961 the county council had made an effort in recent years to keep it clear of vegetation so that walkers and hikers could enjoy the countryside.

She put her best foot forward. After thirty minutes she stopped, rested for a minute, then started back. What had she in the fridge for lunch? Cheese, ham, a salad perhaps. A nice cup of coffee and a chocolate biscuit. The prospect of a reward put a spring in her step and soon she was back in sight of Dunmurry. She had encountered few people this lunchtime; a couple of holidaymakers going in the opposite direction, that was all.

But now, at the bridge stood a boy, watching her as she approached. Strange, she thought, it's a school day. And with his old-fashioned dungarees and side parting it was no child she recognised. She drew nearer and the boy addressed her.

'Please, can you help me find my brothers?' He spoke in a reedy West Cork accent. Miranda looked at him, puzzled.

'Why, where are they? When did you last see them?' The

boy looked at her strangely for a second, then replied.

'I don't understand you. Where are my brothers?' Miranda thought that maybe her American accent was to blame, though it usually created no difficulties.

'Do you live near here?' she annunciated clearly. 'Are you lost?' Again the boy looked at her blankly, and said 'My brothers have left me.'

Miranda didn't know what to say or do, but perhaps she ought to take the child home, perhaps call the Guards to report the matter.

'Look, come with me.' She held out her hand to the boy who continued to look at her, no longer speaking. Miranda took a step closer but the boy ran past her quickly and into the adjacent field. Miranda ran the few steps to the edge of the field and peered in, shouted, 'Young man, young man!' But there was no sight nor sound of the child. Suddenly she was alone again.

Once inside Miranda rang the Garda station in Bantry. They took the details and promised to call her again should any local children be reported missing.

Miranda poured herself a glass of wine that evening to consider matters. She really wanted to talk to someone. The episode with the boy had disturbed her. This was of course not the first time that she had encountered strange happenings at Dunmurry. As she sipped her second glass it occurred to her that these things might possibly be connected. The nightly visitor that passed through the main room at night she sensed to be a child rather than an adult. Could the boy by the river and the presence in the room be the same thing?

Restless now, aware that her head might be full of

nonsense, she wondered what to do. If anything at all. Did the things she had experienced exist only in her own head? Was she going a bit potty? God she was only 25! Anyway, perhaps the boy had been familiar with the fields and had simply taken fright and had hidden himself again. Maybe he was a bit simple.

Just in case, she called the Guards again, but no local child had been reported missing.

The next day found Miranda in restless mood. Joe had emailed to say that he'd been held up in the States and needed to fly to Chicago to see an editor. He wasn't sure when he would be back.

She went for a run down and back along the damp road, showered, made some coffee. She hated to admit it but she was getting bored. Even when Joe was here working in his office with the door closed, it was different. She would buzz around doing little jobs, maybe potter into Drimoleague for some fresh bread, make Joe a coffee. She never felt alone. But she did today. It was early July and she hadn't heard anything about substitute teaching. She simply wasn't going to be able to live in this big house all day with nothing to occupy her.

Maybe she ought to join the golf club, although she hated the idea of being 'a lady who lunches'. She wanted to do something worthwhile. She needed a project.

She squinted at the newspaper, found her reading glasses. That was better. Then she put her feet up and read for a while. She stopped in the middle of an article about the Health Service and private health, thought, and flicked back a few pages to a display advert she remembered skimming over earlier. Here it was, laser eye surgery.

Generally Miranda's eyes were fine and she only needed glasses for reading. Wouldn't it be nice not to need them at all though? She'd thought about it before, indeed discussed it with Joe back in the States. He was fine about it. Few of their friends hadn't had some elective procedure carried out, including laser eye treatment. Without exception all were pleased with the results. But Miranda hadn't been that bothered and the subject had lapsed.

Twenty minutes later she had refreshed her memory on the basics of laser eye surgery. She emailed Joe to say that she was thinking about making an appointment with an optometrist. Joe would be fine with it but she ought just to let him know.

Next, she looked up optometrists in Cork city. She called two, one of which could offer her a preliminary consultation the next morning as they'd had a cancellation. She suddenly felt a lot better, full of purpose. Something to do. It would be her first trip into Cork city, which was quite strange really considering they had been here in Ireland six months now.

Energised now, she decided to start a second project, trying to find out what was going on at Dunmurry as regards to the strange visitations. She would love to find out more about the history of Dunmurry. Padraig had been strangely unforthcoming, and she didn't really know anyone else in the area to ask.

On a whim she called the Dublin legal firm through whom they had bought the property. She eventually managed to speak to an assistant. Yes, he confirmed, the property ownership history would all be on their file. Yes, of course the Hunters could have details – could he check the email address that they had on file for them please? He would try to get onto it shortly. The legal assistant was as good as his word. Towards lunchtime, Miranda received an email with a number of attachments which she eagerly printed off. And before long there it was, the outline of the house's ownership history. It had been easier than she imagined.

Apparently constructed and first owned by a man named Murray in 1901.

1932 purchased by a James Fitzgerald.

1948 purchased by Olive and Kathleen Murphy.

1954 apparently purchased by Cork County Council and sub-let.

1975 bought in the name of Dunmurry Hotels Limited.

1985 jointly owned by a Mr & Mrs Shwarzer.

1987 owned by United Properties Limited, presumably as a sub-let.

2004 purchased by a privately-owned limited company.

Miranda was delighted; and this information had been sitting on their file all along! But after a while she realised that this information, interesting in itself, hardly advanced her quest beyond first base. If she wanted to solve the mystery of their night-time visitor, and of the small boy, then she would need much more information. For now though she put this project to one side.

Miranda drove herself into the city the next morning. She'd underestimated the snarling traffic mess and one-way systems but she was able to find a space in a multi-storey across the river from Patrick's Street. The wind and rain whipped down the river making her umbrella unmanageable, so she buttoned her coat to the throat and battled alongside the morning shoppers. Cork, for all its charm in the sunshine became a miserable place when the weather whipped in from the Atlantic.

She was a little early but was thankful to escape from the elements, pushing open the wooden door of a sturdy Georgian building on the South Mall. She followed the sign for the optometrists to the second floor, growing ever more nervous as she did so. But a little more than an hour later she was sitting, smiling happily, in the nearby Imperial Hotel with a rather handsome optometrist. She had filled out an extensive questionnaire and had then undergone a thorough eye test with an assistant. Andrew had then introduced himself as the surgeon and had looked through the test results.

'Now Miranda, I've another appointment in twenty minutes but I'm gasping for a coffee. Why don't we pop next door quickly and have a chat?'

And so they did, in a quiet corner of the Imperial where Andrew was clearly well known to the staff. He said that, subject to verifying the test results there was no reason why Miranda couldn't have the laser surgery necessary to make the slight correction that was required. They agreed a provisional date for the left eye procedure, in a week's time.

Andrew said that things were very quiet at the moment. In the Tiger years there were long waiting lists for this type of surgery but, to be honest, times had changed. People generally weren't so ready to splash out on expensive treatments. It was the right time for her to come as the procedure could be done quickly and indeed at reasonable cost.

Miranda was charmed. Andrew gave the impression that, at this moment, she was the most important person in his life. She looked at his sharp blue eyes and admired the faux-careless cut of his fair hair, parted to the right.

'... and won't it be great not having to wear glasses for reading?' Miranda felt herself go red as he smiled directly into her eyes. But then he had to hurry back to surgery and

Miranda finished her drink and floated along the South Mall, a silly grin on her face and oblivious now to the rain which swept the grey city.

Two days later Joe returned to Dunmurry, business sorted out and with plenty of writing and research to be getting on with. Miranda was delighted to have him back though he seemed a little too eager to sit down in his office and close the door. A year ago, Joe would have swept her up in his arms and carried her straight to their bedroom. Not any longer, but perhaps she just expected too much. Their days proceeded as before – maybe a run together in the morning, dinner in the early evening either at home or at the Drimoleague Inn. Lovemaking which Miranda thought was becoming somewhat mechanical despite time apart. She was becoming restless.

At least her eye procedure went perfectly. Joe drove her up to Cork and he spent a couple of hours in the Crawford Art Gallery whilst she was undergoing surgery. She reappeared, somewhat disoriented and very pleased to be able to rely on Joe for transport. She would need to go back in a few day's time for a check up and, if all was well, the right eye procedure shortly afterwards. Today they had lunch at the Farmgate Restaurant in the English Market before heading for home.

Andrew had been all business to Miranda's slight disappointment. Maybe it had just been her imagination the first time. Still, she had enjoyed Andrew's attentions. Not that she would ever dream of cheating on her lovely husband but, hey, an admiring look and a compliment now and again didn't hurt.

They made the same trip a few days later. Andrew pronounced the first procedure a success and Miranda now had perfect vision in her left eye. But she had got used to her moderate sight when reading and the treatment of the left, and subsequent differentiation between the right and the left, had left her feeling rather distracted and worried.

The right eye procedure was fixed for a week's time, but then came a crisis. Joe said that he had to attend a meeting in New York and this would clash with the appointment. They had their first major row. Already on edge, Miranda took a dim view of her husband disappearing again so soon, though it was only for a couple of days. Why on earth couldn't they fix up a telephone conference, even a video conference or something? Why did a successful writer like Joe have to jump every time there was something to discuss? Why didn't they bloody come to Dublin or Cork if it was so bloody important? But Joe was firm and Miranda seethed. That night she pointedly turned her back to him and wouldn't acknowledge his presence.

The icy atmosphere was unbroken as Joe left for the States and Miranda was left to fend for herself as far as her eye procedure was concerned.

So Miranda arrived in Cork once again having taxied into Bantry and then catching the bus into the city. To the Hunters, money was little object and Miranda could have whistled up a helicopter ride had she so wished. She certainly wouldn't be able to drive for a few days. But a bus ride was both a novelty and an enjoyable experience. She watched the beautiful Cork countryside pass by at her leisure and enjoyed the background chat of her fellow passengers and the soft West Cork accent that she had grown very fond of.

One advantage of travelling by bus was that she was

deposited in the heart of the city centre without the need to battle the one-way systems to a car park. From the bus station it was just a short walk to the surgery.

And two hours later it was all over. This time under Andrew's expert hands, she was less apprehensive and indeed almost enjoyed being pampered and attended to. And she was happy that he sat with her and chatted awhile afterwards. It was with a sigh that she shook his hand and left, probably one more check-up to go and a last chance to see those smiling eyes and raffish blond hair!

It was the shortest of walks to the Imperial Hotel. She had decided on a bit of shopping and a rare overnight stay rather than flogging back to the west that day.

Miranda checked into her suite, dozed awhile then, refreshed, set off to explore the city centre, protective dark glasses and all. She had seen nothing of the city itself since settling in Ireland. Dublin she was fairly familiar with – they had spent some time there talking with contractors and interior designers during the renovations phase. Cork was, however, a bit of a mystery to her.

First of all though, she was famished. She knew the Farmgate from last time and found her way there for a late lunch. The English Market, within which the Farmgate was situated, was rather quieter at this time of the day. After lunch Miranda spent an hour wandering around the myriad food stalls, craft shops, jewellers and boutiques before emerging blinking and unfocused, into Cork's bright streets.

She wandered down busy Patrick's Street, made a few purchases in Brown Thomas, then down the eclectic Oliver Plunkett Street. Along Grand Parade, North Main and the quays. Gratefully Miranda arrived back at the Imperial in the early evening, tired but happier than she'd been in a while.

Later, treating herself to a glass of wine before dinner, she was surprised to see Andrew at the hotel bar in the company of a couple of male friends. She had no intention of disturbing him but was nevertheless pleased when he spotted her and gave her a cheery wave. And even more so when, a few minutes later, he came over and joined her at her table.

'Well hi, Miranda, how are you feeling? A bit more normal now?'

'I'm feeling great thanks Andrew. I know my eyes will be perfect once it's all settled down. Thanks to you.'

'So, no more reading glasses. You could of course wear neutral glasses if you felt naked without them.'

The way he said that made her shiver – she hoped he didn't notice.

'So, what are your plans for this evening? You're staying in town, right?'

'Yes. No plans. A bite to eat here and an early night.'

'OK right. There are better places to eat in Cork you know. It's a bit hotel-y here.'

'It'll do for me. I'm not that bothered.'

'Well I could show you a great place, but if you're not bothered …'

Oh God, how to say 'yes please' without it seeming like she was throwing herself at him, she wondered.

'Isn't that against your code of ethics or something?' she laughed.

'No, I won't be drummed out of the club, it's perfectly alright.'

'In which case that would be very nice, but I insist on paying, OK?'

Inwardly she shouted 'yes!' as the goal hit the back of the net. Outwardly she smiled sweetly as if she were doing him a big favour.

'You drive a hard bargain Mrs Hunter. Let's go.'

To Miranda's relief it was only a short walk down to the Lee boardwalk, and to the Boardwalk Restaurant. It was a breezy but dry evening and the city lights rippled on the river surface and the small craft moored alongside rocked gently. A whoosh of aromatic smells greeted them as they pushed open the glass doors to the restaurant. Miranda was relieved of her coat and they were escorted to the bar area and left to peruse the menu.

The place was only half full but it was early on a midweek evening. In these difficult economic times she guessed that any restaurant would settle for that. Warm and hungry, she started to relax, but was still uneasy as to Andrew's marital status. Miranda had noticed from the outset that Andrew didn't wear a wedding band, though that didn't necessarily mean anything, if it ever did. Best to get the subject out of the way.

'So, no wife or kids at home wondering where you are?'

'Ha ha, footloose and fancy free. Does your husband know you're dining with a strange man, Miranda?'

She was relieved and disconcerted in even measure. She would have been discomfited at finding out that Andrew had a wife, maybe kids at home. But she hadn't stopped to consider her own position. The fact that she was married, albeit her husband was thousands of miles away, hadn't occurred to her really. Still, Joe wouldn't mind her having a casual bite to eat with her eye surgeon would he?

'So, not even a steady girlfriend?'

Andrew looked at her in that disarming, easy way she had got used to as his patient.

'No, not at present anyway.'

'Are you in the habit of taking your patients to dinner?'

'No of course not. Only the pretty ones that can pay!'

She laughed.

'Well I'm not sure if that's a compliment. Do you live in the city Andrew?'

'No so far, Ballincollig.'

'All your life?'

'Pretty much, though I studied in Manchester. I'm happy to be living and working in Cork though. How are you? How are things out in the bog?'

'Hmm, good. I think. I'm not so sure that Joe is as enthusiastic as me though. He's just jetted off again for a meeting.'

The maître d' arrived and took their orders. Shortly they were shown to a table overlooking the river.

'The maid and her lover the wild daisies pressed, on the banks of my own lovely Lee,' Andrew quoted. Miranda looked at him in surprise.

'Wow that's lovely. Did you just make that up, like a poet?'

He laughed. 'No silly! It's a bit from our own Cork anthem – you mean you haven't heard it?'

'No. I'm ashamed now, like a real incomer.'

'I'll sing the whole thing to you sometime.'

There was something vaguely seductive in everything Andrew said. Miranda was sure, judging from her own reaction, that he had no problem winning women. And here was she, a happily married woman, hanging on every word he had to say. Had she been single there was every chance that she would have been his latest victim. As it was, she was happy to be spending an hour or two in his company.

Miranda gasped, for a different reason, as their starters arrived. Seafood chowder. She had expected an apertif but they had been presented with huge bowlfuls.

'I'll never eat all this, never mind another course afterwards!'

'Then leave what you don't want.'

She finished it all. The thick, beautifully flavoured sauce with treasures of the sea, perfectly textured *al dente*. She even mopped up the remnants of the sauce with a bread roll.

'Well I declare that's the most beautiful thing I've ever eaten. But can we ask them to delay serving the main?'

Sipping wine whilst they relaxed and waited she smiled as she sensed Andrew looking at her, weighing her up. 'No Miranda, don't even think about it,' she told herself.

She groaned as the main arrived, but it seemed manageable. Waving away the offer of extra vegetables and potato she was pleased that she'd ordered chicken which, without the trimmings, was light on the stomach. Meanwhile Andrew tucked into his Angus steak as if he hadn't seen food for a month.

Both refused desserts, but Miranda ordered a port and Andrew a brandy. There were no arguments over the bill as she paid with plastic, then they exited the restaurant onto the breezy quay.

'My turn next time, OK?'

Almost without thinking Miranda linked arms with Andrew as they walked back down the Mall. She was full, warm, slightly drunk and happy. As they came to the entrance of the Imperial Hotel she turned to him.

'Thank you, Andrew, for a lovely evening.'

'Thank you, Miranda, after all you paid.'

They lightly kissed.

'But Andrew, I hope you don't mind if I don't invite you in. You're lovely and all that but ...'

He stepped back and looked at her.

'You think I invited you to dinner just to go to bed with you? It never crossed my mind Miranda.'

'Oh I know but ... I'm sorry ... I ...'

'No, I'm sorry if I gave you that impression. I must cop on. Now goodnight and have a safe trip home tomorrow.'

He turned and walked away. Miranda's face fell as she watched him go. How much of a fool was she?

10

After Orla Spencer's disappearance questions started to be asked of the nuns at Dunmurry House. At first, it was just whispers among the local community that the girls at Dunmurry were being treated badly, worse than their supposed behaviour deserved. There was talk of a husband and wife demanding the return of their daughter. They had received a letter from her, smuggled out via a delivery boy as correspondence was forbidden. The letter complained of the degrading treatment meted out to the girls and she begged for her parents to take her home.

But in those days the Catholic Church was the effective civil police force in the land, hand in glove with the politicians and policymakers. Those few that questioned the actions of the Church and its priests in particular were denounced and shunned by their neighbours. When a local investigative journalist uncovered some of the practices prevalent at Dunmurry, she was quickly ridiculed and silenced.

But the seed of doubt had been sown. Gradually, referrals to the home dried up and some of the nuns transferred elsewhere. In 1973, the last Mass was said there, the few remaining girls were transferred to a home in the city and the building locked up and offered for sale.

Times had changed in the Bantry area. The town and surrounding districts were experiencing an economic boom.

The Gulf Oil Company had constructed a huge oil terminal on Whiddy Island out in Bantry Bay. During the construction phase, and later when the terminal became operational, the town was awash with engineers, labourers, executives with money burning holes in their pockets. Existing businesses thrived, new ones sprung up. It was impossible to get a hotel room during the week or a table at a restaurant at the weekend. A damp and breezy fishing port had become a boom town.

Prices soared as did demand for property in and around the town. Roads were improved to cater to the increased traffic. Money changed hands and overnight, agricultural land was rezoned for development. Everyone took their cut.

It was not long before Dunmurry House was bought by a local businessman determined to make hay. He refitted the building as a hotel with a high-class restaurant offering nouvelle cuisine at fancy prices, bringing in a well-known chef from Dublin.

At first trade flourished. The restaurant was popular, the hotel operating at 80% capacity, profit margins healthy. The road to and from Bantry was constantly busy as the incoming workers and locals with unaccustomed money in their pockets looked to enjoy themselves. The owner, one Ronnie Parkes, and his wife made sure to take a personal interest in the running of their new venture. They were high-profile with their guests and diners, greeting each personally on arrival and checking that everything was satisfactory during their stay. The restaurant was awarded a Michelin star, rare for Ireland.

But as night follows day things changed, though slowly at first. The level of pricing was unsustainable once the novelty of the place had worn off and people found other venues. The management had to introduce fixed price and early bird menus. The Dublin chef was offered, and accepted, the chance to head up a new restaurant in Rathmines.

With more hotel beds now available in the area, Dunmurry found it more difficult to attract the businessmen and instead started to focus on less lucrative packages for holidaymakers in order to put heads on beds. The Parkes now spent most of their time overseas enjoying the fruits of their investment.

And guests started to speak of a weird atmosphere and, at night, strange noises and presences. More than once the night manager had to check out residents in the middle of the night whilst one couple had elected to sleep in the lobby area rather than their assigned room.

Suddenly the hotel was loss-making and staff cuts and new initiatives weren't working. The business struggled through Christmas 1978 by offering 'turkey and tinsel' breaks, but early in 1979 came the final straw. An explosion and fire at the oil terminal killed 50 people.

The money dried up, businessmen cut their cloth, the good times were over. Bantry returned to being a rather more spruced up fishing port and market town. Dunmurry Hotel ceased to trade. Once more the old house, together with its secrets, was boarded up to await its fate.

11

It took no time at all! To Miranda's astonishment she found what she was looking for almost immediately. What she imagined would be days in a dusty library or archive was half an hour on the Internet.

The Southern Star has been the leading provincial newspaper in West Cork since 1892. Happily their archives have been digitised and made accessible online for a reasonable charge. And by trying combinations of search phrases she came across a story dated March 1946.

Gardai from Bantry and Drimoleague are leading the search for John Fitzgerald, 6, missing from his home in Caherogullane, Bantry since yesterday.

Then another piece, several days later.

Bantry Gardai say that they have no news on the whereabouts of John Fitzgerald, 6, missing since 3rd March from his home Dunmurry, Caherogullane townland.

A further hour searching brought up no further mention of the disappearance. She was nevertheless euphoric that she had what could well be a major clue to the goings on in the house.

And didn't Padraig say that the Fitzgeralds had upped and left for Dublin? He hadn't mentioned anything along the lines of what she'd just discovered, though he must know the story. She must sit down with him for another cup of tea to see if he would loosen up a bit. What was he hiding? Maybe he was just trying to protect her in some way.

Now, maybe if she tried calling the night time visitor by his name, John? Would that make any difference, have some effect? If so – and it was a big if – her next step would be to try contacting the Fitzgerald family. Assuming for a moment that the presence in the house was the same as the small boy by the river, then she must let the family know, if she could. Quite why she wasn't sure, or what it would achieve but she had to move on with her research.

She slowly realised the enormity of the task ahead. Finding Fitzgeralds in the sparsely populated townlands of West Cork wouldn't have been difficult, but in Dublin and probably beyond? A needle in a haystack.

However, the haystack might at least be made smaller if she could obtain some better details of the persons she was looking for. The mother and father must be presumed deceased. In any case it was the brothers who were the most important to her. Hadn't the boy by the river been searching for his brothers?

She stood up, stretched and went to make fresh coffee. She knew that she wouldn't be able to rest until she had at least exhausted all avenues of enquiry.

Again Miranda was amazed at the information which could be obtained from the comfort of her own home with a broadband connection. There were more genealogical websites than you could shake a stick at. The most comprehensive ones demanded a fee though and Miranda fished out one of her many cards again.

It was frustrating and slow going with searches continually coming up with thousands of matches. Invited to 'refine your search' she would do so only to be met with the message 'no matches'. She howled with vexation but attacked the keyboard once more.

And then, miraculously, she had them. Late into the evening there they were, transcribed onto her notepad.

James Adolphus Fitzgerald D.O.B. 15 September 1936
Daniel Adolphus Fitzgerald D.O.B. 9 October 1937
John Adolphus Fitzgerald D.O.B. 5 February 1940

All were listed as living at Dunmurry, Caherogullane townland. It all matched up! John would have been six when he disappeared in March 1946!

Exhausted she switched off the laptop. Tomorrow, she would continue. Joe was due back from New York as well. But tonight she had an assignment.

Her phone alarm was set for midnight. Tired but determined to pursue her quest she threw on her dressing gown, grabbed yet another coffee – she had left it percolating in readiness – and sat down in the usual spot in the big sitting room. The main lights were off with only lamplight providing low illumination to see by. It was the first time she had done this for two weeks or so and she hoped her visitor hadn't abandoned her now that she was a little closer to perhaps helping him.

Knees drawn up on the sofa, coffee steaming on a side table, Miranda tried to relax and not move though her instincts were alive and sharp. Shadows cast into the far corners of the room, shapes indistinguishable in the half-light. These were much the same conditions as when she'd seen, or imagined, the young boy before. Imagined yes, but it had been as clear as day to her.

Or was her brain messing with her thoughts and mixing in the very real encounter she'd had with the boy the other day. That was a strange thing all right. She wondered if maybe …

The small hairs suddenly rose on her neck and back. Her eyes focused on the wall to the right, next to an armchair, that was where he had come from before.

Maybe a minute passed then here, now! He came from the wall. Her eyes were wide but she saw nothing, just the lamplight playing against the armchair. Though all around was silent he made no sound. But he was there. Without question. And yes it was the same boy. He moved, walked, glided slowly past her across the room. Miranda's head and eyes followed him, the rest of her stock still. Except her heart which she could feel thumping in her chest. On he moved, then stopped where he usually had before. Now, she had to try.

'John?' It was barely a whisper, again more firmly, 'John?'

He watched, or at least it appeared to Miranda that he was watching her. Had he heard her? She decided to try again, not believing that she was doing this.

'Hello, John? What do you want?'

Nothing, no answer. Long seconds, maybe minutes passed by. Then, to her astonishment, a faint, misty shape started to form. She closed her eyes quickly, shook her head to clear it. When she opened her eyes the boy-shape was still there, partially formed. But she could certainly see him, and he her. He made no move. She had to try again.

'What's your name?' She asked tremulously.

The boy remained still, gave no answer. Miranda frowned and, strangely, was rather irritated. She repeated her question in stronger tones, an order.

Again silence then …, she wasn't sure she'd heard.

'Jonno.' It was merely a whisper, a gasping sound.

'John?'

'Jonno.' A firmer voice this time. The shape seemed to

grow more solid, she thought she could even make out his features. Then the shape faded again somewhat.

'What do you want Jonno?'

Silence, then

'Will you help me find my brothers?' The same as the little boy by the river had asked! What ought she to answer?

'Yes Jonno, I'll help. Now rest.'

Then the misty image moved on, faded, as it passed through the opposite wall. But as she watched it go Miranda was sure that she heard a quiet

'Thank you.'

To celebrate Joe's return they decided to head out to Bantry for dinner. Taxi, of course. There was no shortage of drivers who would jump at the 30-mile round trip from Bantry out to Dunmurry and back, then hang around as long as necessary to deliver the Hunters home again. They had quickly got themselves a name as good tippers. It was said that they didn't really understand euros, being Americans and all. They'd throw you any manner of bank note as a tip without bothering to check its denomination.

In truth, Joe was cuter than that but he had no difficulty in acting the part of a gullible Yank. But it was the case that both he and Miranda were comfortably off and could afford to spread a little beneficence around.

But Joe looked a little tired tonight, Miranda thought, as they got ready. Not his usual sparkling self when they were socialising. But there again he'd only landed in Shannon eight hours ago.

They'd left themselves time for a drink before dinner and happily dashed through a rain shower into a bar on the Quay.

They both enjoyed the pub scene in Ireland and judged it preferable to sipping aperitifs in the restaurant. This place was busy, it being a Friday, but Joe had no problem in whistling up a pint and a half of Guinness. Irish bartenders are unique in that, whatever the crowd, they somehow ensure that no one is kept waiting beyond the obligatory 91-second settle.

No point in trying to find a seat, they weren't staying long. A few words and a joke here or there with people half-recognised or indeed complete strangers, a glance at watches and back out into the rain laughing at the good nature of it all. Umbrella up and a quick step up the hill around the corner to their favourite Italian restaurant.

Miranda was happy and content. She had her man back and held his arm tight. Yes she was able to live happily and productively on her own but having Joe beside her made her whole. She looked at him with fondness as he ordered for them both and asked the maître d's opinion of the wine on offer.

They were shown to their favourite table away from the bar and kitchens where it was a little quieter. It was one of only two tables with a window through which, over damp rooftops, they could see the harbour lights twinkling in the rain. As they nibbled little triangles of pizza and sipped the first of their wine, Joe filled her in with some of the blanks from his business trip. He said that he had considered extending his trip by taking a visit to Martha's Vineyard, catch up with people a bit, though in the end he hadn't.

At the mention of her home island Miranda suddenly felt a little homesick in spite of what she considered to be her wonderful new life. And she momentarily thought that maybe Joe wanted to go back. Well, if so then it would become apparent sooner rather than later. And what would her reaction be? She had no idea.

They shared an Affetatto Misto, a selection of Italian cold meats and pickles. Simple and satisfying. As the rain intensified, blurring the nightscape through the windows, their main course arrived; Dover sole in a lemon-butter sauce with accompanying side dishes of vegetables.

Miranda wondered when she ought to bring up the developments concerning the Dunmurry ghost and her subsequent researches since Joe had left on his short trip. However, tonight didn't seem to be the time. It was a perfect evening. Joe still appeared tired but that didn't matter as they appreciated their food and each other's company. To introduce spooky tales would jar the atmosphere. It could wait.

Irish coffee was, well, a bit touristy but Miranda loved it. Joe made do with a large Courvoisier XO to round off the evening. The bill arrived and Joe proffered a card to pay, not even glancing at the total. A quick phone call ascertained that their driver was standing by. Leaving a 20 under a side plate they made their way out of the restaurant, into their cab and homewards through the rain.

It was wrong to encourage him, nevertheless Joe's mechanical lovemaking and immediate relapse into deep sleep left Miranda unhappy. There was something not quite right between them. Nothing she could put her finger on, maybe her imagination. Hadn't they had a great night? She dozed fitfully but found herself staring at the dark ceiling listening to the raindrops on the window panes and the louder plops as the puddles outside were refilled by the flow from the gutters. Would Jonno be downstairs, searching for her, enquiring after his brothers? Tomorrow she would get onto the case again.

*

And while Joe worked, Miranda continued with her quest, searching for any sign of the Fitzgerald brothers. Irish death records drew a comprehensive blank. This was a good thing insofar as search 'fails' went. She didn't wish to discover that Jonno's brothers had died, though admittedly they would be a good age by this time, 77 and 78 respectively.

Of course, even if she had read the Irish records correctly, they may have died elsewhere, but she hoped that one or both may still be alive.

If indeed they were alive it appeared that neither was to be found in Ireland. No amount of people-searching worked. It was of course conceivable that they were off the grid, in a care home perhaps. But otherwise Miranda had exhausted all avenues as regards Ireland.

Running out of ideas Miranda composed an enquiry and sent it off to a couple of Fitzgerald family history websites and, for the moment, shelved her project. It was time to renew her efforts to find something useful and productive to do, something that paid a salary. The new school year began in a few weeks' time and she was determined to pick up her old teaching career.

12

Well, if that don't beat all,' I said to Janie. I'd read the letter twice and even a third time before it began to make some sense.

'What don't beat all? Who's it from? What's it about?'

Well it's not so often we get mail these days. Mail with a stamp on it that is, and this had a British stamp on it, delivered by the US Mail. Sure, we get official letters talking about this and talking about that. The occasional bill in a window envelope. Figure that nothing worth reading ever arrived in a window envelope. The bills get sent off to the accountant who I presume will tell us if we ain't got any money left, but most of 'em are paid by the management company who own this little complex.

But a proper letter, in an envelope, handwritten, with a stamp with Her Majesty's head on it addressed to me: Mr James Fitzgerald, B28 Fairbreeze Heights Complex, Tulsa, Oklahoma, USA. Don't that beat all?

'Here, read it for yourself.'

'I'm busy. Read it out.'

'It's from my downtown sweetheart, I guess I ought not to read it to you.'

'Then don't bother.'

'OK here goes.' I unfold the two-page typewritten letter again.

'It's from Doris Marychurch, 28 Sycamore Avenue,

Fakenham, Kent, England.'

'Kent? England? What does she want, money?'

'If you'll stop interrupting a minute you'll see. Here goes.'
Dear Mr Fitzgerald,

I hope this finds you well. 'Heh heh, if only.' *Please forgive me for this unsolicited intrusion. My husband Mark is a Fitzgerald and is researching his family tree.* 'Well doggone.' *He recently received a communication from an American lady living in Ireland who is also doing research. She says that she is most anxious to connect with brothers James and Daniel Fitzgerald, formerly of Dunmurry House, near Bantry, Cork, Ireland.*

My husband believes that you might be the first of the brothers aforesaid. 'Whatever that means.' *If you are interested perhaps you would get in touch with me. Mrs Hunter does seem particularly anxious to speak to you.*

Once again please forgive … 'blah blah blah. There now, what about that then?'

'Well I never. Will you write back, honey?'

'I don't rightly know. I'll think about it.'

And think about it I did. My memory might be fading, along with my body, but some things remain clear as a bell. But it's been many a long year since I cast my mind back to those days in Ireland. And there's someone still living in that old house of ours! Well there's something to get you thinking.

I remember those days well enough. The big house, school, our big car, church on a Sunday. Back then Bantry Town was where the action was and we'd go there at every opportunity. There was nothing for growing lads to do at Dunmurry, only to make our own fun and games, out in the road, the fields, by the railway, the river.

But it was so long ago, during the Emergency we called it in Ireland then. Ireland was neutral of course but we wanted the Allies to win. We'd run around, taking it in turns to be the Hun or Allies. We'd swap sides but the result was always the same, the Allies always won!

And then we were gone, gone from Dunmurry. Mam and Dad couldn't bear to stay. Jonno just got lost, disappeared. For the first hour or two we just thought it was part of a game. But suddenly it wasn't.

They were an awful few days. Mam cried non-stop. Me and Donal helped with the searching until we were exhausted. You see we dare not go home to find Mam still crying. And worse, Dad cried too sometimes and that was too much to bear.

One weekend the removal vans came, the house was emptied and we were off to Dublin on the train. We never went back, any of us. And it's fair to say that I, for one, rarely thought about them days very much once we'd left. But now this letter and the memories come streaming back in like rain through a cracked window pane. Strange what the human brain can store away to be brought back unexpectedly.

But I reckoned those days were best left alone and so I put Mrs Maychurch's letter in a drawer and forgot about it.

But doggone if she didn't write again two weeks later. Handwritten envelope, stamp and all.

Dear Mr Fitzgerald,

I really am so sorry to bother you once more. I normally wouldn't but Mrs Hunter wrote again asking if I'd heard anything concerning her enquiries. I really didn't know what to do. I hope that you'll forgive me for being a nuisance but she does seem rather insistent, desperate even. I haven't of course given her your address. You can of course write to her directly should you wish.

I'll leave it entirely up to you though and I won't bother you again 'blah blah.'

This time Janie read the letter and re-read the previous one.

'Well?' She always was a woman of few words which is why I guess we've been married forty years.

'Well what? Why would I bother? What's in it for me?'

'Because you're a good man Jim, that's why.'

Well I can barely write now, and no, I wouldn't have replied. But when Janie pulled up a chair next to mine, pen poised over paper, I had little choice.

Dear Mrs Hunter,

I have been asked to write to you. Yes I am the James Fitzgerald you seek, formerly of Dunmurry House. I have no idea of the purpose of your search. If it is about the broken window I didn't do it! (That was a joke, ignore him – Janie). My brother Daniel who we called Donal is indeed still alive, as last I heard, and living in Australia.

By all means write again though I cannot imagine how I can be of assistance to you. I have no money. And no I don't have email and have no intention of acquiring same.

Yours truly

And that was the end of that? No indeed not. It was only the beginning.

Dear Mr Fitzgerald,

Thank you so much for your recent letter. I hesitate, not quite knowing how to start. And you may well consider me a madwoman and throw this letter in the bin. I have no control over that but simply ask that you read to the end. Then I'm in your hands.

Some months ago, my husband and I uprooted from Massachusetts to Ireland where we bought and refurbished an old house in the West Cork countryside. We've been very happy here. I now find that it once belonged to your family. Isn't that amazing after all these years?

I understand that there was a tragedy in your family concerning your younger brother, in 1946? I'm sure that any condolences will mean little at this time but I send you mine anyway. It must have been a hard time for your family.

But now, this is the point at which you might think me quite mad. I think that I have seen, and even spoken to your brother Jonno. There, I've said it, for better or worse. Several times, at night, he has manifested in the downstairs drawing room. On the most recent occasion I could see and hear him quite clearly. I spoke his name 'John' but, when he didn't respond, I asked him his name and he replied 'Jonno'. On asking him what he wanted he said 'Please would you help me find my brothers,' to which I agreed.

Further, several weeks ago I spoke to a young boy out by the river and he asked me the same thing. I assumed he was just lost, but then he had gone before I could do or say anything else.

Though these happenings have troubled me I am in no way frightened. I have (it would appear) an open mind on the subject of ghosts, spirits and suchlike. And if they are to interact with the living it seems to me that Ireland is the perfect place!

So now you see, or at least I hope you do. If Jonno is to rest then he must see you and Donal again. If that is not possible then perhaps a message from you will suffice.

Now you may throw this letter in the bin and think no more of it. But I ask that you read it through again and share it with

Donal – I assume, possibly wrongly, that your brother is still alive. If you decide you could travel to Ireland then I am happy to make all the arrangements and my husband and I are well able to pay your travel and other expenses. It would not cost you a cent.

    I am, yours truly
    Miranda Hunter

I've gotten to thinking, is it age that does it or is it the fact that your days are numbered? When we're young we all look forward. We want to move our lives ahead – a new job, better car, bigger house, more fabulous girlfriend. Heh heh, just don't mention that to Janie will you.

But there comes a time when you don't look forward no more. Sure, what's for dinner, what time does the Drillers match start, how's the allotment coming along? But you can't get excited about the future is what I'm saying. Who cares where they're holding the 2022 Soccer World Cup? Who's bothered about who'll be President in two years time? Not me anyhow.

Y'know, last week Janie 'n I went downtown to see some exhibition, a heritage thing, about the forming of the great state of Oklahoma. Y'know what? We were about the youngest there and I'm 77! All right, maybe I exaggerate but you get my point. The young people around here, around the world I guess, don't want to look back at the past. And I don't blame them neither.

But when you get to a certain age, I guess it's only natural to look back, maybe consider your life. Maybe even tell your memoirs to one of those nosy writer types so they might put you in an article like you was in a museum.

So I've got to writing a few notes, or dictating them to Janie more like. And d'you know? There's more stored away in this old head of mine than I thought. It's just a matter of opening the right doors.

Yes the memories are starting to flow though I don't know who all will be interested. It's wonderful what can be done when time presses. When you've been told you won't see next Christmas.

But maybe I would never have started only for getting that letter from Miranda Hunter. The strangest thing that letter is, and I'm not rightly sure yet what to do about it. Though I know that if I don't do nothing then nothing will be done. So let me sleep on it. Hopefully, I'll wake up tomorrow, at least for a while.

Dunmurry was my first memory, the first thing I remember. It would have been during the Emergency, the war with Germany. Not that I had any notion of what the war was really about. It was about the good guys and bad guys and it was too far away for us kids to be worrying about. They say that there were shortages of this and that but I never noticed no shortages. I guess I had a blessed childhood, though that never stopped me wanting more I guess. Like all young men.

There was me, I was the eldest. James, though it was only Mam that ever called me James. Mam was always around the house and gardens. Rarely if ever left the place without Dad, to my knowledge. I never saw her drive so I guess she never learnt. There weren't too many cars back then, not in our part of the world anyway. And you never saw a woman driving, nosiree.

There was always one cleaner woman around, sometimes two. Well, between Mam and the cleaners that house was kept in apple pie order and we boys knew better than to mess with it. If we wanted to sit quietly and read, that was OK. Mam tolerated our presence. But young boys rarely want to sit and read do they? I guess some things never change. So we spent much of our time outside, in the gardens and outbuildings. The outbuildings especially if the weather was bad, which it usually was. Before Donal was old enough to play with I used to wander off quite happily, though with instructions never to leave the grounds. Of course that changed as we got older. Maybe Jonno would still be with us if it hadn't changed, but maybe what happened was God's will.

I was sent off to school when I was five. It was a small Protestant school a few miles down the road, towards the town of Drimoleague. There were both boys and girls, some older, some younger. In the bigger Catholic schools, I guess they were able to split the children a bit better but our school seemed to work OK.

I wasn't that pleased about having to sit next to girls, though thinking back I guess the girls weren't so happy neither! But it meant that there was no horsing around and we concentrated on our reading and writing and sums. At playtime it was difficult of course. Us boys would get together and play chasing games, or tag, or even soccer if we could find something to kick, like a pine cone or a bottle top.

Of course there was no football or baseball in Ireland. The Catholic boys had their own sports – hurling with big sticks and Gaelic football where you were allowed to catch the ball. I think I joined in occasionally but as I say they were really games for the Cathy Cats, not us Proddy Dogs, heh heh.

And at three o'clock, there would be Dad outside the school gate in his big car. I used to jump in proudly and wave to my friends as we headed back to Dunmurry.

I don't know that I ever really loved my Mam or Dad, or if they loved me. They were never unkind and Mam would look after me if I grazed my knee or suchlike. I used to kinda enjoy being sick as I got my Mam's attention and maybe the little bit of love that she had to give. But she sent me back to school the minute she knew I was OK again.

Dad was a proper old-fashioned father. Kids out of sight and out of mind was his philosophy. Most times he was away 'at work', wherever that was. Out in Bantry I guess judging by the number of people who knew him when we went to church on a Sunday.

When at home, he would sit quietly and read and woe betide anyone who made a sound within his hearing. When he disappeared into his study to smoke, we would breathe a sigh of relief. If we came across him in the house or the grounds his eyebrows would go up in surprise. It was like he couldn't rightly remember that we were his children.

Donal was always there, only a year younger than me. Even though he was always a bit brighter and quicker on the uptake I was always the leader by virtue of seniority. We got on well and rarely argued. OK, to get it out of our systems we used to play-fight now and again, rolling around and kicking and punching. More than once, both of us would end up with a black eye or bleeding nose, but after a cooling-off period we were playing together again as if nothing had happened.

One summer, Mam got fatter and fatter. One day Dad took her away and an older woman came to look after us. Then Mam came home and showed us our new baby brother. After the initial surprise we decided he wasn't much fun and, thereafter, took little notice of him until he was able to walk and talk a bit.

Naturally, I suppose, Mam and Dad became even less bothered about me and Donal and what we got up to once we were out of sight. We got to exploring the area to the south of Dunmurry, and of course the railway and river that ran parallel towards Bantry in one direction and Drimoleague and all points east to Cork city. Once we realised that there were no serious restrictions we would spend many hours of daylight, evenings and weekends, messing around back there. Many was the toy boat we made to send off floating out of sight.

As the train tooted and the rails rumbled we would stand aside and wave at the driver, the passengers and the guard and they'd always wave back.

Sometimes other boys would join us but not many lived out our way, in the country. It was one of those boys, Eamonn, who told us about the fairy fort. We were agog and naturally wanted to know all about it. Eamonn told us that it wasn't so far away, over to the north of Dunmurry, in a field. No human was ever to go there as, without a doubt, they would be captured by the good folk who would cast a pishogue – a fairy spell – upon you before letting you go, if you were lucky.

Naturally me and Donal wanted to go there at once and we double-dared Eamonn to show us where the fairy fort or rath was. Like commandos we scuttled down the road which ran past Dunmurry so as not to be seen by Mam or Dad. On as far as a little house beside which ran a lane, little used. In those times only the main roads were of any quality and this little lane was little more than a cart track.

We hesitated a little I guess. It was the first time we had been this far down the road on our own. Remember I was only six or seven and Donal even younger. But even though Eamonn wanted to turn back, I told him to show us how to find the fairy rath.

So slowly we crept down the lane, the only sound being the occasional lowing from a nearby farm. At last, we came to a spot where the ditch alongside the lane was rather lower and we could look into the field.

'There,' said Eamonn, pointing to the far corner, maybe a hundred yards away. Well we saw a grassy mound, no more.

As we had come so far we decided, at least, to go a little closer. We climbed into the field and cautiously crept nearer, foot by foot. We stopped at every sound, at every bird or leaf that moved. But not a single fairy did we see. At last we came to the rath and, in relief, climbed to the top. What wonderful views we had of the countryside all around!

Delighted with ourselves for having bravely conquered the fairies we ran off home, though we never said a word to our parents. We visited once or twice more but the rath was of no further interest to us. Not compared to the adventures available nearer to home.

Even Jonno disappearing was a bit of an adventure for us boys. Mam cried, Dad marched around grimly, no one took any notice of us at all. We were allowed to come and go as we pleased, especially as it was assumed we were doing our best to find Jonno. We had told the Guards and the other searchers all the places that we knew, where we would go and play. The search went on for a week or so to my recollection. Everywhere in the surrounding countryside you'd find groups of people with sticks, swishing here, poking there. After a few days, frogmen arrived to search the river, especially to the east where anything in the water would have been carried. But the river was clear and you could see to the bottom. I suppose it gave the frogmen an excuse to get some practice in though.

Donal and I explored further and further afield, way further than we had ever been from the house. We knew Jonno would never have come this far on his own but it was said a bad man might have carried him away. So we wandered, laughed and played, poking and whacking with our sticks, looking in any likely hedges and ditches. Then home we'd come, tired and hungry, to find Mam still crying with neighbours hushing her and handing her cups of tea.

Then one evening the head Guard, a sergeant maybe, took Dad outside. They were calling off the search. After that things happened quickly. The next thing we knew we were packed off to Dublin, hardly time to say goodbye to our friends.

We grew up into young men in Dublin. We lived first at Clontarf, then later in Sandymount. I guess living next to the sea, watching the activity at the Dublin Port and the ferry port at Dun Laoghaire made us realise that there was a world outside Ireland.

I suppose we were both bright enough because we did well at Belvedere. Both of us played rugby – well you had no choice at Belvedere, though Donal was better. He developed into a big, strong lad and eventually propped for the First XV. I did a bit better at the studies and I took a particular liking to the sciences.

Mam died in 1951. You could say that she gave up after Dunmurry, but she certainly never summoned the strength to fight her illness. Dad continued to take little interest in us. He saw to it that the school fees were paid and that we had an allowance. Otherwise he worked away in the city at something or other connected with cattle exports – he never shared his world with us. Along the way he became involved in local politics and fell in with the Fianna Fail crowd which was to serve him well in years to come.

'There Janie, shall we carry on tomorrow?'

But this where my reminiscences will end, though there is much still to tell. You see, I buried Janie a week ago today. She was killed in a pile-up on the Red Fork Expressway. Died instantly they say, which is some consolation. I only wished I'd died alongside her. The police called around to report her death. Two young policemen, felt awful sorry for them. I wouldn't do their job. Now here I am alone in this place, the TV my only companion. Only consolation is that I'll be outta here soon, feet first.

You hear it said often enough but ain't it true. No matter if you're rich or poor, king or beggar, no matter what you've done in life we all end up six feet under, pushing up the flowers. Or feeding the flames, whatever your preference. You appreciate the circle of life only when you're about to complete that circle. I only hope they got the morphine ready when the time comes.

I've no affairs to settle. What I have, and it's not much, is willed to the Red Cross. No children you see. No point in leaving it to Donal anyhow. He ain't got no family either to my knowledge and what money he has he'll waste. He seemed happy enough out there in Australia last time we spoke, which was some years ago now. He's in good company there, everyone throwing sheep around by day, drinking themselves silly at night. Though I guess Donal ain't doing much sheep throwing these days.

I'm exactly a year older and I'm guessing that Donal won't make it a year after I'm gone. You'd think we'd want to meet up while we got the chance but neither of us has any notion of doing that.

Funny thing, now Janie's gone. I can get up by myself, get dressed and undressed. Thing is I don't want no carer coming in, messing about, fussing over me. If I can't have Janie I'll have no one.

Anyhow they could hardly get in the door right now. It's right entertaining that pile of mail underneath the letter box. Why would I need mail? What are they going to do about their stupid bills? They ain't going to cut off the electric now are they? Cause a scandal and letters to the paper when they find an old man frozen to death. Let the lawyers sort it out once I'm gone.

Now to get me a little sleep, perhaps get a bit of the Drillers match later.

Miranda was both pleased and apprehensive to receive a reply. It was a envelope addressed with a flowing, female hand with a selection of US Postal stamps. She might have wondered why a woman had apparently written a man's letter but she was too eager to learn the contents to worry about that.

Dear Mrs Hunter,

I thank you for your letter which Janie and I have read through several times. It has brought back a lot of memories, things that I had completely forgotten about.

Indeed what happened way back then was unfortunate. But, being young lads, me and Donal seemed to get over it quickly enough. Indeed so did our parents. We all seemed to close the book on Jonno and rarely talked about him afterwards. I guess moving away from Dunmurry helped a lot.

I don't know what help I can be to you. I am quite sick and in no state to be gallivanting back to Ireland. What I will do is contact my brother Donal in Australia to see what he says. I can't promise you anything at all however and suspect Donal won't be at all interested.

You must understand that we have other lives now, though some of us for not much longer. I am sure that what you are experiencing will go away in time of its own accord.

With best wishes
James Fitzgerald.

Miranda was disappointed though hardly surprised. But having solved the mystery and made improbable contact with Jim it was frustrating that it might all come to nought. What more could she do now?

There was one last hope in that Donal might show more interest but it didn't seem likely.

In the meantime she had other concerns. For the first time Miranda was having second thoughts about this great Irish adventure of theirs. Although they had not discussed the matter it appeared to her that Joe had changed. Not greatly, but he appeared to be elsewhere. He was easily distracted now and she wondered if he, they, would ultimately be happier back in Martha's Vineyard among their friends and family. This was a conversation they needed to have sooner rather than later.

13

Only that you've put good money over this bar for years Donal. One more, that's all. Behave yourself, hear?'

'Sure gaffer, understood. Apologies.'

'Yeah, 'til the next time.'

Donal took his beer back to his corner with bad grace. He knew that he was in the wrong but refused to admit it. But, at age 76, at least he was starting to learn which side his bread was buttered on.

The group of young lads had forgotten about him, though now one turned and winked in his direction. Donal tensed and started to rise from the cheap, torn vinyl seat. Then he copped on, sat back down, smiled and winked back at the young man. He rubbed his almost bald head, stroked his stubbly chin and chuckled to himself.

Time he stopped fighting. Anyway no one wanted to take him on these days. Too old. 'Sit down grandpa!' they said. He still found himself in the occasional rooty toot with some other old fool, a crowd either laughing at them, trying to separate them or egging them on. It was good sport for the punters, like watching women fighting with handbags.

Anyway he seemed to be more content these days, not so inclined to argue and take offense. He was beginning to see that the other man might have an opinion which was just as valid as his own. To his grudging surprise he found that people would take time to talk to him, joke with him, if he didn't try to knock their blocks off every time the conversation took a wrong turn.

Taking his grimy old hanky from his pocket he wiped the sweat from his face and forehead. That face could tell a tale with all the lumps and bumps on it. His sweat-stained T-shirt covered a body once honed and hard, now not so much. His upper arm muscles were less pronounced though his gnarled hands and fists could still wreak damage on equal or lesser opponents.

He'd stopped working six years ago, the year he turned 70. Not out of choice but the company made it stick. He supposed he ought not to complain. It was young men's work and he struggled to keep up with them. They'd kept him on for longer than they had a right to. If he'd had a lighter job, sitting on his arse, then maybe he'd still be working. Either that or gone mad with the tediousness of it all.

He pulled at his lager, a small gulp, making it last. Fiddled with the beer mat. The young lads were drinking up, leaving. One of them walked over, offered him a high five of peace. He accepted.

Last orders. The gaffer would probably relent, he'd behaved for 20 minutes, but Donal didn't really want another. Times past 'last orders' was almost an instruction to buy, even if he was already full to the gills. Christ, he must be growing up.

The pool players battled on – click, click, curse. The dowdy roomgirl collected glasses, 'drink up please'. People drank up, picked up jackets, left in twos and threes with hearty goodnights. Impatient to be off, the girl started to spray and wipe tables. Taking the hint, Donal picked up his glass. She thanked him, picked up the beer mats, sprayed and wiped.

Donal stood, knocked back what he had left and plodded to the bar leaving his glass on the newly-clean top.

'Thanks gaffer, g'night.'

'G'night Donal, take care.'

Donal pushed through the door, briefly surveyed the street, up and down. Taxis, revellers, drunks. He turned left and was soon swallowed up by the warm Darwin night.

14

Joe announced that he had to go away again. Miranda wasn't surprised and received the news with resignation. She had been waiting for it. It was entirely legitimate, the launch of a new business magazine based in Boston. Joe had a financial interest in the venture and had been working on it for a number of months.

Joe asked her to come and she was tempted. It would be an opportunity to travel up to Martha's Vineyard and this was an attractive proposition. However, they had more or less decided to spend two or three weeks there over Christmas and New Year. Neither did she want to abandon Dunmurry and Jonno just yet, while an answer, a solution may yet be found.

But it was really time that she and Joe talked, heart to heart. More than once Miranda had raised the question with Joe of whether he was really happy based in Ireland. Joe had said all the right things. Yes, he loved it at Dunmurry, but the nature of the game was that meeting his partners and business associates face to face regularly was necessary. No, he didn't want to sell up and go back to Massachusetts.

He wasn't having an affair. Of that she was sure. There were no signs whatsoever and on that score she was content. But on the other hand he seemed to be somehow slowly shutting her out. Before, when they first met, she was the centre of his world. He took interest in everything she did, took care to build his life alongside hers so that they were a truly united couple. Miranda felt that this was no longer the case.

OK the bedroom thing was understandable. They were no longer in love's first flush. Quite often neither of them was 'in the mood' and when they were it was all a bit dutiful.

Mostly it was the disinterest. He wasn't cruel, never criticised, never questioned. When she talked about her day he would nod, smile, say a few words. No more than that.

And, as to her success in tracing the history of the house, and getting in touch with the Fitzgerald family in particular, he was plum not interested. She felt that Joe looked upon her efforts as a little hobby like quilting or stamp collecting.

As a result she hadn't yet mentioned her conversation in the drawing room with the ghostly boy, Jonno, though she had of course told him about the strange meeting by the river. There was, she thought, every chance that Joe would wonder if she was going crazy and if she ought to see a specialist. No, that would have to wait.

The more she thought about it the more she realised that maybe this heart-to-heart talk would do more harm than good. They still had a lovely life, though not as lovely as it might have been, or might yet be. She was a lucky woman. No, best to leave things as they were, at least for now.

And, if the time came, she would just up and ask Joe straight out whether he still wanted to live with her in Ireland, or if their great adventure had run its course.

But now was not the time. Not yet. There were too many questions and she could never leave without answering them.

Miranda gloomily re-read Jim's letter. Her heart fell again as she read it through. He wasn't going to help. Too old. Too sick. How could he simply show no interest in his own brother, his younger brother? He couldn't even be bothered to send a message for her to pass on. What now? There was this other brother in Australia but it sounded as if he, too, would not be interested.

God, she needed someone to talk to. Bloody Joe was bloody away. Again. Maybe she'd buy a cat. A cat would take no notice of her either but at least it would be there.

Crossly, she marched into the kitchen and emptied the dishwasher with much crashing and banging. Men, what was it with them? Not an ounce of empathy for anyone or anything that didn't suit their immediate needs. Joe with his bloody work, Jim in Tulsa who wouldn't get his backside out from in front of the television, Andrew who apparently got his kicks out of flirting with married women without following through. After banging a couple of chairs into place on the tiled kitchen floor she glared out of the window. At least it was dry. She would run.

Stomping upstairs she found her gear. Sports bra and technical T-shirt. Lycra tights that came below her knee. White socks and good, supportive Nike running shoes. She had a small selection of running jackets and today chose a light, red shower proof one. Finally she yanked her hair behind her and tied it into a simple pony tail.

She banged the front door shut and zipped the keys inside the jacket. Jogging around the drive she exited the gate. The wind whistled down the road from the west though the trees and hedges dissipated the strength a little at road level. Clanging the gate behind her she set her watch – 20 minutes out, 20 back. She set off towards Drimoleague. The first couple of minutes she hit a good tempo, wind at her back, before settling down into a more controlled cruise. Already that early effort, that concentration on her forward speed, had served to calm her down mentally. She relaxed, enjoying the wind in her hair, the distinctive smells of the Irish countryside, the silence broken only occasionally by the mournful lowing of a cow or a piece of farm machinery at work in a distant work shed.

So peaceful, so lonely. And she reflected that, back in the States, a lone runner would be regarded as eccentric at best, an escaped lunatic at worst. Here no one bothered you only to say 'hello' or 'good morning'. The driver of the occasional car would lift a single figure in acknowledgment as he or she pulled out to give you a wide berth.

Almost reluctantly she stopped as the watch ran over the 20-minute mark. She turned and headed back to Dunmurry, crossing the road to keep facing any oncoming traffic. The wind pressed against her and she leaned into it, working her arms and knees a little harder. Through a farm gate a dog barked ferociously in her direction but the farmer lifted a gloved hand to her in friendly greeting as he went about his labours. The dog reluctantly acknowledged her as no threat with a muffled woof.

As she approached Dunmurry Cottage, she was pleased to see Padraig sitting outside, sheltered in his small porchway. She decided that the run had served its purpose and decided to greet the old man.

'Good morning Padraig,' she puffed.

'Good morning Mrs Hunter. Now you look as if you might like a cup of tea?'

Grateful for the chance of some company, for someone to talk to, Miranda smiled and pushed open the wooden gate. As always, Padraig's garden was in apple-pie order and was now coming into full growth as a result of the season and his diligent caretaking.

Miranda hadn't really taken to the taste of tea, though she had tolerated it when nothing else was to hand. She enquired about the availability of coffee and eventually Padraig triumphantly held up a coffee jar though it appeared nearly empty. She winced as he dug out some of the contents and put them in a mug. God, how long has that coffee been there? I'm the only visitor he ever has I think.

Miraculously, and with the addition of milk and sugar, the coffee was at least drinkable though maybe she would, for safety, stick to tea in future. At least that was turned over regularly.

In the absence of anyone else, of any other ideas, Miranda decided to confide in Padraig. She was confident that the old man would at least listen without judging her or thinking she was crazy. Maybe he could even suggest a solution as to how she ought to proceed next.

So she took a deep breath and told him. He listened carefully. She related her experiences with the ghost – or whatever it was, of the boy. And of course the strange occurrence out by the river which, it seemed, might be related. At last she paused.

'And you think the young boy is Jonno Fitzgerald?' They were the first words he had spoken since she'd started telling her story.

'Well yes, he said so when I asked him. And it all seems to fit, doesn't it?'

'Well I never. Though now it doesn't surprise me.'

'Nothing surprises you does it, Padraig? I suppose you're part of this lonely world and some things are more real for you. What ought I to do now do you think?'

'What of the brothers, Jim and Donal?'

'I was coming to that. I've traced Jim anyway and corresponded with him. He's not interested and thinks I'm potty.' Padraig looked pensive, worried even, Miranda thought.

'Well now, Jim Fitzgerald alive after all these years. Here? In Ireland?'

'No, in America. Not in good health and not interested.'

'And Donal?'

'Australia, the last Jim heard.'

Padraig sipped his tea. Miranda was hoping for a suggestion because she really didn't know what to do next. But minutes passed and he sat staring blankly ahead, occasionally sipping from his cup. He seem struck to silence. At last she was forced to continue.

'Do you think a priest might do an exorcism or something?'

She was startled at his reaction after all the minutes of brooding. He half jumped out of his chair, his cup jumped off the saucer and clattered to the ground, followed by the saucer. Then he slowly sunk back, regaining a little of his composure.

'No, no! No priests, no exorcism.'

'Padraig, I'm sorry. I didn't mean to upset …why …'

'No, no, best to let things be. Let them be.'

'Look, you sit there and I'll tidy up. Can I make you another cup?'

But she left soon after, puzzled, with more unanswered questions than ever.

With trepidation Miranda presented herself for her final check-up at Andrew's surgery in Cork. To her utter relief he was his familiar, friendly self. There were no problems with her eyes and their professional relationship was over. But Miranda was determined that their cold parting of a few weeks ago be put to right. She wanted to leave Andrew on good personal terms.

She admitted to herself that there was a little more to it than that. Andrew was an attractive man who had paid her a lot of attention. She was somewhat starved of such attention and wanted a little more of it before leaving him for good.

'Andrew, I owe you an apology. About the other night, you know...' She spluttered the words out, felt the heat around her neck. God she was like a schoolgirl!

'Miranda! Of course there's no apology needed. A misunderstanding was all. And I owe you but sorry, I've other arrangements tonight.'

She was crushed, doubly humiliated.

'But tomorrow's a possibility, if you want?'

'Er yes. Great. Tomorrow. Yes.'

'OK fine. Look forward to it. Are you staying at the Imperial? See you at the bar at seven?'

Feeling like a fool, again. What was she doing? Now it was either waste a day in Cork or to drive the 50 or so miles home and then back again tomorrow. Just to have dinner with a man. Annoyed with herself she nonetheless popped into the hotel on the way back to the car park to book a room for the following night.

And 24 hours later she was back again. The drive really was nothing, not with the main roads these days. She had spoken to Joe earlier. They'd had a long chat but somehow she omitted to mention that she was driving back to Cork on a date.

And she'd decided that whatever happened would happen. She was a grown woman and would be happy to defend her own actions. The days were gone when wives were expected to stay at home and wait for their husbands to breeze in.

The city was wet and miserable again today. By arriving in the early afternoon she had avoided the worst of the traffic, but now she had time to burn. The English Market was an attraction as always and she spent some time there. The nearby Crawford Gallery, especially the Harry Clark collection of stained glass work, was a pleasant surprise to her. The city of Cork was growing on her despite the fact that it always seemed to be raining!

Miranda took her time getting ready for dinner. Expensive underwear. She reminded herself that a woman feels at her best in expensive underwear. A beautiful, translucent blue blouse which she'd bought in Dublin but had never worn, together with a plain pearl necklace. A simple peach skirt. Killer heels. She looked at herself in the mirror and was pleased with her efforts. A dab or two of Chanel No.5 and she was ready to rock and roll.

She felt all eyes follow her as she made her way downstairs and into the bar area. Walking tall, eyes ahead like a model on the catwalk. Her heartbeat was way higher than normal but settled a little as she sipped the gin and tonic delivered to her table. Andrew was late and she was beginning to get concerned before he made a sudden appearance, out of breath.

'Sorry, sorry Miranda. Wow, you look gorgeous! Another drink?'

He brought over their drinks and sat down, giving her a little kiss on the cheek. She was pleased to see that her efforts were producing a reaction. The lone males in the bar turned away when the cutie's date arrived but still cast glances of admiration from time to time.

Why did she never do this for her husband any more?

Maybe that was why he was losing interest in her. Anyway, time to consider that later. Tonight she was going to enjoy herself.

Andrew was, by contrast, dressed as slapdash as ever though everything he wore he did so with style. Even his hair, mussed up from rushing through the rain, looked as if he were modelling for a magazine. Simple white shirt and tweed jacket leading to his slim hips on which stylishly hung navy chinos. He probably has lots of girlfriends thought Miranda. No doubt he was with one of them last night. But tonight she was happy to claim him for dinner.

'So, where are we eating?' she asked.

'I've not bothered booking anywhere. Not to worry, nowhere will be full on a Wednesday,' he assured her. He put his hand on her knee, maybe a second longer than was necessary to reassure her that they weren't going to starve. She didn't object.

They talked easily over a second drink. Andrew asked lots of questions about her; things that they'd touched on previously but about which he sought further details. Whilst listening to her talk, Andrew looked into her eyes and actually seemed interested in her. It was a nice change and Miranda chattered away happily.

Eventually they set off into the damp evening. Miranda felt her face flush slightly and she reminded herself that she'd downed three drinks already. She wasn't used to drinking and told herself that she must take it easy for the rest of the evening.

Down a side street onto the wide Patrick's Street and over the bridge into MacCurtain Street they strolled, and Andrew steered her into Isaac's Restaurant. Less posh than the Boardwalk it was nonetheless popular, though they were easily found a table for two. Outside, Cork went about its business; traffic speeding by, theatre-goers arm in arm, young people seeking takeaway food and a bit of craic perhaps.

Dubiously Miranda went along with Andrew's suggestion of Clonakilty black pudding for starter but surprised herself by actually liking the unpromising-looking medallions. She followed this with a king prawn and rice dish while Andrew tucked into a steak. All the while he paid her the best of attention. Their hands touched affectionately now and again. By the time the bill arrived, they were firmly clasped.

As they walked back across the river Andrew held her close. They stopped in the middle of the bridge and Miranda gasped at the beauty of the river flanked on either side by a mixture of old and new buildings and the streetlights that glittered through the drizzle. Then she gasped anew as Andrew pulled her to him and offered his lips. She was helpless to resist and responded eagerly, her knees all but giving way.

They were oblivious to the hurrying figures around them anxious to be at their warm destinations. In due course, they both followed their example and left the wet streets of Cork behind them.

'Stay! Do it again!' She grabbed his arm but he slithered from her grasp, slipped out of the king-sized bed. He turned and stood naked before her, grinning.

'Come back to bed, please. It's early!'

'Miranda it's one o'clock. I've got a busy day tomorrow.'

'You don't love me,' she pouted.

'Of course I don't Miranda. It's just sex. Don't tell me you didn't enjoy it.'

Oh my God, she *had* enjoyed it. She had no idea sex could be as good. Twice. Andrew was a master. She was surprised there hadn't been complaints from other guests so enthusiastically had she responded to his lovemaking.

'That's OK. I'll let you sleep. You can go straight to the surgery in the morning.'

But he was climbing into his pants, trousers, shirt. Already forgetting her.

'Are you forgetting me already? Now you've had your wicked way?'

Fully dressed now he sat on the bed and held her.

'Of course not. I've had a great evening with you. You're a lovely woman. I can't wait to see you again.' She beamed, relieved.

'When then?'

'Call me. Email me when you can come to town. OK?'

'Yeah, OK.'

A last quick kiss and he was gone.

Oh my God. She slumped back in her pillow, body tingling, missing his touch, her senses still heightened. So this was what an affair was like. Why hadn't she tried it before?

Slowly her heartbeat settled and her body returned to some form of normality. A sense of guilt shadowed across her mind, but not so strongly. She still loved Joe but he couldn't give her what Andrew could. And no doubt he was having his own fling or two while he was away. That's what men did. Why should she feel guilty when he was at it as well?

Not sleepy, she raided the bar fridge for a bottle of wine that produced a nice glassful, dutifully ticked the charge sheet and returned to bed. She mustn't do this again. She'd had her last eye check-up, now she'd forget Andrew. But she knew her body would probably betray her.

And what about Jonno? What was she going to do now, what was her next step? And why had Padraig acted so strangely when she had suggested exorcism? Should she and Joe just sell up and go back to the States?

Suddenly exhausted in body and mind she put her half-empty glass to one side and was quickly asleep, soothed by the soft Cork rain tap-tapping against her window pane.

Padraig brooded. He gazed into the coals as they glowed in the range. Then he brooded some more. He wished the American woman, pleasant as she was, would go away. Leave them. Sell the house. There were so many things she didn't understand, and couldn't be expected to. And in not understanding she was in danger of upsetting the order of things. She was in danger herself. She was getting too close for an incomer, an incomer who had connections to the modern world outside of Cork, of Ireland. She was getting too curious. And Padraig was troubled as to how that would turn out for them, for the old inhabitants of the townland.

Her talk of Jonno had surprised him, but only insofar as she, an American incomer, had encountered him. Of course Jonno wandered through Dunmurry when the moon was in the right place. One or two others too. Most people knew better than to hang around Dunmurry after dark. They wouldn't come to harm but it was best that the old world and the modern world kept their distance. It was for everyone's good.

Yes, Padraig was surprised that Miranda had somehow bridged the two worlds. This could have unintended consequences. He must think on this further. Think about what might be done.

15

Joe returned to Dunmurry three days later. She was surprised at how, all things considered, she was pleased to see him. He was her husband, her soul mate. She held him fondly as they inspected the grounds of Dunmurry. As ever it seemed there was drizzle in the West Cork air. But, like snow to an Eskimo, it was just part of the scenery. Around here they thought you a bit simple, amadán, if you passed a comment such as 'wet weather we're having' or 'looks like rain again'. Miranda, if not Joe, had begun to accept rain and drizzle as the norm and, by default, picked up hat, raincoat and brolly when stepping outside.

It was the occasional sunny day that was a cause for surprise and comment. Today was not one of those days. Pleased to simply be together again they slowly walked the gravel path, inspecting the bare flower beds, the condition of the dormant grass, the trees which had been recently pruned.

The boundary walls were sturdy enough, constructed back in the day when good labour and materials were cheap. In places a little maintenance work needed to be done but it wasn't enough to rouse a stonemason to give them an extortionate quote.

And in any case the whole idea of a boundary wall was an anachronistic one. Back in the day the grand houses of Ireland came with walls, the better to make a statement to the tenants, the peasantry. They shouted of separation of they, the landed gentry, from the native people who only existed to do their bidding. The lord and his lady considered the peasants envious as they peered over and around the walls, through the gates. Impressed even if they had occasion to actually walk or ride through these gates up to the big house.

But in truth the best that ordinary folk could do was pay a certain deference born out of years of subjugation. As they went about their hard days, envy of their betters never came into it; more a sense of hostility against those they didn't consider to be part of their community.

Dunmurry was hardly 'grand' but still it had its walls. They served little purpose. To the south the river was the 'de facto' boundary of the property, to the north the road. To east and west was farming land of little quality. Perhaps the cows would have made a beeline for the well-tended Dunmurry grass in the absence of the walls. Maybe then they were there after all to deter the livestock rather than the great unwashed.

It was significant that the property itself was largely intact as originally built, with extensions and improvements. Many was the grand property in Ireland that had been torched as symbols of British rule during the troubled times of the early 1920s. It had been left untouched as there had always been a bed there for those in need who were fighting for Ireland's freedom. The Tans had ransacked the place more than once as had the security forces during the Civil War, but had ultimately left it in peace.

But, for all her happiness in being with Joe again, Miranda's thoughts strayed often to Cork city and to Andrew. Yesterday had been their third and latest encounter; a stolen hour at his consulting rooms before she picked Joe up at the airport. It had been wonderful. Of course she knew by now that their meetings had little to do with love – Andrew had made that clear on the first occasion. But he was warm, intelligent and witty. And amazing in bed, or even on a couch on the South Mall! She was a cheat, a harlot, a floozy but she couldn't resist him. And he was hers, for the time being at least. She shivered at the thought of Andrew and Joe held her closer against the damp afternoon.

It was Joe who found it the following morning. He called upstairs in an unusually formal and stern voice.

'Miranda, come down and look at this.'

'Oh my God, what?' she thought frantically, 'he's found out. Someone has told him. Who …?'

She threw on her dressing gown over her naked body and went downstairs to face the music. She would deny everything. No, she would claim it was a one-off and beg his forgiveness. Oh God why had she been so stupid?

Joe was sitting at the kitchen table. In front of him an envelope, a piece of paper.

'You ought to sit down before you read this.'

Numbly she took the note from him, still trying to find the appropriate form of response. What she read came as a strange sort of relief.

YOU ARE NOT WELCOME HERE. LEAVE WITHIN ONE WEEK OR ELSE.

'What … what does it mean Joe? Who is it from?'

'That isn't all. This was with it.'

Joe held the object out to her. A bullet. A silver bullet.

'Oh my God!' Her hand flew to her mouth.

Within the hour the Guards had arrived from Bantry.

Miranda had wandered aimlessly around the house. Joe mooched in his office until they arrived.

It was two young officers, a man together with a woman that looked liked she ought to be in school, thought Miranda. They poked the envelope, note and bullet with their pens. They groaned and rolled their eyes when Joe and Miranda admitted they had handled all three.

The male officer questioned them both together, then separately. Two hours later, he had their complete recent history including lists of everybody they knew and anything which might have led to this incident. They told everything they knew, which was little.

Miranda kept her two secrets deep within her though. Andrew had nothing to do with this, that was obvious. But whilst the ghostly Jonno was possibly relevant she wasn't about to tell them all about that. She knew that she wasn't mad but didn't all madwomen protest the same?

They left after a good look around. The gravel path did not retain footprints so there was little reason for the SOCOs to call. They carefully bagged the three items and took them away. They would be in touch.

'They think it's me!' Joe stormed into the house the following afternoon. The Bantry Gardai had asked him to come in earlier.

'Huh, what?'

'They think it's me. The note. The bullet.'

'But that's mad. Why on God's earth would you do it?'

Joe took deep breaths and sat down. Miranda kneaded his neck muscles the way he liked it, then poured him a coffee. Eventually he recovered his composure.

'Now, tell me what they said.'

'It's their working theory. They don't suspect anyone else. Not from the people we told them about.'

'Well, neither do I.'

'And they're saying that if it's not anyone we know then why should anyone we don't know want rid of us?'

'That's their job, to find out!'

'Well they're looking for no one. Unless they find any prints on the bullet other than ours.'

'But why you Joe? Why on earth …?'

'Well. They seem to think that I'm less in love with Dunmurry than you. That I'm looking for an excuse to leave.'

'So you sent yourself a threatening letter? That's the craziest idea ever.'

There was silence. Was it such a crazy idea? There was no doubt that Miranda adored Dunmurry and her new life, Joe maybe not so much. Could it be …?

'Miranda, it wasn't me! Though I can see what they're thinking. The question is, what are we going to do?'

'What! You're not thinking of leaving? Of being chased away? Nothing's going to happen.'

'I think we ought to consider our options, is all.'

The next few days were hard for them both. Joe was of the mind that they ought to leave. Miranda was distraught at the very idea. But Joe's line hardened. He didn't want to stay in danger and, even more, he didn't want Miranda harmed in any way.

And it was fair to remember that Ireland was no stranger to violence, and threats of violence, assassinations. They were ingrained in the country's history. Even in modern times it would be foolhardy to dismiss such things with an airy wave of the hand. Just because there seemed to be no rhyme or reason for the threat didn't mean that it could be disregarded.

Therefore it was, with heavy heart, the Hunters boarded up Dunmurry, put the more valuable items into store, and took a flight from Shannon to Boston. It was exactly a week since they had received the unwelcome letter and gift.

They had reached a compromise. For the present they would keep ownership of Dunmurry. Their time away would be treated as a winter break and plans would be made to return in the spring. There would be plenty of time to discuss and refine these plans in due course.

Miranda, almost as an act of defiance, paid another visit to Andrew. The sex was as wonderful as ever but, as she'd expected, he was not exactly heartbroken to hear that she was leaving.

And on their last night in Dunmurry, Miranda sat downstairs and waited for Jonno. As if affronted by her betrayal he did not appear to her. But she imagined he was there somewhere. As her eyes drooped and sleep beckoned she spoke to him.

'Jonno, can you hear me? I haven't forgotten you. I will keep my promise. I will find your brothers. Be patient and I'll be back.'

As they drove off towards Shannon, Padraig, meticulously tending his garden, looked down the road and watched them go.

16

Well, just as I imagine I'm going to die peaceable Janie pokes her nose in again. More trouble dead than ever she was alive, that woman.

The care workers, two of them, had to virtually break in here. Can't blame them anyhow, it's their job. They got bosses telling them what to do. And though they're damn busybodies their hearts are in the right place. I can't rightly be annoyed with them.

I told them, yes the Doc could come and see me. Doctor Felix though, no one else. Truth is I've been getting pains that the painkillers can't kill no more. And I can't hardly make it to the bathroom without getting out of breath and hanging on to the wall. I've no problem with dying but I'd as soon go peaceable.

So Doc Felix will be around later. But in the meantime those damn care workers Tom and Geraldine – Tom and Jerry I calls them – went through my mail. Saves me doing it anyhow. They throws most of it out, makes a neat pile with some others.

Then Tom hands me something, says he thinks I ought to read it. And isn't it a note from Janie. It's attached to that last letter from that darned Miranda Hunter blathering on about Jonno. Anyhow Janie says – here's the note.

My Dearest Jim,

Please don't be cross with me. I know you have your own mind and we've discussed this before. Please call this woman and hear her out. We're here on earth for only a short time and it behoves us to do some kindnesses if we can.

There may be nothing in it but the woman sounds very anxious and disturbed. She went to a lot of trouble to seek you out.

Write to her again, or call her. Her number is there. To contact her does not commit you to doing anything else.

Jim you're a good man. I know you'll do this as much as you know I'll love you always.

Janie

Well that woman wrote like she knew she was going to die before me, yet last time I saw her she was as chipper as a new-born lamb. But it's too bad. It's too late now. I ain't interested. But, God help me, it's as if my Janie was talking to me from the other side. I'll sleep on it.

Miranda was enjoying a catch-up with a few old friends when her iPhone rang. Putting her plate to one side she apologised, looked at the caller display, frowned and hit the red button. Annoyingly, the same thing happened again. She switched off the phone.

It was 24 hours later when she remembered the call. Having a few quiet moments she checked the caller display again. Strange, a US number but not local. About to switch off again she accidentally hit the dial button, sighed and decided to let it ring. How did a call centre get her number? She was about to cancel the call when it was answered.

'Hello?' An old chap, not a sales call. Unless they were employing old chaps these days.

'This is Miranda Hunter. I missed a call from you last night?'

'Oh, Mrs Hunter is it? Oh my, I'm sorry, I was asleep. Thank you for returning my call.' God who was this old fool, she thought.

'How can I help you?' she snapped.

'Mrs Hunter, my name's Fitzgerald. Jim Fitzgerald. You wrote to me?' Oh God, of course now she remembered.

'Mr Fitzgerald, Jim. I'm so sorry for being abrupt. I'm delighted that you've called. I didn't expect to hear from you really.'

'Well I'm kinda surprised I did and everything. Only for my wife I wouldn't have.'

'But you're in Tulsa, is that right?'

'Yes Ma'am, Tulsa, Oklahoma. I've promised my wife that I'll try to assist you if I'm able. I'm not rightly sure of what I can do though.'

'Yes, about Dunmurry. I'd almost forgotten. You see I'm back in the States right now, Boston area. Maybe I can come and see you, to explain everything?'

'Well Ma'am if you wish. I ain't going no place myself.'

'I'll fly over, it's no problem. I have your address, Fairbreeze Heights? Would the day after tomorrow be OK for you?'

'I'm sure I can get my secretary to clear my diary Ma'am, heh heh!'

'Then I'll call you when I'm in town. I look forward to meeting you Mr Fitzgerald. And your wife.'

'You too Ma'am.'

Joe was bewildered and not a little miffed. What was he to think of his wife flying off to meet a strange man? Miranda had little choice but to expand on the matter of the Fitzgeralds – Joe had taken little interest in her research.

Again she thought it was high time that she told him about Jonno's ghost, but still she demurred until it was absolutely necessary.

Still, Joe grumbled so Miranda put her foot down.

'Now listen here, Joe Hunter. I've come back here with you to Massachusetts because you asked me to, and because you're my husband and because I love you. The least you can do is humour me and let me have a bit of freedom to do my research. I've never stood in your way.'

And without waiting for an answer Miranda sat down to check out flights from Martha's Vineyard to Tulsa.

During the long flight from Boston to Dallas-Fort Worth Miranda pondered why on earth she was doing this. She was being driven by her heart to help Jonno to rest, but her head told her that this was a hopeless task. She had located one brother but apparently he was too ill to travel. The other brother, Donal, had last been heard of in Australia. Dead or alive, she had no idea. And even if he was alive was there any better chance of persuading him to travel to Ireland?

A cautious bookmaker might give odds of 100-1 against her getting both brothers back to Dunmurry. And, even if that happened, would it provide the closure that Jonno needed? It was all very unlikely.

But yet, but yet. Miranda's heart was indomitable. She knew what she had to do. If she failed in her mission then at least she would have been true to herself. The thought of six year-old Jonno wandering around Dunmurry would forever trouble her otherwise.

*

She had something of a wait for her connection at Dallas-Fort Worth. While she sipped an orange juice she phoned Jim and arranged to call up to him that evening. And after an hour's hop north to Tulsa, she gratefully checked in to the Renaissance Hotel, set the alarm and napped.

Showered and refreshed, Miranda grabbed a cab and quickly arrived at Jim's place. It was over to the south of the city and was, even in the darkness, a pleasant-looking low-rise complex of sheltered apartments. Finding the concierge's office she was given walking directions while her presence was phoned through to Jim. Two minutes later he was welcoming her at his door and, five minutes later she was sitting in his apartment.

Jim was much as Miranda had imagined him. Average height, clean shaven, balding, slim. He was dressed in a check shirt and jeans, comfortable brown shoes. He was a model of politeness as she had surmised from his correspondence and their short telephone conversation.

She accepted his offer of coffee and noticed him wincing as he carefully sat down opposite her. She had decided to come clean with Jim, put all her cards on the table. She could do nothing else. This was her last chance of persuading him to come back to Ireland with her.

Well, I might be a crabby old man and difficult to get on with but I still appreciate the sight and smell of a good looking woman. And especially when they decide to visit in my own home. So I'm sorta on my best behaviour for once, try to act polite like.

I owe it to Janie to hear this Miranda Hunter out. I don't mind admitting I'm a little intrigued. Hearing from her has taken me back many years and has awoken memories which had been almost buried. Now I can just recall hoping that they'd find Jonno just so that Mam would stop crying. She went to her grave not knowing what happened to him. If there's a chance that I can do something about it – yes I know it's a bit late for it – then I'll do what I can.

This Miranda tells me her story all over again and I don't say much. I expect I'm too used to letting women do all the talking. From the beginning, the way I understood, she and her husband done bought Dunmurry there a year or two back. That in itself didn't surprise me none. Even back when we lived there we'd get the occasional rich Yanks stop by, looking to see if the house was for sale.

Then Jonno starts appearing to this Miranda. Or so she says. Her husband don't see him though, or won't. And the last time they had a conversation the two of them, just like that, like they were neighbours. He asks her to help find his brothers, and she promises that she will.

Now I've been around, heard stories and tales, some of them tall, some not. Those that tell of sea serpents and mermaids and spirits and suchlike are usually taken away by men in white coats, sooner or later. Or so it used to be the case. These days they mainly let them carry on the crazy talk and just keep an eye on them so they live normal lives like anyone else. Maybe this Miranda is romancing, seeing stuff that ain't there. But tell me this – how else did she know about the Fitzgerald family except that Jonno gave her a clue?

This Miranda now, I listen to her, watch her. She don't look crazy to me like I thought the first time she wrote. And now she's saying that Jonno won't rest until he finds me and Donal. See, that makes sense and all. Happen the day he disappeared he was probably looking for us in the fields, up and down the river.

Now there's a new twist! The reason she and her husband are back in the States is because they're being threatened. 'You are not welcome here.' She tells me that they've not fallen out with anyone. So what can it all mean? The Irish police are investigating but her husband Joe has insisted that they leave. Leastways until things get cleared up.

Now the story had been told she had to ask the question.

'Jim, thank you for listening to me. You haven't treated me like a madwoman. Now I have to ask you that huge favour again. Will you come back to Dunmurry with me? Will you speak to Donal, ask him as well?'

Jim sighed. He suspected this was coming. But he knew it was impossible.

'We'll Ma'am, I sure would if I could. Problem is, I'm old and ill. I'll be joining Jonno in Hell before too much longer. I'm not able for the journey. Why, a trip downtown would probably kill me. It just ain't possible though it grieves me to say it.'

She slumped forward, defeated. Her eyes brimmed and, despite herself, the tears silently fell onto the carpet. Embarrassed she fished in her handbag for a tissue. She tried to speak but no words came. Instead she stood up ready to take her leave.

'I'm sorry Ma'am, I truly am. Even if I wasn't sick, I couldn't afford to go.' She composed herself enough to say

'Money would be no object, Jim. We're rich.'

'I'm sorry Ma'am, I truly am.'

'Well, thank you for seeing me Jim. Thank your wife as well.'

'Janie was killed two weeks ago Ma'am, but it don't make no difference.'

Back at the Renaissance Miranda ordered a room service meal, then a bottle of wine. It was over. She'd never return to Dunmurry. She just didn't have the strength to start all over, trying Donal in Australia. Then later, desperate to find some comfort she swayed downstairs and drank at the bar until she had to be gently helped back to her room.

She was roused late the next morning, her head splitting, light pouring through the curtains. It took her a full minute to locate the source of the shrill noise. It was her iPhone. With shaking hands she located the phone and hit the green.

'Hello.' It was part gasp, growl and grunt.

'Miranda, good morning Ma'am. Jim Fitzgerald here.'

'Oh, Jim.' She rubbed her eyes, tried to find some moisture in her parched mouth.

'When do we leave?'

'Huh, leave? I'm sorry I ...'

'Well I spoke to the Doc this morning. He agrees the trip might kill me. But I'm dying anyway.' As he spoke Miranda slowly hauled herself to the surface and arranged her brain into some sort of basic working order.

'Jim! I'm so grateful. But I understand your position. I can't make you come.'

'Happen I'll make it if my doc comes with me. Can you arrange for that?'

'Wow, yes of course. I'll make all the arrangements. Tell me when you can both fly up to Boston and I'll make the reservations.'

'Well now, I'm quite looking forward to seeing the old place again after all these years.'

'And do you think, I wonder ...'

'Donal? I'll see, I can't promise anything. Don't rightly know if he's dead or alive. But maybe seeing me will be enough for Jonno.'

17

Ha! They've got you at last, you old bugger!'
Donal looked up in surprise from his regular
corner seat. A smartly-dressed policeman stood in
front of him, an envelope in his hand.

'Donal Fitzgerald?'

'Yeah? I ain't done nothing.'

There was raucous laughter from nearby tables with a few
more witty comments thrown in. This was good sport. Early
evening in the Cricketers Bar and the lagers were going down
nicely. Donal knew everyone there and, though he preferred
to drink alone, at his own table, he was on friendly terms with
most of his fellows.

His slow brain desperately tried to scan over the past few
days. Try as he might, he couldn't remember any particular
misdemeanour – at least none other than the usual. Being
a pest, he'd got a little string of minor convictions, it was
true. Mostly disorderly conduct with fines and bindings over
being the end result. He'd spent the odd night in the police
cells and didn't care to make a habit of it, far less end up in
one of the more secure State establishments.

'Relax Donal. I'm only a messenger boy. Here, this is for
you. Time you got a phone, man.'

The policeman handed over an envelope, mock-saluted
and walked out of the bar followed by low-level jeers from
the assorted company.

It was true. He had no phone, landline or mobile. He'd never owned one and was not inclined to invest in one at this stage of his life. Why would he want a phone? And he had no address. Well, strictly he had one but couldn't remember what it was. His latest accommodation in a long list was a single room in a townhouse in a run-down part of Darwin. The only people that mattered, the benefit people, had had to look up his latest address with the help of a map and Donal's directions.

He wasn't about to open the envelope in present company and stuffed it into his pocket. It was unlikely to be money so it held little curiosity for him. He stood up and marched to the bar for a refill.

It was late the following morning when Donal remembered the envelope. As was his wont, he'd woken late, showered and decided to shave, it being a Saturday. About to fry a breakfast of sorts, he remembered the policeman and then, by association, the envelope. He found it, ripping it open with no great interest. It was on a police letterhead and poorly typewritten.

Mr Donal Fitzgerald,
We have received a message from your brother James, who presently resides in the United States. He requests that you call him as a matter of urgency. The number is ———.

Donal stared at the note, extremely surprised. It must have been ten years or more since he had spoken to Jim. And, as he recalled, they'd had some sort of argument. He was still alive then, probably in better shape than he, Donal, was.

He wondered what might be so urgent. Their parents had died years ago and they had no other close relatives, to his knowledge. It couldn't be that urgent.

Nevertheless, he was now curious. There might be money in it. He'd give the old bugger a call.

The Cricketers opened at midday and Donal was outside as the doors were unlocked. Ritchie looked at him in surprise.

'Morning, Donal. This is early, even for you!'

'Morning, gaffer. Just want to use your phone if that's OK?'

'Usual, Donal. One dollar.'

'Ta. Can you dial this number for me, gaffer? I'm not au fait with modern gadgets.' Ritchie squinted at the number.

'That's not local, that's international. Five dollars that'll be, and keep it short.'

Donal grudgingly fished out a five-dollar note, handed it to Ritchie who shuffled behind the bar, pulled out the old phone, dialled and handed the receiver to Donal. The bar was empty which is why Donal had chosen this time to make the call, otherwise the details would have been all over Darwin within the hour.

'What's that noise?' Ritchie had a listen.

'International dialling tone. It's ringing.'

Donal held the phone to his ear. It continued ringing. He was about to lose patience, reclaim his five dollars, when the call was answered.

'Hello?'

'Hello, who's that?'

'Jim Fitzgerald. Is that you Donal, you eejit?'

'Yes.'

'You're ringing me. How would you not know who I am?'

'That's the way you speak to your younger brother? I've a

mind to put the phone down. It's costing me five dollars this!'

'Well, now then, Donal. You're alive then?'

'I guess so. How's yourself anyhow?'

'I'm grand. You'll be wondering why I asked you to call.'

'And how. No one knows where I live.'

'Well I know you're still in Darwin. I got in touch with the police there. I guessed they'd find you.'

'Well they did that. Now, what do you want?'

'Right. Do you remember Ireland, Dunmurry, the house?'

'Huh? Vaguely, I guess. Did we used to live there one time? Hold on Jim, the gaffer here wants another five dollars. Call me back will ya? The Cricketers Bar, Darwin.'

A trip! A journey back to old Ireland! They'd send him a ticket! Good God, wasn't that something? He'd never been on a plane. He'd arrived at Sydney Harbour in 1956 and had never left Australia since. In fact, he'd not left the Darwin area for a dozen years or more. And now they were offering him a trip to Ireland. A celebration was in order. A lift of the little finger and a pint of 4X was on its way.

A week later it was a quiet, subdued figure that stepped into the Cricketers Bar as the bolts shot back and the doors creaked open. Ritchie looked at Donal with a scowl but was preempted from barring his further progress by the miscreant himself.

'Gaffer, sorry about last night. If there were any breakages …'

Ritchie looked at him, his scowl remaining. Donal took this as a good sign. At least Ritchie hadn't turned him around and kicked his arse back down the road as had happened more than once previously. It can't have been that bad. But he had the foggy remembrance that riotous things had happened the night before involving singing, fisticuffs, spilt beer. He had decided to come and face the music, get his apology in quickly.

'Oh Donal, why do you do it to yourself? You can't possibly enjoy acting the eejit, brawling and that. You're an old man now. The young ones just laugh at you.'

'Sorry, gaffer.'

'Sorry my arse. Fine chance of me doing this place up, spending a few dollars on carpet and that. Place would be ruined in five minutes.'

'I know. You're a fine man to put up with the likes of me. It won't happen again.'

'It will, Donal, then I'll have to bar you, let someone else take the pain. How now, you're looking smart?'

'Give us a half and a whiskey there, gaffer. I'm off to the airport.'

'What, plane spotting? You've not stepped across the city limits in 20 years to my knowledge. Meeting someone are you?'

'Off to Ireland, gaffer, that's what I am. See my brother Jim.'

'Good Lord, you're the sly one. A brother in Ireland? And where did you get the money for that gallivant? You have trouble enough paying up your tab here on a Friday.'

'This woman sent the ticket. I don't really know. Just wants me to go to Ireland. Place I lived as a kid.'

'Well, that beats everything. That explains the smart get-up of you. Here, have a whiskey on me.'

*

Several whiskeys later, Donal thought that he had better be on his way. Although his plane ticket had arrived, he had not let Miranda know that he wasn't a man of means. However, he had a little put by and had drawn most of it out in the hope that it would last him as far as Ireland anyway.

The taxi stopped by Donal's room and he picked up his battered suitcase containing much of what he owned. The jacket and trousers that he wore he had picked up cheap enough a couple of days previously at a charity shop.

As Ritchie had said, it had been a good few years now since he had been beyond the city limits and he was somewhat disappointed when he found the taxi driving into the airport terminal. He was just starting to enjoy himself looking at all the activity as they sped up the Stuart Highway. He paid off the taxi, found himself confronted by a neat and modern building, and correctly guessed that 'Departures' was his most likely bet. The smell of aircraft fuel and the noise of jet engines all around was a novelty to him. He had never been to an airport before, far less as an intending passenger.

Once inside, Donal looked about in bewilderment. People rushed past him in every direction, screens flashed and scrolled. Donal had fondly imagined that he would immediately have seen a single queue for Dublin which he could join. Instead, as he read the nearest screen he became increasingly concerned. Kuala Lumpur, Cairo, Melbourne, Singapore. Dublin he couldn't see at all.

But then to his relief he saw 'Restaurant and Bar.' This he understood. He brightened and followed the arrow to the right. He hardly recognised the establishment he arrived at as a bar. Clean, shiny, bartender in a smart uniform. Only the beer taps and bottles on the shelves told him that he was in the right place. Crikey, he'd have a few suggestions to make to Ritchie at the Cricketers!

Two beers later Donal felt fortified enough to resume his quest. This time he was emboldened to enquire of two women in green uniforms. They looked as if they knew what they were doing and were familiar with this place.

The women looked doubtfully at Donal's paperwork which Miranda had sent him. The consensus was that, for Dublin, he should join the queue at Gate 15, Quantas flying to Singapore. Donal had no interest in going to Singapore but at least he might get further directions. He joined the queue.

Twenty minutes later he had reached the head of the queue and was called up to the desk to be greeted cheerfully by a small, bronzed girl, smartly presented, make-up, neat hat.

'Good afternoon, sir. May I see your ticket?'

'There you are, Ma'am. All the way to Dublin, Ireland.' He was starting to enjoy his journey, but it wasn't to last.

'Sir, this ticket hasn't been validated.'

'What?'

'It hasn't been validated.'

'What does that mean? The woman said that I could travel anytime with it.'

'Yes but you can't just turn up and fly. You need to book a seat and quote the reference number etcetera.'

'Where do I do that then?'

The queue was getting fidgety. The check-in lady called a male colleague who took Donal into a nearby office. He soon ascertained that Donal had no clue whatsoever. The term 'online' meant nothing to him.

The man, young and helpful, escorted him to the Quantas

sales desk. He explained to the staff there that Donal wished to travel to Dublin, then he left him in their dubious hands.

But yes, they told him that the ticket was valid and paid for. And yes, the connecting flight was leaving for Singapore in two hours. Would Donal like to book for Singapore through to Dublin? Donal nodded eagerly.

'May I see your passport please sir?'

'What?'

'Your passport?'

'But ... I don't have ...'

'You don't have a passport?'

'No, no one told ...'

'I'm sorry sir, you can't fly without a passport.'

Two hours after leaving the Cricketers Bar, Donal was back there. For the first time in his life he felt alone. Alone and stupid. Stupid and distraught. Nursing his lager in the corner, served to him by the afternoon girl, Donal put his head in his bony, gnarled hands and silently wept.

Chantilly regarded him warily. Not her favourite customer. Steady enough when sober but a bloody nuisance after a few drinks. If she'd had her way he'd be barred, take his dubious custom elsewhere.

She had mentioned it before to the gaffer but he'd been firm on the matter. 'He's OK is Donal. Yes he can be a pest, I know that much. Many's the time I've kicked him out. But giving a man his ticket, that's a tough one, Chantilly. Bloke's worked hard all his life, not like some shirkers nowadays. He's earned every cent of his pension, and, what's more, he spends most of it here. He doesn't go to other bars. Donal's OK. Let him be.'

The few other customers ignored him. A couple of old fellas were playing dominoes, click clack. An old lady with her shopping supped a half down the other end. One lone drinker perched at the bar in the slow mid-afternoon.

And Donal sat at his usual table, head in his hands, elbows on the table, shoulders shaking gently.

Chantilly checked unnecessarily for waiting customers, lifted the hatch and wandered over to his table.

'Everything OK, mate?'

A surprised Donal peered through his fingers, saw the chit of a barmaid, gulped what may have been an answer and resumed his former position.

'Well, fuck you too!' She went to turn away on her heel but something made her hesitate. Donal looked up again and removed his hands from his face, sat up straight, blinked at her.

'You stopped crying like a Sheila now?'

Donal looked at her. It had been a long time since a young person, a woman at that, had addressed him so directly. A short little thing, cropped hair dyed yellow, pixie face, silver stud in her nose, arms folded over her red T-shirt, jeans rolled up just below her knees. Crikey, Donal thought, kids get away with anything these days.

She abruptly turned and walked back to the bar, reached over and grabbed a few tissues from a box. She marched back to the table and held them out to him. Stood back warily in case he exploded. The dominoes players glanced across, though with minimal interest, before resuming their pushing and tapping.

Donal wiped his eyes, blew his nose.

'Another?' Chantilly pointed at his near-empty glass. He took the final swig and held it out to her. She served the man sitting at the bar, then poured a glass of lager for Donal along with a Coke for herself. She took them over, placed them on the table and sat herself down in a chair across the table from him. He fumbled in his pocket.

'Nah, it's OK. That's on me.'

'Well, thank you, Miss,' Donal managed.

'Hey it talks! I thought you were from the deaf and dumb home. So, you doing OK, Donal, ain't it?' His eyebrows went up, the glass half way to his lips. This wasn't the banter he was used to with the night-time crowd. He guessed he had better attempt conversation with this alien creature who came in peace.

'Yeah, it's Donal, Miss …'

'Chantilly.'

'Miss Chantilly. Thank you kindly for the drink.'

'No worries. You're not normally in at this time mate?'

'Nah. Things have gone a bit wrong for me today.'

'Y'going to tell me?'

'Today I found out I know nuthin' about nuthin', that's what. I'm a loser. I can't even get on a plane by myself. I'm just a useless old man …' Hurriedly, she pushed the tissues towards him and waited patiently. Eventually he told his story and she even understood some of it.

'So you ain't got a passport and you want to go to Ireland – did I get that right?'

'That's about the size of it. Never had one, not that I recall. Lived in Oz for 60 years, never needed one. Now I've lost the chance of seeing Ireland again, where I was born, and my brother Jim.'

'If getting a passport is your biggest worry mate, then I'm happy for you. Post Office, couple of days, if you pay the extra.' She treated him to a happy smile.

'Are they expensive?'

'Not cheap. You got any money?'

'A little. Depends. I guess I could borrow a little more.'

'And you say you have a ticket, already paid for?'

'Yep, here in my pocket. The airport woman says it needs validating or something.'

'Must be an open ticket. Donal you'll be home and dry once you've got the passport. Look, I'll help you if you like. Meet you outside here in the morning, say 10 o'clock?'

'Ah now that's kind of you, Chantilly. I feel like an old fool but I guess I do need a little help.'

'Well, there's a first!' she chortled, 'A man admitting he's not perfect! No worries. Glad to help mate.'

'There is one other thing that's worrying me though,' Donal began, 'I don't know if you can help?'

'What's that?'

'I need to call Ireland, speak to this woman. Tell her there's been a delay …'

'Look, use the one behind the bar. Ritchie won't know. Make it quick though. Blimey you've got a woman paying for you to fly half way around the world. You're a sly dog.'

Donal was delighted with his room at the Dublin Airport Clarion. Light and airy on the third floor with views away over the city and the hills further south. He was pleased now that Chantilly had persuaded him to retire his battered suitcase and instead purchase a holdall, more easily carried and more respectable in a place like this.

He supposed he ought to be tired but he'd snoozed on and off as the Quantas jet made its way over land and sea to eventually deposit him in Ireland where he'd been born in

1937. He hardly felt like he'd come home though. The Aussie outback and frontier town of Darwin were all he'd known for 60 years. Anywhere else was a mystery to him.

He'd never have got here in a million years without Chantilly. She'd marched him in and out of offices, up and down stairs, helped him fill out forms. She'd sat with him in an internet café to validate the ticket that Miranda had sent him. She'd written down his itinerary, the times he could expect to be in Singapore, Dubai and finally Dublin. She'd made sure that he'd packed the right stuff and that he had all the essentials. What was in his bag was radically different from when he'd first packed.

Finally, she'd accompanied him to the airport, made sure that both he and his bag were checked in correctly. Despite his protests she'd pushed what dollars she could spare into his pocket. Then, with a small push, she'd put him in the security queue, begged him not to drink too much, reminded him to check the screens and listen for the announcements. And then, like a mother bird, she let him fly and hoped for the best.

In the Arrivals Hall at Dublin Airport a bewildered Donal wandered to and fro trying to find a telephone. Eventually he found one, but once more had to swallow his pride. He asked a passing woman if she would kindly help him call the number he showed her. His growing belief in people's inherent kindness was fortified when the woman, learning he had no credit card, inserted one of her own so that he could make his call.

To his relief Miranda picked up the call and told him to go to the Avis desk where they would look after him. A smart young man at the desk directed him to the adjacent Clarion Hotel with instructions to return to the desk in the morning to be driven down to Cork. Light of heart he found the hotel easily enough, checked in and found his room. He enjoyed this unaccustomed luxury for a while before deciding a drink would make things even better.

He somehow made sense of the lifts and, after wandering around corridors and being confused by mirrors, Donal found the hotel bar. Thankful again to his Good Samaritan for sorting out some euros for him at the bureau at Darwin airport, he waited patiently for his first pint of Guinness to settle and then took it away to a table.

Curiously he took a sip. Heavy, sweet, warm. Not unpleasant. He took a swallow and leaned back. This was the life. Flown across the world and put up in a hotel for nothing. He wasn't yet at all sure exactly what Miranda wanted in return but he supposed he'd find out in due course.

The bar was quiet, shiny, sterile. Not the kind of place Donal felt comfortable in though he was neatly dressed, shaved, hair combed. He wanted to drink in a proper pub. After making enquiries he left the hotel bar and set off through the airport complex, following the directions he'd been given. Sure enough, ten minutes later, a welcoming sign proclaiming 'Healy's' greeted him as the road left the airport taking traffic towards the city centre.

Pushing open the door to Healy's he peered in, then with glad heart he joined the merry throng inside. A few levels below the Clarion, Healy's was still a few levels above the Cricketers Bar. Confident now he marched to the bar, ordered his Guinness, waited knowingly like a local for it to settle before taking it to find a seat. They were far and few between tonight but an old couple waved him to a spare place at their table. Immediately he was in his element, chatting away, telling them tales of the Outback.

But, as it had so many times before, his night took a wrong turn. Donal found himself, two hours later, turfed out on the roadside. He was in the right, too. The other bloke had started it with his taunts of sheep and corked hats. Donal was thirsty and made to re-enter the bar. Then, wisely, he thought better of it. He weaved his way back to the Clarion, though not caring to try for another drink there. By a miracle he not only arrived at his room but managed to open it with some manner of card they had given to him instead of a key.

He threw his boots and jacket off and lay down on the huge, soft bed. And before sleep overtook him he promised that no more would he drink too much, at least not until he had done what Miranda wanted him to do.

Whatever that was.

18

Miranda couldn't believe it. In the space of 48 hours her project had gone from 'no hope whatsoever' to 'full steam ahead'. Both Jim and Donal had agreed to travel back to Ireland. It appeared that Jim was quite poorly but she'd hope for the best with that. It was a perfect solution to have his doctor accompany him though. That took a lot of worry off her shoulders.

Of course, Joe thought it was all quite insane. Miranda seemed oblivious to the death threat, the reason they'd left only 10 days or so ago. No, she seemed determined to not only go back but to arrive there with some sort of three-ring circus trying to catch a ghost!

But he had given up trying to dissuade her. She was both adamant and determined. Joe reckoned that the sooner this was all over, the better. Their relationship had deteriorated over the last few months, that was obvious to both of them, though they never talked about it. Joe was certain that Ireland, or rather, Dunmurry was the cause. Things would be better once this baloney was dealt with one way or another.

Jim and his doctor, Felix Barnard, flew over to Boston and put up at an airport hotel there. Felix had more than a drop of Irish blood in him and, being without any dependents, was quite happy to take a sabbatical from his downtown practice. Miranda would pay his fares, put him up at Dunmurry and pay him a reasonable daily rate whilst in Ireland.

Donal had been couriered an open ticket Darwin-Dublin though they had yet to hear from him recently. He didn't sound like the kind of guy you could rely on so Miranda had her fingers crossed on that one.

Flight reservations made for the three of them, Miranda prepared to leave Martha's Vineyard once more. The tone was subdued as she and Joe ate in a French-style bistro in Edgartown the evening before. Miranda was alarmed. She sensed the loss of connection between them at this time. So much had changed since their idyllic evenings in Bantry when they had first arrived there. It was probably all her fault with her recent preoccupations. But maybe if Joe had shown more commitment towards her and their new home she wouldn't have become quite so obsessed.

What she did know, however, is that she had no intention of losing him. She still loved him and believed he still loved her. But, as they sat silently across the table from one another, neither could express what their true feelings were. Miranda only hoped that, once all this was over, things would return to how they had been before.

She was relieved to find Jim and Felix in the lounge at Logan International the following evening. Felix looked about 30 years of age, tallish with prematurely greying hair. She warmed immediately to his friendly manner and it was clear that he would be a good companion for Jim. The two of them joked and bantered as they waited for their flight to be called.

Ignoring Miranda, Felix told Jim a joke about the two Irishman flying home from America. The captain announced that, with three of the four engines having failed, they would be arriving late at Shannon. The one fella turned to the other and said, 'Bejaysus if the last engine fails we'll be up here all night!' As Joe laughed and spluttered Felix had to hurriedly find his nebuliser and apply it to Jim's mouth. It reminded Miranda that Jim was on borrowed time.

Unusually, Miranda was foregoing first class. In deference to Joe's feelings about the whole matter, she thought it politic not to be overly extravagant. He was the major earner in their marriage though Miranda was comfortably off in her own right. To all intents and purposes they shared non-business expenses. Their accountant kept track of things and let them know if he considered anything was amiss.

Soon enough they were over the Atlantic, everyone settling in for the trip. Miranda sat in an aisle seat with no one to her immediate right, Jim and Felix in the row in front. They clearly enjoyed each other's company, laughing and joking. Felix was careful to keep watch though and more than once he settled Jim down with the nebuliser.

As the meals clutter was cleared away and the lights dimmed, Miranda had plenty of time to think things through. The time for doubt had passed though and she was committed to this action plan.

It was as yet a fairly unformed plan. There was no template for dealing with spirits that wandered through old houses. Fortunately, Jim at least was open minded enough to consider that her description of events wasn't the figment of a madwoman's imagination. She had not reacted like a '30s film star, running around screaming with disheveled hair! On the contrary she had acted in a controlled manner, then had described events exactly as she had experienced them.

She had not been overtired, drunk or under the influence of mind-altering substances. It was a while now since she'd last smoked grass and had no wish to experiment with anything stronger. And although she enjoyed a glass of wine she preferred to wake up in the morning with a clear head.

But what if Jonno didn't appear? Or if Jim or Donal didn't see anything? She had no Plan B at present to back up her tenuous Plan A.

She hoped that Donal would show up as promised, within the next few days. She had left a message with whom she assumed was the manager at the Cricketers Bar in Darwin. It had hopefully reached its intended recipient. It asked Donal to travel to Dublin as soon as possible where he would be met and brought down to Cork.

And after that who knows what would happen?

There was little activity now in the cabin. Felix and Jim appeared to be asleep. Her mind was racing so fast that Miranda doubted that she would sleep at all.

But the next thing she knew was the change in engine tone and the morning light through her small window as the big plane tracked in and down towards Shannon.

Well, it's kinda hard to believe. Only yesterday or the day before I was at home in Tulsa. Now here I am like the President himself in the back of a limousine being driven through Ireland. There's Felix beside me, keeping an eye on me but I feel good. Miranda there is up front with the driver, turning around and chatting, describing the passing countryside like she was the native, not me. Why, she ain't been gone from the States for less than a year but she appears to love the place.

It's true what Johnny Cash sang about them forty shades of green. One minute it's raining and you get all the dark shades – the fields, the trees, the hills. Then the sun appears and it's like a miracle how the land is lit up with bright greens and yellows.

I guess I dozed off a little, missed a few of the sights. Limerick town is a bleak-looking place though, not so much green about Limerick. We're doing a fair lick towards County Cork and Bantry and Dunmurry and I'm pleased I came. I wonder if Donal made it yet.

Felix is like a big kid, whooping and pointing at every cow and ruined castle which we pass by. I guess those ruins are no more or no less ruined as when I grew up hereabouts. Charleville now and the roads say Welcome to Cork. The main road leads to Cork city but we ain't going there, not right now anyhow.

Roads are quieter now, narrower. These are the roads I associate with Ireland. There weren't no wide, fast roads way back then. No one was in a rush to go anywhere anyhow. I hope this driver knows what he's doing.

I remember the town of Macroom. The signs point to Dunmanway now, then Drimoleague. Memories. Bantry up ahead but we ain't going there just yet. I hope we can while we're here, while I'm still able.

And hey, we're here! The limo pulls up outside the gate and the driver goes to open it. But I want to walk! Miranda understands and she and Felix help me out of the car. I can't believe this. Seventy years since I stood here, outside these gates. And it's the same, or appears to be. The house is as I remember – it's been well looked after, looks like from here anyhow. The trees, the lawns, the gravel path … it's like stepping back in time, like I was a boy again.

Crunching up the path, just as it was. And hey, we're expected. The big old front door opens for us, a housekeeper I expect. Miranda goes in, fusses over me, I'm fine. Now. I can't say the inside of this place rings many bells. The interior's changed a lot I guess. Not that I rightly remember what was here in the first place, but I'd know if it was the same. You get my understanding?

Big, modern kitchen to the left but we're shown into a living room to the right. Beautiful place, sink into an armchair. Felix inspects the pictures, the ornaments, not so modern, respecting the age of the building.

Accept the offer of a cup of coffee and Miranda whistles up the order to 'Mary' who must be the housekeeper. Something stronger is offered but I need to treat alcohol sparingly in my condition. Maybe later. Coffee arrives on a tray and is placed, with some biscuits, on a coffee table. Felix sits down and joins us.

No Donal, not yet anyway. Miranda will try to contact him later. Nuisance him not having a phone like everyone else. If this little thing is going to work then I reckon it stands the best chance with both of us.

Miranda shows us to our rooms – Felix and me are next door to one another and Miranda has given me a little bell to ring should I be in trouble or anything. That is indeed a comfort. If I'm going to go I want the Doc by my side to see that I go peacefully. Hopefully I'll last until this job is done anyhow.

This big bed sure is comfortable. It's been a long journey so I guess I'll lie down awhile.

Miranda was tired in body too of course but her mind still raced. There was probably no going ahead without Donal though, in his absence she would just have to try. Impatiently she checked yet again for incoming calls and messages that she may have missed – nothing. She didn't want to bother the staff at his bar again, not just yet. Hopefully he'd arrive in Dublin before too long and she'd have the limo company pick him up from the airport. Patience is a virtue, she kept telling herself.

She called Joe. Yes he was 'fine', he was always 'fine'. And as always he was pleasant. He had accepted her need to pursue this rather strange project at Dunmurry but had little personal interest in it. He was quite content to wait until it was all resolved, Miranda returned home and they could discuss matters.

Miranda felt very lonely after hanging up. Yes Joe had told her he loved her, but did he mean it? It seemed that they had drifted gradually apart after those idyllic first few months. She still loved him intensely but it felt as if he was just going through the motions in return.

But was this the story of all new marriages? She had discussed this at some length with her old friends back in Martha's Vineyard. There was no consensus. One or two were of the opinion that, indeed, marriage did not improve over time. Others, however, declared that they were in love with their husbands, and they with them, as much if not more than ever.

Miranda wanted to be loved. Maybe when this was all over they would grow closer once more.

In the meantime, she had idle hands. She had no idea of when Donal would arrive, if at all. There was only so much entertaining and sightseeing she could do with Felix and Jim, though it appeared they were the best of companions. She probably ought not to worry on that score.

Mary, the temporary housekeeper, left for the day after ensuring that there was plenty of food in the fridge and freezer. They wouldn't starve.

There was silence from upstairs. Miranda looked curiously at some half-forgotten books on the shelf. She chose one, tucked up her feet on an armchair and began to read.

19

She wasn't particularly fascinated with history. At school, stories of the Pilgrim Fathers and the settlement of the eastern seaboard had left her yawning. The pioneers who conquered the west, the subjugation of the Native Americans, War of Independence, Civil War, the Presidents of the USA. She had barely scraped pass marks at school.

It seemed perfectly natural for her though to choose a volume entitled *A Short History of Ireland*. Here in remote West Cork on the edge of Europe she had the strangest feeling that history was moving on more slowly, reluctant to change gear. The very reason the three of them were here right now was directly linked to the 1940s for example. Maybe it was time to get a little background to this strange place.

She read with surprise that the earliest inhabitants of the island of Ireland, Partholan and his followers, came ashore at Bantry Bay, no less! She wished she'd known that fact during the time they'd lived there, and visited since. Certainly no one had thought to mention the fact to her. This was about 2,680 BC. Unfortunately, Partholan's descendants were completely wiped out by a plague 300 years later.

Ireland was then disputed and fought over by the Nemedians and Fomorians, but the combination of warfare and another plague again left the island uninhabited.

The third occupation was by the Firbolgs, a small, swarthy race, about 1,900 BC. They are credited with the first division of the country into provinces. These remain broadly intact today though the ancient province of Meath has long been merged with Leinster. Each province had its own King.

A great battle took place at Moytura, Mayo where many were slain as the Tuatha De Dannan were victorious, ending the Firbolg's reign. Many of the stone circles and cairns in the area date from this period in Ireland's history.

At a time of almost perpetual warfare the Gaels or Milesians occupied the land around 1,700 BC after further great battles at Slieve Mish, near Tralee and again at Tailtin in Meath. This was the age of bards, druids and brehons of which little written record remains.

The first great Irish king of whom we know was Cormac MacAirt who ruled in the third century AD. He was the first king to establish a pan-Ireland army thus creating, for the first time, order and establishment. It was he who established the tri-annual *feis* or parliament at Tara, County Meath. There laws would be enacted, the annals of the nation read, genealogies recorded, taxes assessed and disputes settled.

Miranda's drooping eyelids shot up as her phone rang, and just as Felix and Joe appeared from upstairs. She quickly remembered which century it was she lived in, grabbed the phone and answered it notwithstanding there was no caller display. It was a man whose voice she did not recognise.

'Hello, Miranda speaking.'

'Hello, who's that?'

'Donal! Where are you?'

'Dublin airport. Someone had to show me how to use this bloody phone, begging your pardon. What should I do now?'

'Donal, hold on there, Jim's here, wants a word with you.'

Jim had heard the phone and conversation and had struggled across the room as quickly as he could. He grabbed the phone.

'Donal, is that you?'

'Who do you think it is? How are ya?'

'Well, OK I guess. Where are you?'

'The airport. Look put Miranda back on will you?'

'Hello Donal,' Miranda began, 'I've organised a car for you.'

'A car? I guess I can still drive one. I'll try.'

'No, I've arranged a driver. Now, you're to go to the Avis desk and tell them who you are. They'll put you up in a hotel nearby and drive you down here in the morning. Is that OK with you? It's all paid for.'

'Blimey, you must be rich Miranda. I hope it's the penthouse suite. Right, Avis desk is it?'

'Yes. Enjoy Donal. Call me back if there are any problems. We're all looking forward to seeing you tomorrow.'

It was a cheerful trio that sat down to dinner that night, dished up from what Mary had prepared earlier. Miranda opened a bottle of wine. She happily drunk most of it as Felix was teetotal and Jim was simply too ill to risk more than a glass. He seemed to be bearing up well, though Miranda was very pleased that Felix was with him. She was a hopeless nurse with no medical knowledge or aptitude.

'So, are you going to tell us the plan Miranda?'

'Jim, I think I'll wait until Donal arrives. I need the agreement from both of you to do anything.'

'Fair enough. I'm not particularly eager to get to grips with spooks and that, even if it may be Jonno.'

'Felix, do you think I'm bonkers?' She looked directly at the friendly doctor.

'Frankly? No. I don't think anything at all will come of this but there's no denying your determination to see this through. Did you really see something?'

'Only the last time. But I spoke to him Felix. We spoke together. I swear.'

'Well, I'd rather not be involved with whatever plans you've got, if that's OK.'

'No Felix, that's fine. It's Jim and Donal he wants.'

Felix and Jim had taken the car and gone out for the evening. Miranda eagerly picked up her book again. From ancient history she turned to myth and legend. To fairies; the gods of Pagan Ireland said some.

Fairies take many forms but are always capricious and inconsistent in their behaviour. They are easily offended and always like to be known as the 'good people'. At the same time they are easily pleased, maybe with a little milk on the window-cill, a horse-shoe above the door.

They live between heaven and earth and love feasting, fighting and loving. May Eve, Midsummer Eve and November Eve are their special days. At Midsummer, it is said that they often steal away mortal brides. On November Eve, *Samhain*, they dance with ghosts and witches because it is the end of the summer.

It is said that certain of the Irish country folk are able to see the fairies, converse with them. It is further said that sometimes the fairies can take human shape, if it pleases them.

Commonly the fairies live in forts or raths which may have been the burial place of unchristened children.

And there are sub-species of fairies. The Leprechaun

makes shoes continually and has grown rich. Should you catch one, don't let him go, though he will promise to lead you to his crock of gold.

The Pooka and Banshee are other forms of fairy, the Fairy Mistress another. She seeks the love of mortals and, refuse or consent, you are her slave.

Miranda turned to the section on ghosts.

Like the fairies, ghosts inhabit a world somewhere between this life and the next. Something prevents them from fully crossing over – maybe an earthly longing or affection, a duty unfulfilled, perhaps unrequited anger against something.

Those that have died suddenly may become haunting ghosts.

Miranda stopped reading to reflect. Some things seemed to be falling into place. Astonishingly this old book of legends and superstitions, which would be scoffed at by many, was telling her exactly what was going on with Jonno. There was still no telling how he had died but one could presume it was sudden. And also he clearly had affection for his older brothers, much as they seemed to have almost forgotten about him. Might she then be on the right track? Might finding his brothers release him happily into the next world? She read on.

When the soul has left the body it is drawn away, sometimes by the fairies. Such souls are considered lost. If a soul eludes the fairies then it may be snapped up by evil spirits.

A ghost is compelled to obey the commands of the living.

The souls of the dead sometimes take the shape of animals or insects.

Before putting the book aside, reluctantly, Miranda noted with some interest that the ancient festival of Samhain was only days away.

20

He was one of the lucky ones, they said. No one on the oil tanker was said to have survived, and few that had been in the vicinity. In the days and weeks that followed the vivid images of the explosion, the booming, crashing, cracking noises, the awful screams, were with him constantly. Asleep or awake he couldn't escape them. And the pain, the searing pain in his face. He felt it yet though they had treated it as best they could.

At the Bantry General Hospital they had done their best, treated and sedated him, then had him moved up to Dr Steeven's in Dublin. A number of weeks and several operations later, they said that he could go. But his face was a mess from the flames, misshapen, one ear gone, lips swollen and askew. But he could walk and talk after a fashion; his hair was growing back in places. They needed the bed.

He walked out of the hospital into a chill spring air, anxious to get back to Bantry, back to his family. He had enough money in his pocket and a voucher for the train and bus home. Sure, his face was bad but weren't there enough quare looking people wandering the streets? It was a short walk to Heuston Station and it was surely his own imagination that the few people he passed averted their eyes. But the shock in the eyes of the polite woman that sold him a copy of the Independent in the station foyer told him the truth of the matter. In a quiet corner he slipped on the balaclava that one of the nurses had kindly found for him. Checking himself in the mirror in the gents he decided that the balaclava covered the worst of it.

All he had now was the choice of going around scaring people with his injured face or to look as if he were a member of a terrorist organisation on his lunch hour. Slowly the euphoria of his release from hospital evaporated. The reality of his new life started to sink in. It was no longer any use pretending that people wouldn't notice, or at least wouldn't make it obvious. Already on his short walk he had seen the way that eyes glanced away, expressions froze. Previously comfortable with his identity, Eamonn, sitting there waiting for the Cork train, started to realise that his life had changed that awful night, and not for the better.

As the train rumbled out of Dublin and picked up speed southwards Eamonn experimented with the balaclava. He tried to find an acceptable halfway house between a total cover up which might provoke worry and even a Garda intervention and full disclosure of his injuries. In the washroom he tugged the balaclava here, pushed it there, regarding himself in the mirror. There was going to be no lasting solution. The remainder of the journey he spent studying the scenery, unwilling to pretend sociability, until the hills of Cork came into view and the train rumbled through the tunnel into Kent Station.

Normally he would have enjoyed the comfortable and scenic bus journey from Cork out to Bantry, the weather crisp and clear. He would have been looking forward to seeing his wife Molly and his two young boys Oscar and Dan. But he had forebodings. His wife had visited him only once in hospital, when he had been high on medication, and she hadn't stopped long. She knew that he was coming home but hadn't exactly sounded enthusiastic about it. But surely it would be OK, Molly whom he'd known and loved for years and his two rascally sons who loved going to the park with their Dad and having a hit around with the hurleys.

Jumping off the bus in the familiarity of The Square, Eamonn hoisted his holdall onto his shoulder and headed off on the short walk home. People he knew walked by him, unknowing. He went to speak to them, then stopped himself and walked on. The little town was quiet. The disaster had cut off much of the bustling economic activity overnight. Eamonn wondered if things would eventually start up as before, if he would be able to apply for his old job back. His hands were still in good working order thank God, shielded from the flames that night being thrust in his protective overalls against the icy weather.

But now he walked up his garden path. The door was off the latch. Pulling off his balaclava he pushed the door open. His wife Molly stood there. Tears brimming she walked to him and hugged him, then stepped away. His boys stood side by side and looked at him. They tried, oh yes they tried. They had been well prepared. 'Hello Dad …' But then, both together, their bottom lips trembled, their eyes dropped to the floor and they sobbed. Eamonn walked to them, hugged them, but there were no words between them. Their mother ushered them out of the room.

They tried for weeks but the affection from his family was no longer there. Molly did her best but stiff formality was the best she could manage. They slept together mainly because there wasn't a spare room, but she wouldn't let him touch her, apologising to the best of her ability. His boys no longer came near him, begging to be taken to the park. They sidled away whenever he was around. His old friends were civil in the main but no longer wished to prolong a conversation. The pub staff served him but, by their coldness, made it abundantly clear that they would prefer it if he would take his custom elsewhere.

One morning, before the sun arose, Eamonn slipped out of the front door, holdall on his shoulder with sleeping bag rolled up and attached, and walked away.

The first night he stopped at a little B&B. The second night, the weather being cold but dry, he laid out his sleeping bag inside the walls of a long-abandoned cottage and had his first experience of sleeping under the stars, surprisingly comfortably. He moved on each day with no destination in mind. He knew that he was not wanted and he hoped that, in time, he would come to terms with this new reality and find a new life of his own. It would be a lonely life but that didn't concern him. He wished Molly and the boys good luck but now considered them a part of his old life, best forgotten.

He had a little money and, though he didn't need much, he occasionally drew a few euro from an ATM at a roadside garage or convenience store. On occasion he would do odd jobs in return for a cup of tea or a sandwich. The tramp of yesteryear, wandering from place to place, was gone but Eamonn found that he was treated courteously as long as he didn't outstay his welcome. He travelled slowly north into Kerry and, during the fine summer, began to enjoy his new, simple life. The Guards checked on him occasionally, even brought him in twice, but in the end decided to let him go on his way. He was doing no one any harm.

He didn't linger in any one place, conscious of his stricken features and the effect they had on others. He hurried in and out of shops, buying only a little bread and cheese, maybe a bottle of water though Nature has granted the west of Ireland plenty of that commodity for free. He became content in his own way and missed the comforts of home life not at all. As the leaves started to fall he wandered eastwards and back into Cork, though only the occasional road sign let him know this. The countryside was his oyster and each county alike to him.

As the first storms of winter started to batter the country he found himself, one afternoon, in the environs of Bantry once more. Despite his new life and his adaption to it, he was nonetheless well aware that an Irish winter was not best spent out of doors. No matter how well-chosen the doss the damp chill permeated both sleeping bag and clothes at night and the day was spent sheltering from the elements. It was not as carefree a life as it had been during the summer time. He wondered if, after all, he should head for Cork and find himself a hostel for the winter. He didn't want to live among other people again, with all that entailed, but maybe it was the only sensible option.

But for now, it was late afternoon and Eamonn was looking for somewhere to hole up. Walking by the Dunmurry Hotel he laughed and wondered if he might treat himself to a night of luxury. It was only when he had walked by that it struck him – the hotel seemed very quiet. Closed perhaps, it being November. Curiously he retraced his steps, opened the creaky gate and wandered up the gravel path ready to apologise and be on his way if challenged. But there were no lights on despite the gloomy early evening, no parked vehicles. And indeed it became quickly obvious that the big property was closed, shutters closed on the lower windows.

Eamonn had come across old, empty properties before but was loathe to break into them for a doss. For one thing it would be an excuse for the Guards to lock him up, and for another he had been brought up to respect the property of others. Just because it was temporarily unused did not give another person the right to occupy it, especially by forced means.

Nonetheless, Eamonn thought there might be a shed or something around the back. Cautiously he walked along the front of the big house and down the path that led to the back. Still no lights, not a sound. He came to the grounds at the south of the property. These had been well kept despite the fact that there were now clear signs of neglect. Further down to the left there were a number of outbuildings. And, happy days, the doors of two of these were unlocked. Eamonn was in luck. This would do him royally for tonight. As quietly as he could he pulled the holdall from his shoulders with relief. The concrete building was half empty and cheerless but there was rubber matting of sorts which Eamonn was able to use as groundsheet. Building a sort of a nest with his own belongings together with bits and bobs from the shed Eamonn settled down safe from the elements and as content as a knight of the road could be.

Eamonn stayed the next night too, then the night after that. It was the first time he'd spent three nights in one place. It didn't sit well with him and his wandering instinct but he felt strangely at home, unaccountably welcome, and he therefore delayed his departure. He forayed out to search for a little food but returned to Dunmurry in the evening. And on the second night he happily found an overlooked case of whiskey beneath tarpaulins in another of the outbuildings. Eamonn had never been much of a drinker and, even upon this discovery, he limited the pleasure to the night time when he found it helped him to sleep.

On the third day, he decided to touch up the weather-worn white paint of the timber window frames of the house. They had started to peel and Eamonn, who had always been something of a handyman, found the necessary items, together with a stepladder, to both smarten up the frames and to give them some protection against the coming winter. Whilst doing so he found a window open on its latch and, by dint of a few belts with a trowel, he gained entrance to the main hotel. Indeed it was remarkably intact with much of the furniture, beds etcetera having been left in situ. Whether temporarily or not Eamonn was unable to say. It did appear however that any items of real value had been removed. Wandering around, Eamonn noticed that deterioration was beginning to set in – dampness in particular. He resolved that, if he were to remain here for a while then he would pay for his board by trying to rectify these things if he could find the tools and materials to do so.

So each morning he would arise, go and wash down at the river. He would make up his mind to move on that day, but still his holdall remained as his pillow. If he needed provisions he would step out the few miles to the nearest convenience store and collect them, along with items like wood sealant, brushes etc. During the hours of daylight, whilst at residence at Dunmurry, he busied himself with little jobs, anxious lest he be accused of mistreating the place if he were to be discovered. Every day he made a point of doing something to aid the old property, even something as seemingly trivial as tightening the screws of a curtain rail.

He could have made himself very comfortable in one of the bedrooms but he didn't even consider it. Each night he made himself perfectly at home in the outbuilding, treated himself to a few sips of whiskey and considered the future. He never thought back, to the days of his former life. To do so would only invite unhappiness and despair. No, he looked forward. He was still young and strong. He just needed to find himself a place in life where his disfigurement would count for nothing, where people wouldn't avoid him or avert their eyes.

And often in the late evening, in the time between drowsiness and sleep, he would sense someone outside, on the path, in the garden maybe. But when he checked there was no one and he would think no more of it.

One night just before Christmas, Eamonn was awoken by noise that had permeated his sleep. Becoming fully awake he heard voices, raucous laughter. Shaking himself free of his sleeping bag he pushed open the shed door. The noise, and intermittent flashing light, was coming from the front of the property. Eamonn padded down the side path and peered around the wall. It was a group of lads, drinking from bottles and cans. They were mainly sprawled under the trees on the other side of the drive. Their car was parked askew on the gravel, door open, some manner of music blaring from its radio. The lads joked and laughed but otherwise seemed harmless enough.

All the same Eamonn squatted down, out of sight. Kept an eye on them. He wasn't afraid to confront them if they threatened trouble. And indeed, a while later, they seemed to be ready to move on, hurling the last of their bottles and cans across the lawn. But then one of them seemed to suggest something that the others agreed with, cheered. Two of them fiddled with the petrol tank, a bottle, a rag or cloth. The group grew quieter, urging their mate on. Suddenly Eamonn realised what their intention was. Too late. The cloth was lit and the deadly cocktail launched through the glass of a first floor window with a crash, to renewed cheers. Eamonn charged at them screaming and shouting. The group were on their way anyhow but, at the sight of the disfigured apparition hollering towards them they panicked and threw themselves into the car, trying their best to cover their faces lest they be recognised later. The engine fired into life and the car fishtailed down the gravel drive, screeched onto the road and accelerated away.

Eamonn, glancing up, saw flames licking the curtain inside the broken bedroom glass. Dashing to the back, he entered the property and took the stairs two at a time. He found the room and saw, with horror, the flames engulfing the curtains and starting to spread across the ceiling. His experience at Whiddy had left him with a deep fear of fire but now he charged across the room and desperately grabbed the undamaged edges of the curtains and dragged them away from the rails, onto the floor. Looking around desperately the only helpful item he could see was the double mattress on the otherwise bare bed. He grabbed it, lifted it with a roar, and threw it on top of the flaming curtains. To his relief, this seemed to stop the conflagration. Still flames licked around the edges. Eamonn managed to find a nearby bathroom and, to his relief, the water still ran. In the darkness he found two glasses, the best he could do. By ferrying glasses of water from the bathroom he managed at last to douse the remaining flames. He sat, exhausted on the bed frame for half an hour until he was certain there was no chance of the fire taking hold again.

His hands were burnt and starting to hurt but, from experience, Eamonn knew that this was nothing and they would heal. He retreated back to his shed, took an extra large swig of whiskey and did his best to sleep.

A few days later Eamonn woke up, unspeakably depressed. It was Christmas morning. Last night he had finally given in to self-pity. With the help of the whiskey he had lain in the dark reliving his life before the accident. He thought back to his carefree early life in Cork city, his parents, their house in Tivoli. Children still played in the streets in the hills above Cork; no one thought to lock their front doors. They had nothing to rob. His Teddy Boy days. His engineering apprenticeship at Cork Steel. Turning out at football and hurling for St Finbarr's. Meeting the first and only love of his life, Molly, at a club dance.

When the oil terminal had come on line at Bantry he had applied for, and got, one of the many jobs going there. Molly had gone with him and they had been married, and she quickly thereafter presented him with two lovely boys. The money was so good they were able to put a deposit on the small house in the town centre. Life was good and the best ahead of them. Then came the explosion. His life as he knew it had come to an end. And all his wanderings since he had left home had only led him to this; to the conclusion that life no longer had anything to offer him.

Depressed beyond belief, hungover as never before, he dragged himself and his half-empty bottle of whiskey into the main house. He also took the length of good, strong rope which he had found in the shed. Taking a slug at the whiskey he made his way upstairs, to the room with the broken window. He had dumped the fire-damaged curtains and had boarded up, as best as he could, the window. In tears now, he apologised to the house for not protecting it and for being unable to fix the glass properly. It was his only regret, he had no others.

As he worked on the rope he took further slugs of the whiskey. He wasn't afraid but the alcohol was a comfort in his final moments. No regrets. Soon he had a serviceable noose made with the good, strong new rope. There was plenty of it and he threw the loose end several times over the solid beam that ran under the ceiling, tying it off. No fear, suffocating was quick and easy. Without hesitation he took the nearby chair, stood on it, squeezed his head into the noose and kicked the chair away.

He found himself, half-conscious, on the floor. He examined the rope. The knot had slipped. He couldn't believe it, he had tested it well. Before he could lose courage he re-made the noose, hung from it by his sore hands to test it, stood on the chair and once more launched himself into oblivion. To his utter amazement and disgust, just as he was blacking out, he crashed to the floor a second time. When he came to his senses he found the knot intact but the strong rope had unaccountably snapped.

In a daze, a surreal world, he worked once more towards his own destruction. He wouldn't be beaten. A final gulp of whiskey, the rope tested this time almost to destruction, he repeated the process for a third time. This time he smiled to himself through the agony as the rope held and he drifted into unconsciousness.

When he came around for the third time it was in the sure knowledge that he had passed over. But he coughed uncontrollably and slowly sight returned to his eyes. Only by degrees did he realise that, unbelievably, he was still of this earth. The rope was still intact, around his neck. Hardly able to move, his body ached from head to toe, his throat horribly constricted, the coughing non-stop. The proof that he was still alive was the near-empty whiskey bottle on the bed. With a great effort he grabbed it and drank.

When he finally regained his full senses, he looked about him. Above. The rope was intact but the immensely strong oak beam, rock of ages, had snapped through. In both despair and wonderment, his body wracked with pain, he realised that Dunmurry didn't want to hang him.

The next day Eamonn pulled his holdall over his shoulder, left Dunmurry behind him and, his body complaining in protest, he trudged off towards Cork city. Maybe his mother would take him in, maybe there was yet a glimmer of hope for him.

21

First game of the new year. So early in January that the county council couldn't supply anyone to paint the lines and put up the nets. Here are the keys though, lads. Drop them back in through the letterbox after you've finished.

Trevor and Fiachra had taken an executive decision. The lines were faint but OK as long as both teams agreed to play honest like. They didn't fancy spending an hour in this weather trying to repaint them with the contraption that they hardly knew how to operate anyway. Anyway they had lugged the nets out of the shed. They had made a commendable effort of hanging them at one end and they were now engaged doing likewise at the other set of posts. The first of the cars came in through the gate and up the rutted drive. There was adequate parking behind the groundsman's shed and the two portable cabins that served as changing rooms. There was some semblance of shelter over there behind the hedge but here, out on the field, the lads worked away in a cold sea breeze and a relentless drizzle that had long since rendered their fingers numb as they roped and threaded the heavy netting between crossbar and posts, then back over the supports behind the goal.

Team captain and secretary of 1796 Bar Sporting Club. They had happily accepted the positions at the general meeting of the gaelic football team back in their home pub in the summer. Sure what work was there to do and mightn't there be a few free pints in it? As they narrowed their eyes against the driving rain and worked the netting along the crossbar, rain now dripping down their necks, they both made a decision to relinquish their exalted positions at the next possible opportunity.

Finishing the job adequately, Trevor and Fiachra carried the stepladder back to the shed and made their way to the sanctuary of the home portakabin. A few of the boys were already there, reluctantly beginning the process of togging out in the bleak January afternoon.

'My hands, I can't feel them. I'm off into town to warm them up in the deep freeze in Murphy's Mini Mart', Fiachra complained to whoever would listen.

'Don't plunge them in warm water now. Did you ever feel the pain? You'd be wanting to cut them off you.'

'Can't we just call the game off? Go down the pub? Ask them Trevor. Share the points.'

'Now come on lads, this is our big opportunity. They're the only side worse than us. Beat them and we're on a roll.'

Both teams gathered slowly. In the 1796 hut, the blue shirts and white shorts were pulled out of the kit bag and donned. The smell of embrocation filled the air as muscles were massaged against the elements they were about to be exposed to. Boots were dragged on and, in customary fashion, at least one lace snapped leading to oaths, panic and a search for a spare one that then had to be threaded onto the boot as throw-in time approached.

In the next changing room were the Eastside Reds who made the 1786 team look like a model of professionalism. They were made up of a mixture of old lags who could no longer get a game on any other team, but with a sprinkling of keen young lads. There were two father and son combinations and the youngsters were expected to do the running with the older ones issuing instructions. It was in the lap of the gods if enough bodies turned up to constitute a full team. The old, red shirts were stained and torn with an assortment of sizes including those large enough to accomodate extending waistlines and bellies.

The Reds were firmly bottom of the league but didn't lack spirit. They treasured their reputation as the poor boys of the league and celebrated every point that they were able to garner from time to time. And today they had a realistic glimmer of getting a result against 1786, a team noted for its ability to smoke and booze rather than play with a football.

At this ground, on the outskirts of Bantry, the referee had a choice of changing with one or other of the teams. In this instance the ageing and increasingly ineffective Packie Byrne chose to pull on his boots in the comfort of his own car. Packie had reffed at a good level in his time and even now his spirits rose as throw-in time approached at this bleak outpost of the GAA with ordinary lads doing their best on a Sunday afternoon. The association annually discussed putting Packie out to grass but always concluded that it would be the end of the old fella. He was instead assigned to the lowest levels of football. Even so Packie found the game faster than he could manage, but he did his best and was well treated by everybody.

Packie checked he had everything, the same routine he had used these last 30 years. Watch, plus a spare. Whistle, notebook, pencil, cards, rule book etc. Five to three, he climbed out of his car and trotted onto the pitch. A few keen lads from either side were kicking a ball about. Packie gave a blast on his whistle and, reluctantly, the portakabins slowly emptied themselves of the rest of their inhabitants, a couple of the 1786 Blues still pulling on their fags.

'Howya lads,' said Packie as the respective captains trotted up to him in the middle of the sodden pitch.

'Howya Packie,' replied Trevor and the young captain of the Reds.

'Have you got full teams now lads. Don't make me be counting them with my old eyes.'

'Thirteen Packie, that's it I think,' replied Trevor.

'Well, we have twelve at the moment Packie but we're expecting two more.' The Reds captain scanned the road anxiously as if possibly a few county players would soon drive by and fancy a game.

'Well, just bring on who you want, but no more than fifteen now, you hear? Now Blue, head or tail?'

The Reds elected to play into the elements in the first half. Packie threw the ball into the air and play commenced. The action was desultory at first, the combatants more intent on preserving body warmth than throwing themselves into the fray. It was one of the eager young Reds that brought the game to life with a solo and a kick just wide of the posts. Trevor yelled at his troops to wake up and his marginally more accomplished side gradually took control. Hands securing the ball, neat hand-passing, kicking into the corners, the Blues took a couple of routine points and then, thanks more to the immobility of the Reds' goalkeeper than any quality of the shot, a scruffy goal. 1-2, 0-0 with fifteen minutes gone.

The few spectators stood silently on the sidelines. A couple of old men shared a hip flask against the day that was in it. Girlfriends wondering whether love was worth all of this. A scuffle broke out between two players of either side. Handbags. Packie let them sort it out themselves. The game continued on the far side of the pitch. The Blues notched another point. The young Reds tried hard but got little joy against the more experienced Blues defence, and so the game meandered towards half-time. At least the weather relented a little and, as the breeze dropped the clouds lifted and the rain stopped.

At right corner back, even Trevor the captain was finding it hard to raise any enthusiasm for the battle. With the ball constantly in the Reds' half he took to chatting to those on the sideline, even accepting a swig from the hip flask. His mind wandered. He was looking forward to a quiet pint or two later and then an assignation with a young lady from the office they both worked in. It was time he settled down, started acting responsibly. That business out the road the other week had shocked him. Waking up the next day he found it hard to believe that he had done that – tried to burn that house to the ground. It had seemed an obvious and harmless thing to do at the time, with all the drink in him and the lads cheering him on. Then the apparition from the bushes, the mad drive back to town. He had sobered up quickly as he realised his stupidity.

The next day he had driven by the house and was highly relieved to see that it was still standing, the broken window the only obvious sign of damage. Giving a little prayer of thanks he had, there and then, declared that he was henceforth a responsible adult who would behave accordingly.

Half-time arrived with the Blues still the three points up and the Eastside Reds looking hapless and well worth their position at the foot of the table. During the five-minute break the senior members of the Reds decided on new tactics. They would go direct, no more of this fancy Dan passing that was becoming all the rage. Two of the younger, faster lads that had been trying to stem the flow in defence were sent up the field with a couple of ineffectual older players brought back where they might at least be of nuisance value. Then they would kick down the field at every opportunity. This worked spectacularly well for a few minutes. The Blues were caught unawares and two consecutive points were the result with high fives all around and an outburst of cheering from the sidelines. Worse was to follow for the Blues as Packie, at the edge of his visionary powers, awarded a dubious penalty which was smashed into the net by one of the old lags. Their first goal of the season and it was if they had won the county cup.

As darkness descended, the Blues roused themselves to pull back the deficit and to edge two points in front but missed a number of chances to run away with the match. This was to prove costly as the Reds first pulled a point back then, almost as the final whistle blew, Packie adjudged a wide shot by the Reds to have gone over the bar. Neither the protests of the Blues or the sheepishness of the Reds would change his mind.

'Ah sure now wasn't the draw the best thing lads? They'll maybe call the replay for Croke Park next week.' And Packie disappeared into the West Cork gloom.

Trevor set to with dismantling the netting whilst his teammates got changed, everybody quickly forgetting the match as plans were made and confirmed for later. Only three or four of the 1786 Bar team remained when one of them, Tomas said,

'Where's Trevor? He's a while taking them nets down.' Fiachra, who had studiously forgot to offer to help in favour of getting into his warm clothes replied,

'Yeah, ought to have been out there helping him I guess. Come on, let's see if he needs a hand.'

They went out into what was rapidly growing darkness. They could see, at the road end, the nets were down. They looked towards the other end but could see no movement, so they set off in that direction across the muddy field. Then they saw, though they couldn't quite comprehend at first. Silhouetted against the sky seemed to hang a figure from the crossbar, perfectly still.

'Jesus, Trevor!'

They broke into a run but it was all too late. Swinging gently in the breeze, neck tangled in nylon rope, stepladder on the ground hung what was left of Trevor, both hands still clutching at the rope from which he had desperately tried to wrench himself free. It was already too late by the time they had found a Stanley knife with which to cut him down.

And down the road in Caherogullane townland the big old empty house seemed to heave a sigh of satisfaction as it settled down for the night.

22

'Will ye come down out of there, Elvin,' Padraig sighed. He was troubled and could well do without those two eejits messing around. Elvin happily continued to tap dance on the beams that criss-crossed underneath the cottage's shaped roof. All in brown – jacket, trousers and cap, Elvin was quite at home in the warm roof space and was impervious to Padraig's grumblings.

Things were getting worse, considerably so. The Fitzgerald boys were home. He thought that he'd seen off the curious Americans and hoped to see Dunmurry boarded up again, or better still, pulled down. But she, the woman, had not only come back but she had brought the Fitzgeralds with her. And Padraig doubted that this was a social visit. Not all three together, and a fourth who puzzled him but who was no doubt up to no good as well.

The three men had walked by the cottage earlier. Padraig had made sure the door was locked and the cottage appearing empty in case they thought to pay a social visit. He generally had no problems with social visits and had enjoyed the chat now and again with Miranda when she first arrived. Until she started to get curious. Until she'd met Jonno.

Padraig thought that meeting Jonno would have had her and her husband out of Dunmurry in a flash, but it hadn't worked out like that. Instead, she had started digging. And then he thought that the letter and bullet had done it. But, bejaysus, she was back and so were the Fitzgerald boys.

Kalen came to sit on the arm of the chair and looked at Padraig curiously. Kalen was the most empathetic of the two and was inclined to less divilment when the old man was in bad form. Same brown trousers as Elvin but cap and jacket of forest green. He sat quietly while Elvin continued to caper on the beams.

How would he get rid of the Yanks this time, and their entourage? Why wouldn't they leave him in peace? There were few enough places left in Ireland where they could live in the old way. Thankfully, they'd been left alone for many a long year out here in West Cork. They'd been worried when they made up the main road that development would follow, but that hadn't happened.

They'd been clever enough, and lucky as well he conceded, that no developers had been inclined to purchase land hereabouts. There had been plans put forward but never followed through. Quite why that was remained something of a mystery. When the oil terminal was going strong, everyone wanted to live near Bantry. They'd survived those days and Whiddy blowing up had more or less put an end to it. He hurriedly made the sign of the Cross and Kalen did likewise. It was poor form to see good in the deaths of those 50 poor souls back in 1979. But it had delayed, at least, the economic progress that might have destroyed them all. They'd had taste enough of it with the hotel.

'Be off with you now, you two. Can I cook my bit of dinner in peace?'

Soundlessly chuckling to one another, Elvin and Kalen performed a final leap or two, waved their little hands at Padraig and vanished.

23

Donal finally arrived at Dunmurry in mid-afternoon. From inside they heard the unmistakable clang of the gate and crunch of the gravel under wheels. Jim smiled and, encouraged by Miranda, stood up and made his way to the front door, opened it.

There, getting out of the car, was the brother he hadn't seen for over 60 years. He took a couple of steps forward, then Donal saw and recognised him, hurried to embrace him in a bear hug which lasted a full minute.

Miranda held back, trying not to be tearful at the unashamed display of affection. If all else failed she would at least have had the satisfaction of engineering this moment. Eventually they broke apart.

'You haven't changed a bit,' was all Donal could manage as they made their way to the doorway. Miranda was introduced, then Felix. Finally the three men settled down in the big sitting room whilst Miranda fetched coffee and biscuits. For the next half hour the brothers tried to catch up on over a half-century's news. From the moment Donal had left Dublin for Australia in 1953, when he was 16, they hadn't spoken for many years before their brief calls recently. The occasional card or letter, that was all. Neither was aware of the other's life, any aspect of it, during the intervening years. Miranda and Felix smiled, took a back seat and enjoyed the story time.

Several cups of coffee and a packet of biscuits later Jim

and Donal paused for breath. They needed to speak of the elephant in the room. The reason they were here back in their old family house thousands of miles away from where they lived. They agreed that this was a good time to discuss Jonno.

There was no sorrow left. That had been quickly used up long ago. Even at the time they had been more affected by the way their parents, especially their mother, had reacted. Being only young boys they had been loosely bound by companionship, not by love and affection. Losing Jonno was, in itself, not much worse than losing a pet dog or a favourite toy.

Once they had packed up and left Dunmurry then they had quickly forgotten Jonno. Their thoughts, like all young people, were in the present and future. What was in the past was irrelevant. And it was only now, in these last few weeks, that Jim had been drawn back to those earlier times. Donal had barely begun the process of remembering. He had only the vaguest recollections of Ireland, and Dunmurry. Many years of manual labour in Australia's outback, hard living, hard drinking had dulled his capacity for recollection of things that were gone.

It was Jim who remembered, and being with Donal sparked off more and more memories of those faraway times. It was Jim who would say, 'Hey, do you remember …?'

And Donal would, some of the time anyway, answer, 'Crikey yeah! Wonder how he's doing these days?'

But their childhood friends would be either old, like them, or dead.

Now Miranda brought them back to the present. Felix was an observer, though he had shown himself to be a trusted one. He too was there to do a job and did it with a good nature. He didn't seek to impose himself in things outside his job description which was simply to look out for Jim.

'So,' Miranda began, 'this is the way it is. And remember, I had no way of knowing about your family until I felt I had to do the research. So you know I'm not making this up. I've no reason to. Jonno appears, sort of, out of that wall there. He walks, or moves, across the room and disappears out that side. At first, I only sensed him, but on that last occasion I saw him, and we spoke. I addressed him as John, and the first thing he did was correct me. Jonno, he said. Now how could I make that up? Then he asked me if I would help him find his brothers. I told him I would and he seemed satisfied before fading away. He even said thank you. I tried again to see him before leaving for the States but nothing happened.

'And I met him before that, out there by the river. It was the same boy, I'm sure of it now. He said he was looking for his brothers. Then he just sort of vanished from view. I didn't see him again. So, that's twice I've seen him, in addition to the sensing on a few other occasions.'

Donal whistled. 'And he told you his name, this spook?' he asked.

'Yes, that last time. It's like I was gaining his trust or something. Seems to me like he's wandering. Maybe he can't rest until he finds you both. I don't know but it's my best shot.'

'So you want us to try and meet him, put him to rest. Is that the idea?'

'Yes, Jim. I know it must sound mad but that's the best I can come up with. That's why I've brought you both here.'

'Mad alright, but from what I've seen you've got your head screwed on ...'

'Thank you Jim!' She laughed.

'... and I guess we'll go along with you as best we can. What do you say Donal?'

'No worries mate. Amazed if we see anything right enough but I ain't come all this way to let you down Miranda.'

'When do we do this then?' asked Jim.

'Soon, I need to be sure that we have our best chance. I have an idea though. I'll let you know when I'm sure.'

The light was starting to fade. Jim suggested to Donal that they go for a walk, get some fresh air, try to connect with the locality where they'd spent their early days. Felix tagged along unobtrusively as Jim's shadow. Miranda said that she'd stay in, prepare some dinner.

Off they strode eastwards, slowing down at Felix's exhortations. Donal was clearly physically fit for his age but Jim was not at all well, though he was bearing up, Felix thought. Three months, no more, was still his prognosis. But better that he enjoyed his remaining brief time on earth than by being fussed over in a bed to prolong his life a little. As long as he was able to walk then Felix wouldn't argue.

At ease, though still trying to get to know one another again, the brothers pointed out this and that as they meandered along, more slowly now. Things seemed smarter, fresher somehow. From what they could recall the road itself had been little more than a track, certainly until it got nearer to Bantry. Now it was in good condition and cars, though not in profusion, whizzed by either side of the bright white centre line.

Hedges were trimmed, roadside buildings were neatly kept and brightly painted. The fields presumably hadn't changed much but even they looked neat and the cows well turned out. A young lady, neatly dressed, smiled and said hello as she passed them by. When they were boys she would have been wearing a milkmaid's dress and shawl, carrying a bucket. Time had moved on in their absence.

They came to Dunmurry Cottage with the lane heading behind it through the fields to the north.

'This old place. Remember this Donal?' Donal laughed.

'Yes I do! Some old fella lived there on his own. Grumpy old sod. We used to tease him.'

They laughed companionably and walked on, still chatting. But soon Felix suggested they turn back. It was quite dark now; the car headlights were brighter as they flashed by. He didn't want Jim overtired. Back past the old cottage. Jim glanced towards it, saw the face of an old man in the window briefly, then it was gone. A few steps later he frowned and said

'Donal, there's an old fella living in that cottage, I saw him there, just then.'

'And, so what?'

'It's the same old fella that was there before!' Instead of answering, Donal started chuckling, then Jim joined in until they were both clinging to each other in the roadway, laughing uproariously. At length they calmed down a little.

'What? The same fella as when we were young? Get outta that!'

'No, it can't have been. You're right. A son or grandson maybe.'

'Never saw a wife about the place back then, did you?'

'No. Well, it's odd. Maybe we'll call in before we go back, say hello.'

'Yes we'll do that. Come on now, maybe Miranda has some dinner for us.'

Miranda had done them proud. Though not a natural cook

she had built up a repertoire of basic dishes. Living out this way made cooking at home a necessity. So tonight, it was a sole starter in a butter sauce followed by roast beef with plenty of good Irish vegetables.

She'd had the foresight to purchase a couple of four-packs of Fosters which made Donal's eyes light up. He'd happily cracked the first of these, at Miranda's invitation, as soon as they had come back from their walk.

Jim and Donal had shaken off their initial uncertainty at seeing one another after so long. The news that Jim was dying served to bring them together quickly. Though it seemed hard to believe it was mid-October and Jim was resigned to not seeing Christmas. At present he was, with Felix's ministrations, comfortable enough and able to get around, but Felix had warned him that it would be only a short time before he would be bed-ridden and then the end would come rapidly.

Miranda had decided, and they had all agreed, that tomorrow night would be the night when they would try to meet with Jonno. It would give Donal a chance to sleep properly after his long trip – he was still going on adrenaline. But then, every day's delay would increase the risk of Jim suddenly leaving them.

So this evening they kicked back, ate well, drank a little and let the conversation flow. Memories, long since dormant, were prodded to life. The laughter was warm and companionable. Miranda cleared the table, filled the dishwasher, cleaned the kitchen and, giving her apologies, left the men to themselves. Shortly after Felix did likewise leaving Jim and Donal together.

Jim remarked, 'It's strange to be back. So much has changed, but so much is the same. Glad you came?'

'Yes mate. Definitely. I never thought I would. Never entered my head, but I'm pleased I got here.'

'Not sure I'm looking forward to tomorrow though. This Jonno thing …'

'No, that'll be weird, mate.' Donal paused then continued, 'D'you know, that's the one sound that takes me right back to the old days.'

'What's that?'

'Listen, the train.'

Jim listened, and smiled. Over the sound of the breeze in the trees he too heard the rapid puffing sound of the train as it passed, and then faded, on its way across the countryside.

'Some things never change, do they?'

'Thank God for that mate. Now I guess we'd better get some kip. We may not get much tomorrow.'

If the following evening was going to be eventful, Miranda was not likely to be rested in preparation. Her mind was racing in several directions at once. While she was trying to play the ideal hostess to her unlikely guests there were other issues competing for her attention.

Most immediate of course was the business with Jonno. Whereas on her previous encounters she had felt surprisingly relaxed and unafraid, she was now becoming very apprehensive about the whole thing. More than once during that long night she resolved, once and for all, to call the whole thing off. She would thank the three men for their trouble, board up the house and catch the next available flight to Boston. She had no need whatsoever to put herself through this. She would pick up the threads of her old life again with Joe in Massachusetts. Clearly that was where he preferred to be.

Living in Ireland had been a dream, a fantasy. It hadn't quite worked out like that. Something was most certainly telling them that they did not belong at Dunmurry.

Then she would think again. If she ran away now would she so easily forget the lost, lonely young Jonno? Would she forever regret leaving him wandering around Dunmurry and its environs, searching for his brothers? This was her chance to put the matter to rest. It was a miracle that she had managed to get Jim and Donal under one roof from opposite corners of the globe. Jim was dying and Donal would probably never leave Australia again. No, she had to give this her best shot. But what if no Jonno appeared?

Would Joe have her back? Their relationship had become more than a little strained. The cracks were showing before all this business blew up. Joe's business interests were primarily in the States. She wasn't sure if he loved her any more. What if he was with someone else even as she lay there, uncomfortable and lonely?

And Andrew! Her body shivered involuntarily. She had called him earlier and he'd seemed delighted to hear from her. No excuses about eye check-ups. Yes, of course he would see her if she was in town. They were only just getting to know one another, he'd said. They needed a bit more practice. More practice! He was an expert and left her breathless. She was flattered that he was willing to meet her, Miranda, at such short notice when he must have his pick of Cork girls. It would be the lucky woman who managed to get a wedding ring onto his finger. Maybe...no! Stop it Miranda! You've made your choice, you married Joe, you love him. Until both of you decide otherwise that's the way it will stay.

But anyway Miranda promised herself a trip to Cork as soon as all this was sorted out. Maybe the day after tomorrow even, if it all went well. Again she shivered though not from the cold. It was a warm enough night for late October. Whoever had told her that Irishmen were lousy lovers hadn't met Andrew.

And would she be finding another letter, another bullet soon? It frightened her that someone wanted them – her and Joe, away from Dunmurry. Frightened her and puzzled her. They were no threat. They had spent a lot of money doing up the old place and were living there quietly, no bother to anyone. Maybe if there had been wild parties every night then people hereabouts might have got a bit upset. But an explicit death threat? She supposed that the Guards had made no progress with the case; they'd probably just stuffed the file in a cabinet and forgotten about it by now.

Maybe she'd stop by Padraig's cottage tomorrow. Then again maybe not. She enjoyed their chats but the last time he was a bit peculiar, didn't seem to like what she was telling him about the house. That day he seemed anxious to be rid of her. Well, she wasn't going to make a nuisance of herself. If he called her in as she passed, then maybe. Then maybe not. He had made her feel uncomfortable that last time. There was something about him that she couldn't put her finger on.

Sighing, she sat up in bed. Maybe she ought to go downstairs to see if Jonno would come. Then she would be able to tell him about Jim and Donal, how they would meet him tomorrow night.

Her watch said 2.30am. She was wide awake. She picked up her book. Maybe that would send her to sleep.

November Eve, Samhain, three days time!

Irish witches are born of evil spirits and are often able to take the shape of animals. They are wicked and feared, casting spells on those to whom they take a dislike. Their counterparts are fairy doctors, familiar with the ways of the witches and often able to counter-charm the spell. For example, if a cow won't give milk, or the milk won't make butter, the fairy doctor will diagnose whether or not the cause is natural or through witchcraft, and may cure the problem.

Such fairy doctors are often strange, solitary folk who go about their days quietly and without anger or quarrel.

Miranda's eyes were drooping and she put the book down, lay back and closed her eyes. Only a little while back she would have considered the old book an entertainment, an account of the superstitions of a simple people living on the edge of civilisation. Tales handed down through generations and believed without question, regardless of fact. Such stories gave explanations for many happenings that had no apparent meaning, or which were out of man's control.

But, she wondered, to what extent were they true? Unless she was already mad hadn't she herself conversed with a ghost? And was planning another meeting!

Questions many, answers few. At last she slept.

She awoke with the daylight bright against the bedroom walls and furniture. Slowly she stretched, cat-like, until she felt able enough to walk. She was intrigued and slightly alarmed by the smell of cooking. In her experience, men and kitchens were best kept separated. Throwing a dressing gown over her night dress she plodded downstairs. There were Jim and Donal seated at the kitchen bar chin-wagging over glasses of orange juice.

'Good morning lads! How are you? Sleep well?' The brothers politely answered. At the corner there was Felix, the housekeeper's apron donned, tending to a huge frying pan.

'Morning Ma'am. I assumed the quantity of food in the freezer is to be eaten? I took the liberty …' Miranda laughed.

'Absolutely correct, Felix. I'm impressed at your skills.'

'Full Irish Ma'am? Perhaps orange juice and coffee first?'

'Indeed I will, if you stop calling me Ma'am. Thank you Felix. Orange, please. And please only a fraction of what's in that pan.'

It was a breakfast royale with sausage, egg, mushrooms, bacon and black pudding with seemingly unlimited toast to go with it. The four of them ate and chattered happily, including Miranda, despite having hardly slept.

'Well, how did you sleep, lads? I confess I didn't. I'm worried about tonight.'

'I slept like a lamb anyway,' Donal replied, 'the breeze in the trees and the old train puffing sent me straight off.'

Miranda lifted her eyebrows and looked at Donal curiously. No one else commented and the conversation moved on. Amazingly, most of the breakfast disappeared. Jim remarked that the cholesterol was going to kill him before the cancer did. It was yet again another reminder to Miranda that Jim was living on borrowed time, though he was making very light of it.

The men were making plans to go out for the day. Miranda encouraged them to do so. Felix could drive the car. She herself asked to be excused as she felt exhausted. All she asked was that they were not back too late. Tonight, hopefully, would be the night.

So off we drove. And I don't mind saying it was a relief to get out into the open air again. Not saying Dunmurry ain't a fine house and Miranda a fine hostess, it's just that it's sort of claustrophobic. A bit spooky too. Well, I guess that spooky is no surprise if it's got a ghost marching around the place.

Towards Bantry, the old road we used to take on a Sunday morning. A mite quicker now though with a good road beneath us and only the odd tractor to slow us down a touch.

Strange, after all these years I still get a little thrill by being on my way to Bantry. It is, by any standards, a small town. Set down on the Texas plains it would be what we call a one horse town. Of course it's changed – what hasn't after 60 years? I hadn't expected a time warp. The town seemed to come out to meet us. The neat and tidy houses have spread away from the old town centre. They line the roads and there are housing estates that have sprung up in the intervening years. Back then you arrived bang, into the town. Now it's junctions, traffic lights and the rest. Here on the outskirts is Bantry House, a big old place from the days of the Ascendancy. Smartened up now and charging money to go and see. And Bantry Bay sweeping away to the west. The Square is unmistakable, but busy with motor traffic these days. Back then it was horse and cart, tractors, lorries. But with all its modernity it's still recognisable.

I tell Felix that we'd like to see the church. We find St Finbarr's eventually after negotiating the one-way system. Much as I remember. Churches don't change much. But there's a memorial to those who died in the big oil terminal disaster in 1979, overlooking the harbour.

I need to sit down awhile, I tire easily now. Felix and Donal join me on a bench by the memorial and we chat easy. It's the last time I'll see this place before I meet Janie again. For now a puff of the nebuliser and a couple of pills keep me going. We're off to Glengarriff now, a place vaguely remembered as a child. Donal is quiet but appears to be enjoying himself. It's strange for both of us this trip, in so many ways. Who would have guessed that there would be one final adventure left for us old men?

I've only a few weeks, if that, left to live. Or so I'm told. Only now has it occurred to me that I should be making a list of things to do, a bucket list, a hundred things to do before you die. When I first got the news I wasn't that upset, as you'd think I'd rightly be. No, my first feeling was of guilt. Guilt that I'd be leaving Janie on her own. Then, when she went so sudden, even the guilt left me and I had no feelings about it one way or the other.

I've done most everything I want to do, I've had a good life. The good Lord can take me on up whenever he has a mind to.

But my last wish seems like it was made for me. I ought to have come back to Ireland before now. To West Cork. It's where I was born and maybe it's where I belong. Sitting on this bench here in Glengarriff, looking out over the Blue Pool. Donal and Felix have gone to stretch their legs. I told 'em to go ahead, I'm fine right here.

You can get a boat to Garinish Island from here but I guess it don't go this time of year. It's peaceful, not a breath of wind, a light drizzle. A soft day they call it hereabouts. If I could choose my moment, right now would be good. But here come the boys, back from their walk. It clearly ain't my time just yet.

A mite peckish now, dying or not, we decide to call in to the Blue Loo. They offer sandwiches, though Donal is more interested in the Guinness. Seems he likes his drink, Donal. Also seems like he'd stay here all afternoon if the option were offered to him. But he's happy enough to tag along, maybe leave the booze until after our job's done.

The sandwiches and coffee are delicious. We're about to be on our way when there's a final treat. The bartender offers us sea urchins, cut right open in front of us, fresh from Dunmanus Bay. No charge and hope to see you gentlemen again soon. Well, delicious as they were the old bartender won't be seeing me again, not down here anyhow.

Lord, I'm tired. Felix looks at me anxiously. I don't feel so good so he gives me one of the orange pills. I drop off quickly as Felix drives smoothly, heading back to Dunmurry.

I wake up – one day soon I won't, and there's trouble up ahead. Flashing lights, police tape. We're back at the house with the light fading. What's going on?

Miranda was rudely woken from her gentle dreams with a loud crash. Terrified she sat bolt upright in the chair, heart racing, eyes wide. Wildly she looked about her, unable at first to locate the cause of the noise.

Then she noticed the window and net curtain behind her, the window that overlooked the grounds at the rear and the fields beyond. Shakily she stood up and examined them and, to her horror, she saw a neat round hole in the glass, and the curtain too. And across the other side of the room the wall had been penetrated with what was undoubtedly a bullet. Terrified she ran to the phone and called the Garda station in Bantry. They said that they would send a unit as quickly as possible.

Her mind raced as she ascertained that there was no one outside, no one making themselves visible anyway. Despite her fear she realised that whoever had done this was unlikely to be trying to kill her. It was a further warning.

Still panicked, she tried to reach Joe but his cell rang out. She had no doubt that he would order her home immediately and indeed this was worthy of serious consideration.

She boiled the kettle – wasn't that the Irish way to deal with all situations? If there was trouble, sickness, argument, money worries, a nice cup of tea at least alleviated the problem. Why wouldn't it work for gunshots?

The Garda car arrived within a short space of time, screeching to a halt on the road. Miranda opened the gate allowing them to drive up to the door. A male and female again, this time with bullet-proof vests. They hurried inside and ordered Miranda into the kitchen, away from sight of the south-facing grounds and away from the window. After quickly ascertaining the facts, the male officer, David, went around to check the back of the house. He returned and radioed for back up. Meanwhile the woman, Juliette, taped off the gate, followed by the front door. Miranda returned to the sitting room with David.

He examined window, curtain and wall, taking care not to actually touch anything. Deciding there was little he could do until reinforcements arrived David accepted a cup of tea and asked a few preliminary questions. Miranda took a cup out to Juliette, who was shivering in the drizzle and growing gloom, ensuring that no one came near.

Before long, the second car arrived with two more officers. They quickly started to make a search of the grounds as well as they were able in the semi-darkness. And, when the brothers and Felix returned from their day trip, and were identified and admitted, it was a full house. The kettle boiled merrily, the coffee bubbled, mugs and cups clinked, biscuits were devoured.

It became a group discussion much to David's frustration.

Nevertheless, he ascertained that this latest incident must indeed be connected to the earlier written threat. And still no one, least of all Miranda, had the foggiest idea of who was trying to frighten them away. And she couldn't, for the life of her, think of who they might have upset to want them gone.

At least, she thought, the Guards' working theory of Joe being behind it all could now be scrapped.

Eventually the Guards said that they could do little more for now. They would be back in the morning, hopefully with scene of crime officers from Cork city who would do some forensic work.

Down the road Padraig was trembling. He realised now that he had made a big mistake. By paying your man to frighten that crowd off he had instead brought the Guards down in force to investigate. That was the last thing he had wanted. If they came down here asking questions and searching about then it might mean the end of the community.

There had been searches in the past when people had gone missing – Jonno and Orla had been just two. These had angered the old community but Padraig had persuaded them to stay on. But if uniformed guards came along looking for guns and the like, combing the fields, then the good people might decide to stay underground for ever. This couldn't be allowed to happen. He could never rejoin them. They would reject him. Then what would become of him? He sat and trembled. Elvin and Kalen sat in the corner, chins in hands, watching him.

'So, what do you think? Maybe we should call the whole thing off?'

'Well hell, seems like it's your call Miranda. We'll back you up, whatever you decide to do.' Jim looked at Donal and Felix who nodded their agreement.

'Well thank you lads, I appreciate it. I was having second thoughts, but what happened this afternoon has made my mind up. I'm not going to back out now. We've come too far.'

'So', Jim continued, 'do we have a plan of action? Assuming Jonno appears, who's going to speak to him?'

'I guess we play it by ear,' Miranda replied, 'see what happens. There's hardly a text book approach to these things.'

'Isn't it important that Jonno knows that his brothers are here though?' Felix said little but whatever he said usually made sense.

'Yes that's vital,' Miranda said. 'I guess I ought to speak first though, he knows me now.'

'Yes, then we'll see.'

They sat silently for a while, then decided to rest before reconvening downstairs just before the witching hour of 12. Jonno had always appeared some time after that.

Miranda herself decided to stay downstairs, read a little maybe. Who knew what tonight might bring. Would Jonno appear? Would there be some sort of happy ending? What form would it take? She had staked a lot on trying to solve this unexpected mystery; her marriage in particular. It had been an intense disappointment to her that Joe wanted nothing to do with her quest to put Jonno to rest. It seemed now that he wanted her only as long as she conformed to his idea of her. But she had expected marriage to be give and take. Joe had given her love and friendship, it was true, but he had shown no understanding of her needs in this matter.

He disappointed her, but it now appeared she was disappointing him. Neither of them were wrong, or right.

They had somehow drifted apart. She couldn't foresee a situation in which they would live together again at Dunmurry, or in Ireland.

This would all be resolved shortly, for better or worse. She could think no more beyond tonight. Tomorrow night she planned to see Andrew, but those thoughts would have to be pushed to one side for tonight. How did she ever get into this, and how was she going to get out of it intact?

Donal was wide awake. He still didn't quite figure how he wasn't still in Darwin, Australia. The last few days had been surreal. He'd hardly been outside Darwin in his life and everything that had taken place since he stepped aboard the Quantas jet seemed like some sort of a theatre play with him playing one of the actors. And it was only with a lot of help and providence that he had managed to arrive at Dunmurry to play his part.

But he was not being allowed to settle down and enjoy a bit of Irish pub life. No, he was being expected to be a ghost hunter! Of course Miranda had tried to explain this to him beforehand but he hadn't really understood. All he really understood was that Miranda was anxious for him to meet his brother Jim at Dunmurry and was willing to pay his passage in order to sort out some sort of problem.

It was good seeing Jim again, though they had barely recognised one another. He spoke with an American accent, a bit like John Wayne who he had occasionally watched at the local flea-pit. Hardly surprising though. He said that he had spent most of his life in the oil industry and had done pretty well for himself. They hadn't seen each other and had spoken less than a handful of times, since they had left Dublin in the 1950s.

When this was over he, Donal, would be relieved to get back to Oz. It was the place he knew. Maybe he didn't have much there but that was where he belonged. He'd never married so his life was his own, and he had no intention of changing it at this stage.

In truth a part of him wanted to sneak off right now, get a lift back to Dublin. He didn't know what use he was going to be later. Reckoned he was going to be the one running up the road like Scooby Doo if the spook appeared.

Funny though, he'd hardly had a serious drink since he'd left Darwin. On the plane he'd been happy with a beer or two and, when they stopped coming, he didn't mind. Here in Ireland he'd had a few pints of the famous Guinness. He liked it. A lot. But somehow he found himself drinking at the relaxed pace of the locals. They smiled, chatted and joked. In Darwin it always seemed to be a race against time, get drunk before closing time. It was no wonder nerves got frayed and there were arguments and fights.

But it was his world. He was old and he could never get used to living in the land of his birth again, strange and pleasant though a short trip was.

Jim just hoped that he would get through the night. His chest was worse, his breathing more difficult. Felix had told him that this would happen towards the end. The nebuliser and pills would only keep him going for so long. Once these stopped being effective then Felix would have to start administering the needle; that would keep him drowsy and bed-ridden until death finally released him.

He therefore hoped that whatever was to happen, happened tonight. There was a great danger that it would otherwise be too late and that he would let Miranda down, and of course, Donal. Most of all, much as he was struggling to comprehend this new reality, he would be letting down Jonno. If his spirit was to be released then it appeared both he and Donal were required to play a part.

And after that, what? He may as well die here, in Cork, where he had been born. No point in flogging back to Oklahoma even if he were in a fit condition to do so. He had left his affairs in order with his lawyer in downtown Tulsa, but things had changed. Maybe it wasn't too late to change his will. Felix could witness it and vouch for his soundness of mind.

He struggled painfully out of bed, found pen and paper and started writing.

And in the other room Felix had his own concerns. He too found the turn of events somewhat surreal. It was nothing that hadn't been explained at the outset but the reality startled him. But yes, he had enjoyed his trip after a fashion. His one duty was to look after Jim and for this he was being well paid. He hoped he could keep Jim well enough to travel home to the States but any sort of delay would endanger that plan.

He didn't have to take part in this business tonight but he felt duty-bound to be at Jim's side. He doubted anything would happen. Pleasant though Miranda was, she seemed to him somewhat fanciful. Nothing in his medical training, or indeed experience, made mention of, or allowance for, ghosts and spirits. Still, he would attend and sit in the background and keep his counsel.

But a much bigger worry lurked at the back of his mind and it returned now and again to haunt him. He was being blackmailed. He was married to a lovely lady, Charlene, and he loved her dearly. But he preferred sex with men. And, after a spat with his latest boyfriend Bobby, it had all gone horribly wrong. His refusal to see Bobby again had resulted in very real blackmail threats. Bobby would make sure Charlene got evidence of their affair unless he was paid 200 dollars a week. He had caved in to this demand which, even on his doctor's income, was becoming onerous. Charlene was beginning to query why they were so short of money. Despite Felix's pleas Bobby seemed determined to keep up the demands or even ratchet them up.

The premium rates being paid to him by Miranda for this trip were therefore very welcome, but the respite wouldn't last. He would either have to confess to Charlene sooner or later, or do something about Bobby.

Felix dozed fitfully after setting his phone alarm for twelve.

One by one they gathered in the sitting room. Miranda had arranged armchairs so that they were all facing the part of the room where Jonno was known to cross from wall to wall. In front of them Miranda had placed a small table with a notebook, bottles of whiskey and water, and four glasses. A sole lamp dimly lit that part of the room.

'Now, he always comes from over there,' said Miranda, pointing to the wall to the right. 'You may not see him – I didn't at first – but you know he's there.'

'But you saw him the last time?'

'Yes, eventually. That was when we spoke. The only time.'

They sat quietly, saying only the occasional word. All but Felix cradled tumblers of whiskey like some sort of comfort blanket. The tension grew, no proper conversation being possible under the circumstances. There was no point in possibly postponing the encounter by lively chatter.

There was a false alarm. All four stiffened, stopped breathing, and stared at the far wall. A minute or two passed and things returned to normal. There was silence other than the breeze outside and the occasional passing car. Jim started to say something, then stopped.

The hairs on their necks stood up. The temperature seemed to drop. Their eyes were riveted once more on the wall. Then a shape, an indefinite shape, an outline of a figure... It faded, then returned. It moved slowly across the room.

The men froze, eyes staring, as they followed the shadow's progress. Miranda, more ready for this, tried to relax and breathe deeply. She resolved to speak if the shape looked like it was moving onwards.

Just the size of a young boy, the shadow continued to move slowly. Then it stopped, appearing to have noticed the group.

'Jonno?' It was Miranda, sounding calmer than she felt.

The shape started to take on the definite aspect of a young boy, faded then returned. Then, to their astonishment it seemed to say,

'Jonno.' It was a high-pitched rasp, but clearly audible. The watchers were stock still, the men unable to speak or move. Miranda spoke again.

'Jonno, Jim and Donal are here.'

The young boy-shape appeared to turn towards them, then again the same raspy voice,

'Jim. Donal.'

'Yes. Are you pleased Jonno?'

'Jim. Donal. I cannot leave. I am earthbound.'

'Jonno, what do you mean? Tell us,'

'Until I am replaced. At Samhain, Samhain.'

'Jonno we don't understand, tell us...'

But the boy once more took an ephemeral shape and he disappeared quickly through the wall to the left.

Several minutes passed. No one moved. Then Jim broke the silence.

'I think that's the entertainment over for tonight folks.'

'Well crikey, if I'd not seen that with my own eyes ...'

'I can't believe it. I simply don't believe what I've just seen.' Even the disbeliever Felix was convinced.

Miranda hurried to put the main lights on and refilled glasses. She took charge.

'Right guys, what did all that mean?'

'What's Sowan?' Jim wanted to know.

'Now I know that, I read about it, if my Irish pronunciation is correct. S-A-M-H-A-I-N. It's an ancient Irish pagan feast day marking the end of summer. She grabbed her book and flicked through the pages. Look, here it is. November Eve. It's the night when spirits most easily enter the mortal world. And when souls are said to return to their earthly homes.'

'November Eve? It's the 30th October now, this morning isn't it?' This was Felix, now convinced that things existed outside of his learning.

Donal asked, 'But what did he mean about being earthbound, about needing to be replaced?'

'I just don't know Donal,' said Miranda 'though maybe it's simply as he says. Jonno can't leave until he finds a replacement.'

'So what do we do now?'

'We sleep on it, and we talk in the morning.'

It all seemed unreal the following morning. One by one the earthly inhabitants of Dunmurry came downstairs. Miranda, baggy-eyed, was in charge of the full Irish breakfasts that were proving exceedingly popular despite Felix's protestations about cholesterol levels. He had urged Jim to avoid too much fried food. However, Jim had soon fixed that.

'Felix, good friend and eminent doctor, if I avoid high cholesterol foods will I live?'

Argument over, Jim tucked in heartily though knowing his chest pains would be exacerbated.

No one had come up with any bright ideas overnight. Miranda felt rather guilty in announcing that she would be going off to Cork later and would not be returning until the next morning. They would all talk about what to do then, if indeed there was anything they ought to do. Perhaps they (meaning she, Miranda) might talk to some sort of expert in these matters. Possibly Padraig. He might know what would be best.

After breakfast, Jim announced that he and Donal would be going for a little walk. Surprised though he was, Donal agreed. While they were getting ready to go out David and Juliette, the Bantry guards, arrived together with a white van containing two SOCOs from Cork city. Miranda greeted them and they started work. Amongst other things, they needed to remove the bullet which had lodged in the wall. It may give them a clue or two.

Jim and Donal put on light raincoats, the sky was still heavy. Jim led a surprised Donal out of the back door and down past the outbuildings. They were shooed to one side by the SOCOs who were trying to ascertain where the bullet might have been fired from.

'Remember we used to get out down through this way as kids?' asked Jim.

'Yeah, I guess I do. Was there a gate or something? Leads to the river and the railway.'

They found the gap in the hedge though any gate had long since disappeared. Pushing through they found themselves on the banks of the river, flowing free after the recent wet weather. They stopped and looked across to the fields beyond, the sun doing its best to shine through onto the stubble. Slivers of childhood memories came flickering back. It was a timeless scene. The smell in the air as well as the view transported them back in an instant.

'Come on, over the bridge!'

They marched over the wooden bridge, a rather stouter version than the rickety one they remembered through the mists of time.

'We used to swim here. Starkers! No girls allowed.'

'Crikey yeah, we did sure enough!'

'You'd be locked up these days, put in a register or something.'

They crossed the bridge and started walking along the opposite bank. Jim slowed, then stopped.

'You haven't noticed anything have you.' It was a statement by Jim, not a question.

'Noticed what?'

'The railway line.'

'It's here … it used to be … it's gone!'

'Yes, and …?'

'What's that we've been hearing at night then?'

'Donal there are no tracks. And there are no steam trains any more.'

'Then what …?'

'Then that's our second mystery. Come on, we've got another one to find. My old brain sure is working better now the rest of me is packing up for good.'

The SOCOs were at work in the sitting room as the two old men walked through the house and out onto the Bantry – Drimoleague road, turning right, the way they had walked before. Jim was in some physical discomfort but his mood was determined.

They came to Dunmurry Cottage only to find David and Juliette circling it, trying the doors and windows. David looked up and greeted them.

'Good morning again you two. We were hoping to speak to the owner of this place but he appears to be out. Out for a walk are you?'

'Yes, officer. Hope you have more luck with the neighbours.'

'Do you know Mr O'Leary sir?'

'How would we know him. We've been away 60 years, me and him,' Jim retorted, flicking his thumb in Donal's direction. 'What's his first name?'

'Padraig, the station tells me. Padraig O'Leary, Dunmurry Cottage.'

'Well, good luck with your enquiries.'

Jim marched off, not down the main road but down the lane to the left. Donal hurried after him. When he caught up Jim said to him, 'What was the name of the old fella that used to live there back in our day?'

'Blimey, I forget mate.'

'It was Padraig, I know it was. Now, how old would you say he was back then?'

'He was old, I don't know …'

'78, would you say?'

'His father, grandad perhaps?'

'Donal it's the same man! There's plenty of mysteries around here, aren't there? Come on.'

On they went, down the lane, Donal more than a little bewildered. Jim was way ahead of him in this business. A little further on Jim stopped again, puffing now, holding his ribs. He pointed over the ditch and across the field.

'Now, do you remember that Donal?'

'The fairy rath! I do now that you point it out. We weren't allowed to go there.'

'That's right. But we did though, didn't we?'

'We did, once or twice, for divilment. But it was only an old mound. Nothing there.'

'Never at night though.'

'No. What would we be going there at night for?'

'For nothing. But listen. Did you hear Miranda? November Eve, tomorrow, the pagan feast of Samhain. The night the good people dance with the spirits. You'll come then?'

'No Jim, not in a million years.'

'Well come on then, back to the house. But don't you see how everything is linking up? Who owns the land with the rath on it? Might not there be a good reason that nosy newcomers ought to be kept away, frightened away?'

'And Jonno. How do we help Jonno?'

'We'll find a way.'

24

Miranda happily spent a couple of hours in Cork, picking up some bargains at Brown Thomas, treating herself to home-made soup in the English Market. Then a stroll around the other main shopping streets before making her way slowly back to the Imperial, and to her room.

She wondered what Andrew had in mind for tonight. She didn't really care if they went for dinner or not. She might not have the chance to see him again if, as seemed inevitable, she had to return to the States.

She shivered and dressed carefully in her new BT underwear and perfume in all the right places. A man like Andrew made you feel like the sexiest woman on earth just by thinking about him.

Her heart missed a beat as she saw him in the bar and she kissed him warmly. He seemed a little reticent tonight but never mind, wait until later.

The meal they ate in Washington Street wasn't as nice as she'd come to expect in Cork. It was a bit of a student–y place and she was surprised that Andrew had chosen it. Nevertheless she was determined to enjoy the evening.

She looked into his eyes over coffee. Again, maybe it was her imagination but they didn't seem so warm tonight. Perhaps he was working too hard, or, more likely perhaps, worried about balancing all his girlfriends out. Miranda was under no illusion that she was his only one. He was such a good-looking and hot guy.

It would be wonderful to be with a man like this all the time, she mused. A hard-working professional, respected, loving, great in bed. She sighed. Maybe she could get him to love her. She must try harder then, at the right time, insist that he stopped seeing other women. Then he would see what he would be missing if he let her go.

Then she remembered again that this was Cork and all the pointers were that she would be flying west for good before too long. But there again …

Andrew had forgotten his cards so Miranda had to pay, not that she minded a jot. She had no idea how much money she had but her plastic never failed her thanks to their accountant. Money wasn't everything but it was something else that she could use to lure Andrew to her, to keep him for her own.

They walked slowly back to the Imperial. She wanted to go straight upstairs but he fancied a brandy, so she humoured him and joined him, arm in arm. They stood at the bar and she curled her arm around his slim waist, kissing him fondly. He responded by kissing her on the lips, his hand reaching down to caress her bottom. She breathed heavily through her nostrils, things were looking up.

'So this is your squash club is it Andrew?'

Startled they both looked around, Andrew's hand quickly removed from its resting place. Confronting them was a glamorous blonde with steely eyes and angry voice.

'Oh, Virginia! Miranda, I'd like you to meet my wife Virginia,' Andrew squeaked.

'Your wife?'

'Don't worry darling. You're not the first. Now Andrew, you'll come with me now or you're history. What's your choice?'

He mumbled something, possibly a form of apology, in

Miranda's direction as he followed his wife out of the bar. She watched him go, unbelieving, brandy glass frozen in time, half way to her lips.

Then she glanced about her. Everyone was looking at her. Some sniggered behind hands, others gave her a sympathetic 'sisters in arms' look. The well-trained bar staff carried on as if they hadn't noticed a thing. Then the conversation levels returned to normal.

Tears welling, Miranda place the untouched brandy on the counter, picked up her clutch bag, pushed her shoulders back and, head held high, walked from the room

25

The next morning Felix heard noises coming from Jim's room. Still in his dressing gown, he hurried in. Jim was half out of bed, sweating, deathly pale.

'Jim, lie back now. You're not well.'

'I'm fine … just need a glass of …'

'Glass of water. Coming up. Here, lie back now.'

He helped Jim back into bed and brought him the glass of water. Jim swallowed a little and Felix put the glass down on the bedside table.

'Is it bad?'

Jim reluctantly nodded his head. Felix hurried to get his bag and brought it back to the room. A minute with the nebuliser regulated Jim's breathing, making him feel a little easier. Then Felix considered, looked in his bag and chose a selection of pills. Totally trusting him, Jim swallowed the pills with a little more water. After a while he felt more comfortable and was able to travel to the bathroom and back before collapsing, exhausted, onto the pillow.

'You should have called me earlier, Jim. That's why I'm here. That's what that bell there is for.'

'I'm fine. Never better. You need your rest too.' They chuckled, then Felix became serious.

'I think maybe we should get you to the hospital, Jim.'

'For what?'

'Well maybe you'd be better off in the charge of a team of professionals than just the family doctor.'

'Will I live longer then?'

'Probably not but ...'

'But nothing. All it'll be is tests and questions and more tests. And the end result will be the same. Is that about it?'

'Maybe. I guess so.'

'You have the disclaimer, if that's what you're concerned about.' There was a long silence. 'And another thing Felix.'

'What's that?'

'No needle, no morphine. Not until I say. Understood?'

'Understood, Jim.'

Miranda arrived back at Dunmurry mid-morning. She'd certainly got more sleep last night at the Imperial than she'd originally intended. She had reckoned on a couple of hours between dawn and last call for breakfast. Things hadn't quite turned out that way.

She felt stupid, quite stupid. Men were so transparent that anyone could see straight through them. Yet she had seen nothing, never suspected that her dream lover was just another husband cheating on his wedding vows. A man looking for any available, preferably good-looking, woman to spice up his life. There was she, just the dumb sort that he knew would be an easy lay. She thought she had found her sexual soulmate when all the time he had a bitter wife at home who had just realised that squash matches don't last all night.

On the long road back from Cork she'd had plenty of time to consider where this left her. Her conclusion was that she was no worse off than before, loss of dignity notwithstanding. She'd had an affair, a fling, and she couldn't deny that she had thoroughly enjoyed it. But there was no way that she'd be looking for another. She wasn't a kid any more – she was a 26 year-old woman who was married to a man she truly loved. It was time that her efforts were directed towards saving that marriage. As soon as today, tonight, was over then she would return to the States and try to rebuild things with Joe.

As soon as today is over. How the hell is all this going to pan out? What do we do? If we do nothing then Jonno's going to wander around Dunmurry for ever. Trapped between life and death. What can we do?

Can we somehow provide a 'replacement' for him? That's what he said. He's trapped. We have the obligation to free him. But how? Would a dead cat constitute a replacement, she thought wildly. Hardly. I don't have the answer. Who does? I'll go and visit Padraig, he seems to know everything about the area, the history, how things work. I'll go and see him later, after I've spoken to the guys.

She pulled up in front of the house. At least the rain had eased as she'd driven west and had been replaced by higher clouds but a stiffer breeze. It was quiet, no one about. Maybe they'd gone walking. She put on the kettle. She hadn't got used to the Irish habit of drinking tea at every opportunity. Maybe that was another weight on the set of scales that was telling her that she no longer belonged in Ireland.

She flicked through her book of history, old legends and stories trying to think of a possible answer to their dilemma. Nothing came to her and she put the book to one side in exasperation.

She heard the back door open and the sound of male voices. Felix and Donal came through and she greeted them.

'Where's Jim?' she asked.

'Upstairs. He's not well at all. I'll go check on him,' replied Felix. And, so saying, he headed off up the stairs. Donal spoke.

'Miranda, there's no railway out back is there?' asked Donal.

'Why no, that was back in the day. The last train ran in 1961 I've been told. You'll remember it of course.'

'Yes, but they didn't rebuild it further south?'

'No Donal, there are only the fast inter-city lines left in Ireland these days. Why do you ask?'

'Oh, no reason.'

Felix rejoined them.

'How is he?'

'Not so good. I've told him to stay where he is for now. I'll keep an eye on him.'

Miranda considered. Jim wasn't going to be much help tonight then. Donal was never going to come up with a bright idea and Felix just seemed bewildered by the whole thing. How had she got herself into this scrape, and able to rely on no one but herself?

Abruptly she grabbed her coat and, without another word, left the house.

Padraig was in serene mood, leaning on his pitchfork and surveying his newly dug drills. His garden would be in fine condition for the next owner. Who knows, he might return on occasion to see that they were keeping up the good work.

It was time to go back, this time for good. He had no regrets. He would be missing nothing only a lot of worry, and that he could do without. His bit of gardening, yes, he enjoyed his bit of gardening. But he'd be just as able for that in the other place.

He supposed he should consider himself fortunate. When he passed over that first time he had been given the opportunity to represent the good people in human form. It was useful for the community to have a connection to the mortal world.

This old cottage was old when he first came here. The road beyond was a track, no more. Horses and carts, maybe six or ten a day would pass by. And labourers looking for work on the farms perhaps – he would point a few out to them. The odd tinker pulling his cart, offering to fix your pots and pans.

Towards Bantry there, maybe a mile, was a tavern, an inn. Shanahan's it was called. He had walked there one day out of curiosity, just so no one would have the advantage of him. There it was, laid back from the road, its painted sign swinging in the breeze. It didn't occur to him to go in; knowing it was there was enough.

Then came the motor cars and mechanised farm machinery. They churned up the track so the council had to lay hoggin and gravel down. But still most people used to travel by train, way back of the road there. Who wouldn't with the way you'd get from Bantry to Cork in no time? No one in their right mind would set off along this road here in those days.

The electricity came through here next, see, the poles are still there. Padraig was having none of that malarkey though. What would he be doing with the electric light when he had perfectly sound oil lamps and candles? It still confused the electricity company that there was a place that wasn't connected to their grid.

But now, since the oil terminal, the road is good and fast. No one needs the train any more and didn't they shut it down years ago now?

And no one stops by for a chat with Padraig any more. Apart from the odd one maybe. Which suited him well. Why would he want to be chatting?

But it was time he left, back to where he belonged. They were getting too close and it would be dangerous for all if he were to continue to live here in human form. No loss to him, except for his garden. And there would surely be gardening to be done in the other place.

'Bejasus now, here she comes, the one from Dunmurry House,' he thought. Too late, she'd seen him.

'Hello Padraig. How are you?'

With bad grace Padraig invited Miranda in for tea. He wished he'd not set a precedent that first time but he could hardly claim that he was too busy now. Still, he'd make sure she didn't stay long. He made her the weakest of cups of tea, put three spoons of sugar in (she'd asked for one) and sat opposite her, determined to see her off but not so quickly as to create suspicion.

'Padraig, you've a lot of knowledge of local history, legends and suchlike.'

'Now, maybe so.'

'Yes you have. You've told me lots of things before, about how things used to be. Now, you remember me telling you about the young ghost-boy up at Dunmurry, the one that might be Jonno Fitzgerald?'

Padraig remained silent; she continued,

'Well, he's still around. How would one go about getting rid of a ghost?'

Padraig scratched his head. 'Well, there's a thing now. How would the likes of me know anything about that?'

'Because you've lived your life among the Irish country folk, Padraig. You know the stories, even if you may not believe them.'

Padraig scratched his head again. Of course he knew but

he was hardly going to tell this woman from Americay! On the other hand he could hardly claim to know nothing at all and be thought amadán after a lifetime, several lifetimes, of living in West Cork.

'Well missus, 'tis said that ghosts are souls stuck between heaven and earth.'

'And how do you unstick them?'

'Sure, ignore them. They go away on their own. They crave the attention.'

'What if they won't go away?'

'Then order them, away with ye! 'Tis well known that a ghost must obey a mortal.'

'So they may go away, but they're still stuck?'

'That's the long and the short of it missus. Now, if you'll excuse me …'

'What if the ghost told you he was stuck until he was replaced?'

'Told you bedad?'

This was getting into dangerous territory. It seemed to Padraig that such a thing was the work of the good people. Often they would capture souls because they fell in love with them and were reluctant to have them leave. They might consent after a time if a replacement soul could be found.

'Missus I've little enough knowledge of such matters. Now I am tired and you must please leave, begging your pardon.'

Padraig watched her go. More than ever he wished for tonight to come quickly when he could most easily rejoin the community. He had done his bit these last 200 years.

26

Darkness fell. It was a quiet group that sat in the kitchen at Dunmurry House. Jim had recovered to the extent that he had made his way downstairs. He was wheezing heavily, deathly pale and obviously in pain. Felix attended to him with little or no interest in the extant conversation.

There were no useful ideas. Donal was becoming increasingly anxious to get back to his own country, his own city, his own room and his circle of drinking mates. Only out of a sense of adventure, and a little family duty, was he here in the first place and intended to leave as soon as he could. Probably tomorrow.

Miranda reported back on the scraps of information she had gleaned from Padraig. It seemed the best they could hope to do was to command Jonno to leave the house. If Padraig was correct then Jonno must obey. Maybe that would have the effect of releasing him from whatever spell he might be under.

Clearly, they weren't going to sacrifice a virgin only to end up with the virgin's ghost wandering Dunmurry in place of Jonno! Even Jim sniggered at that idea and this had Felix ministering to regulate his breathing again, easing the pain.

Eventually they decided there was little they could do other than to confront Jonno's ghost again that night. Then what would be would be.

Jim and Felix disappeared upstairs. Donal treated himself

to a couple of cans of lager from the fridge. Man was he going to have a session when he got back to the Cricketers. Then he too went upstairs leaving Miranda on her own.

Miranda too had had enough. Of everything. Enough of being apart from her husband for one thing. Absence certainly wasn't making the heart grow fonder in their case. Only if she and Joe were back together again did they stand a chance of getting their marriage back on the rails. Tomorrow, she would break up this party and prepare to leave herself.

Outside, the clouds cleared and the moon put in an appearance, brightening up the countryside. Samhain, November Eve, All Hallows Eve, Hallowe'en. The night in the year when the spirits are as close to the earth as they would ever be.

But this was now tiresome stuff as far as Miranda was concerned. She no longer cared. It pained her to admit it. She and Joe had fallen for the country at once. It had brought them under its spell immediately, snared them.

But the charm had worn thin. The damp weather was no longer an attractive feature which gave the place its green-ness. It wore you down, got into your bones, made you miserable and inward looking.

The people of Ireland had once appeared wonderful, friendly, welcoming, nothing too much trouble. But when the thin veneer had worn off what was left was a meanness, a bitterness. Any success was begrudged. In the countryside at any rate curtains still twitched, everybody knew everybody else's business. Though if you were from the States looking for your roots for a week you would never notice.

And the pace of life, so slow. In the beginning the peace and quiet was an attraction. You'd love the way they gave directions by saying 'well you shouldn't start from here' and, when asked the distance it was always 'a mile wesht the road' which meant any distance at all. Now you just wanted to slap them. If she had to spend any further time in Ireland it would be in Cork or Dublin where people moved and talked at normal speed and you could buy a designer dress or a Starbucks.

Thoroughly depressed she plumped a cushion, lay back and shut her eyes.

It was late when she awoke, was awoken. It was Felix.

'He's gone!'

'Who's gone?'

'Jim of course!'

'Where to?'

'How would I know? We have to find him. I'll get Donal.'

Well now, ain't it a mighty fine night for a stroll. Might rightly be the kind of night that a young boy would set out to meet the girl of his dreams. He might take a token of his esteem, some flowers perhaps, if he was just a poor boy. Here, I'll pick a couple of these snowdrops for my Janie, the girl of my dreams. Put 'em in this breast pocket right here.

You wouldn't want to be walking in these parts tonight pardners. You stick indoors with your flat TV screens and make sure the door's closed behind you. Wouldn't want anything sneaking in on you like.

Oh Jonno, this is the way you came, wasn't it? While we was all looking for you along the river bank and the railway line and them fields. No one thought you'd have any interest in coming down this way. Nothing to see for a 6 year-old. What brought you down here when we were all playing across the road like we always used to?

Well now, here's the old cottage. I'll rest awhile here. Don't want my breathing to give out just yet. An' my chest is paining something wicked, but these old legs are still working.

Anyone at home? Don't appear so. Neither would you expect the old man to be home tonight. Tonight of all nights. He'll be over there with the rest of 'em. Leastways that's what I'm thinking. If I've got it all wrong an' all they're going to think old Jim finally lost it – the disease finally got to his brain.

But I ain't wrong, it all adds up. As clearly as if there was a flashing signpost pointing down this here lane. Didn't think to bring me a torch though. A good job there's a nice moon risin' so I can just about see the way.

Tarmac helps too. Back in the day this was nothing but a track where the farmer would drive his animals. You'd be sure to hop up on the ditch pretty damn quick and you see them cows trotting towards you! Tarmac now, and no cows, not hardly a car at all I 'spect.

I guess it's hereabouts. If I'm right then it ain't far to go now. I ain't coming outta this field once I'm in. So long Donal, Felix, Miranda, Dunmurry. It was good knowing y'all.

This here climb might finish me off … up … up … there! Life in the old dog yet. Now, this way. Got to keep going 'fore this chest of mine packs in once and for all.

I hear it now, the music, the fiddle. Not loud, the odd note on the night air. And rustles in the grass, the little blighters are watching me, weighing me up. Well I mean you folk no harm.

Yonder now's the mound, you see it? Silhouetted against the sky. That's where I'm bound. You see the light shimmering around it now, the music becoming clearer …

'Hello Jim, I'm pleased you could come.'

'Howdy ma'am. You'll excuse me. I don't know you do I?' By the moonlight I make out a tall young woman, a beautiful young gal with a Cork accent.

'Orla, they call me Orla, Jim. Will you come with me?'

'Surely ma'am.'

'Call me Orla dear Jim, we'll be getting to know each other well tonight.'

Well Jonno, if I'd known it was going to be this pleasant I'd have come before. I hope Janie ain't watching, though if she is I guess she don't mind much. I hope I'll be seeing her soon enough.

They danced, Jim awkwardly at first. It was many years since he had danced and that had been quite a different manner of dancing. Now, as his eyes became accustomed to the light he made out the fiddle player, a little chap half hidden by a hawthorn bush that grew on the side of the rath. No more than eighteen inches tall, dressed in pointed hat, jacket and trousers he picked out the gentle rhythm of a hornpipe, redolent of Ireland's past. Orla, with her red hair and kind eyes smiled at him and he started to fall into step, feeling the pull of the music.

Then the fiddle was augmented by a higher tone as another little man appeared. He marched around the base of the rath playing a tin whistle. And slowly the mound, and the flat ground around, began to fill with dancers.

Another fiddler joined in, and a flute. The little people joined hands and danced in circles. When the tune changed they danced in lines, cheerfully shouting and encouraging. Orla and Jim blended in, the good folk caring not that they were so tall but seeing that they danced in the old way they were happy to have them participate.

On they flew, the rhythm increasing as the quick low, insistent beat of the bodhran encouraged the dancers to greater efforts. Jim was transported. Free of pain his feet moved as quickly as the rest. Somehow his feet knew all the steps, his youth and health returning. Orla, never taking her eyes off him, laughed happily and rejoiced in his gaiety.

As the moon moved across the sky the dance seemed to approach a crescendo. It must surely cease soon, but the good people of Dunmurry danced on.

'I know. I think I know where he is!' Donal spoke as they quickly put on coats and scarves.

'Where then?'

'A fairy fort. We were never allowed there as kids. He reminded me about it yesterday.'

'You think he's gone there?'

'Well, I'm guessing.'

'OK, torches. Let's try there first, if we've no other ideas.'

The three of them hurried down the dark, silent road towards Dunmurry Cottage, Miranda and Donal picking out the way with torches though the moon lit the main road well enough. They knew that, if Jim had collapsed somewhere, there was little chance of finding him until daybreak. And the chances of that were high. As they went they shone their torches into dark corners, fields, hedges.

'Down here, come on!' They had arrived at the cottage which was in darkness, and they now followed Donal down the narrow lane.

'It's about here.'

'What? Where?'

'The fort, the rath, over there.' Donal pointed across the field. 'You can't see it from here, in the dark …'

'Shh, listen!'

And in the silent night they could make out the faint sounds of gay music. And now, across the dark fields, they could see a sort of glow. For a minute they stood in wonderment but Miranda brought them back to the task in hand.

'Come on, but be quiet.' They climbed over the ditch and slowly crept towards the mound.

At last the musicians seemed to tire a little. For hours they had played fast and furious. The speed of the jigs and reels decreased and, one by one, the musicians laid down their instruments until there remained only the original fiddler. He now contented himself with playing melodic, romantic airs as the dancers slowed down.

And gradually the good people separated into smaller groups. Pairs started to leave the party. Soon there were no more than a dozen chatting together, reluctant to leave.

'Come,' said Orla to Jim, 'sit with me.'

Though feeling as if he could dance all night he was nevertheless content to sit with the young lady who had been his constant companion these past few hours.

'Well Orla, I thank you kindly for the dance.' She threw back her head and laughed merrily.

'Good God, what a gentleman you are Jim. Gentleman Jim. I wish I'd met you years ago.'

'Oh? I think maybe you're a little young for me Orla.'

'Just turned sixty I think, but what would it matter?'

'Sixty?'

'I was thinking back to the Lilac Ballroom, in Enniskeane there. How I needed a gentleman that night. Instead it was just a crowd of langers wanting sex and not a please or thank you between them. Jim, you're different.'

'Happen I was brought up correctly, ma'am.'

'Will you call me Orla!' She threw him a fierce look, eyes flashing like diamonds, then she laughed heartily and continued, 'Jim you're a good man. I know why you're here tonight.'

'Who doesn't like a party? Orla, first tell me what *you're* doing here tonight? You're not of the world of these other good people are you?' The fiddler broke into a rolling sea shanty and the remaining little folk nodded their heads in time to the music.

'Ah Jim, it was a blessed day I found them. When I escaped from that hell hole of a convent I was in deep despair. I had no one in the world and I couldn't remember when an ounce of love had ever been thrown my way. I was a nasty, bitter, horrid young woman. I came across this place. The good people took me in.'

'They took you?'

'Yes. They said that they loved me and that I would live with them for seven years and be happy, then I could go free. It was true. I knew love, happiness and contentment for the very first time. And at the end of seven years they kept their promise but ...'

'You're still here.'

'I'm still here, of my own accord. Now Jim, time is short, the dawn approaches. You must listen to me. Listen very carefully. In return for pledging myself to the good people was granted the power to give one gift, one that is rarely bestowed. It … ah now Jack, come here a minute. This is Jack, he's one of our leaders, aren't you Jack?'

'That I am, and full time now bedad. I've become weary of living in mortal form.'

'You're Padraig, aren't you?' asked Jim.

'Was Padraig, no more. Someone will be elected in my place soon enough. So Orla, Jim is going to be the subject of your gift?'

'Yes Jack, if he accepts.'

'No better choice. Now may God fill your hearts with gladness to cheer you.' And he was gone.

'Now Jim, listen carefully. Please consider my gift as I can offer it only once. There is a land, you may have heard of it, called Tir-na-Nog.'

'Vaguely.'

'It is the land of eternal youth, health and happiness. I can take you there.'

Jim was silent for a long minute, then he put his head in his hands and cried. At last, he spoke again.

'Orla, you are sweet and kind. After the wonders I have seen tonight I ought not to be ungrateful, but I do not believe this. Your Tir-na-Nog is a legend, for children. In any case I wish to go where my Janie is.'

Again there was a long silence. At length Orla spoke again.

'Jim, you have a choice. I can take you now from this field and point your way home. You won't live another week and you will have let Jonno down.'

'Jonno! I'd forgotten Jonno.'

'He will be at rest if you will replace him tonight, if you will come with me to Tir-na-Nog. That was what you wanted, wasn't it?'

'But will Janie be there, at Tir-na-Nog?' Orla threw back her head, laughed and clapped merrily.

'All the right questions and answers Gentleman Jim! Janie is there and waits for you now. You will both be young in spirit, healthy and live there happily forever. Jonno will go to his rest. Now, take my hand, say no more dear Jim, come with me.'

By the time Miranda, Donal and Felix got to the mound there was nothing but a grassy hillock with a couple of hawthorn bushes, a few rabbit holes.

The Guards and locals searched for Jim for a week, and found nothing. The older ones of the district well knew that nothing would come of the search, just like the young lad in '46 and the young woman in '70.

Felix returned to Tulsa. Shortly afterwards his blackmailer died instantly after falling from a multi-storey car park.

Donal has become a respected storyteller in the city of Darwin, in demand for his tales of fairies, ghosts and leprechauns. His erstwhile drinking mates wonder what on earth happened to him over there in Ireland.

Donal's Good Samaritan, Chantilly, won enough on the National Lottery to enable her to realise her ambition of studying History at Oxford University, England.

Miranda and Joe are happily settled back in Martha's Vineyard. They have two children, James and Daniel.

*

And down a minor country road in West Cork stands a boarded-up, desirable looking property with a 'For Sale' sign leaning to one side. And occasionally honeymooners slow down and stop outside and the wife might say 'Darling, can we buy it?'

66438967R00156

Made in the USA
Middletown, DE
11 March 2018